PERFECT DAYS

PENGUIN PRESS
NEW YORK

PERFECT DAYS

RAPHAEL MONTES

TRANSLATED BY

Alison Entrekin

PENGUIN PRESS
An imprint of Penguin Random House LLC
375 Hudson Street
New York, New York 10014
penguin.com

Originally published in Portuguese as *Dias Perfeitos* by Companhia Das Letras, São Paulo.

LIBRARY OF CONGRESS CATALOGING-IN-PUBLICATION DATA

Names: Montes, Raphael, | Entrekin, Alison, translator.
Title: Perfect days : a novel / Raphael Montes ; translated by Alison Entrekin.
Other titles: Dias perfeitos. English
Description: New York : Penguin Press, 2016. | Originally published as Dias
perfeitos (São Paulo : Companhia das Letras, 2014). | Description based
on print version record and CIP data provided by publisher; resource not viewed.
Identifiers: LCCN 2015047915 (print) | LCCN 2015043629 (ebook) |
ISBN 978-0-698-18914-0 (ebook) | ISBN 978-1-59420-640-5 (hardback)
Subjects: LCSH: Medical students—Fiction. | Stalkers—Fiction. | Women
screenwriters—Fiction. | Abduction—Fiction. | Man-woman
relationships—Fiction. | Brazil—Fiction. | Psychological fiction. |
BISAC: FICTION / Literary. | FICTION / Suspense. | GSAFD: Suspense fiction.
Classification: LCC PQ9698.423.O6176 (print) | LCC PQ9698.423.O6176 D5313
2016 (ebook) | DDC 869.3/5—dc23
LC record available at http://lccn.loc.gov/2015047915
International edition ISBN: 978-0-399-56435-2

Printed in the United States of America
1   3   5   7   9   10   8   6   4   2

Designed by Amanda Dewey

For my mother

There is always some madness in love. But there is also always some reason in madness.

FRIEDRICH NIETZSCHE

Gertrude was the only person Teo liked. The other students weren't quite as at ease around her. The minute they walked into the lab, the girls all held their noses. The guys tried to be cool, but their eyes revealed their discomfort. Teo didn't want anyone to notice how good he felt there. He'd walk over to the metal table with his head down.

There she'd be, serenely waiting for him. Gertrude.

In the pale light, the corpse took on a very peculiar brownish hue, like leather. On a small side tray were instruments for more in-depth investigations: scissors with curved tips, anatomical forceps, rat-tooth forceps and scalpels.

"The great saphenous vein can be seen near the inside of the knee. It then courses medially to lie on the anterior surface of the thigh," said Teo. He pulled back Gertrude's epithelium to expose her dried-out muscles.

The teacher looked down at his clipboard, frowning from his fortress of notes. Teo wasn't intimidated: the anatomy lab was his domain. The stretchers here and there, the dissected bodies, the limbs and organs in jars all gave him a sense of freedom that he couldn't find anywhere else. He liked the smell of formaldehyde, the instruments in his gloved hands, Gertrude there on the table.

In her company, his imagination knew no bounds. The world melted away, until he and Gertrude were all that was left. He'd chosen the name the first time they met, when her flesh was still in place. They had grown closer over the course of the semester. In each class, Teo discovered new things about Gertrude: she loved to surprise him. He would hold his head close to hers—the most interesting part of her—and wonder. Who did that body belong to? Was her name really Gertrude? Or was it something simpler?

It was Gertrude. Looking at her withered skin, narrow nose, and dry, straw-colored lips, he couldn't conceive of any other name for her. Although decomposition had stripped away her human appearance, Teo saw something in those misshapen eyeballs: the eyes of the ravishing woman she must have been. He conversed with those eyes when no one else was looking.

She had probably died in her sixties or seventies. The few hairs on her head and pubis confirmed his theory. In a detailed examination, Teo had discovered a fracture in her skull.

He respected Gertrude. Only an intellectual could have forgone the adulation of a funeral to contribute to the future, to the training of young doctors. Better to serve as a light for science than be devoured in darkness, she must have thought. She had probably had a bookcase packed with quality literature. And a collection of vinyl LPs from her youth. Those legs had danced a lot. Night after night.

Many of the corpses in the foul-smelling vats had belonged to the homeless, beggars whose purpose in life was to die. They had no money, no education, but they had bones, muscles, organs. And that made them useful.

Gertrude was different. It was hard to imagine that those feet had roamed the streets or that those hands had begged their way through a mediocre life. Teo didn't believe she had been murdered either, killed with a blow to the head while being mugged or bludgeoned to death by a betrayed husband. Gertrude had died of extraordinary causes, something not in the natural order of things. No one would have had the courage to kill her. Unless he was an idiot . . .

The world was full of idiots. All he had to do was look around: there was an idiot in a lab coat, an idiot with a clipboard, an idiot with a high-pitched voice who was now talking about Gertrude as if she knew her as well as he did.

"The articular capsule has been opened and the stratum fibrosum pulled back to reveal the distal and proximal extremities of the femur and tibia."

The girl made Teo want to laugh. And if Gertrude could have heard that nonsense, she'd have hooted with laughter too. Together they'd have drunk expensive wine, chatted about all manner of things, watched films and discussed the cinematography and the set and costume design afterward like film critics. Gertrude would have taught him how to live.

The other students' disrespect for her got on his nerves. On one occasion, in the teacher's absence, the same girl who was now spouting fancy medical terms in a shrill voice had taken some red nail polish out of her bag and, giggling, painted the corpse's fingernails. The other students had flocked around, finding it all very funny.

Teo wasn't the vindictive sort, but he wanted to avenge Gertrude. He could have made sure the girl received some kind of institutional punishment, but it would have been bureaucratic and ineffectual. He could have arranged for her to take a bath in formaldehyde—just to see the look of desperation in her eyes as she felt her skin drying out. But what he really wanted to do was kill her. And then paint her pale little nails red.

Of course he wasn't going to do anything of the sort. He wasn't a murderer. He wasn't a monster. As a child, he had spent many a sleepless night staring at his shaking hands, trying to decipher his own thoughts. He felt like a monster. He didn't like anyone, have feelings for anyone, or miss anyone: he just lived. People would come along, and he'd be forced to tolerate their presence in his life. Worse: he was supposed to like them, to demonstrate affection. He learned that if his playacting seemed real, it was all a lot easier.

The bell rang, and the students were dismissed. It was the last class of the year. Teo left without saying good-bye to anyone. The gray building was behind him now, and as he looked over his shoulder, he realized he'd never see Gertrude again. His friend would be buried along with the other corpses, tossed into a common grave. They'd never share another special moment.

He was alone again.

2

Teo woke up in a bad mood and went to the kitchen to make his mother coffee. The counter was high, and Patricia couldn't reach the shelves. She had to stretch, and her legs would flop about on her wheelchair. It was degrading.

While he waited for the water to boil, he swept the living room of the flat and washed the dishes. He changed Samson's newspaper and filled his bowl with food. As always, he set the coffee on his mother's bedside table and woke her up with a kiss on the forehead, because that was what loving sons did.

At nine o'clock, Patricia came out of her room. She was wearing a simple dress and cloth sandals. Teo had never seen his mother getting dressed, but he imagined it was an exhausting process. He had once offered to help her with a new pair of jeans, but she had refused emphatically, saying, "It's all I have left." Half an hour later she had a dress on, and the jeans were in the trash.

"Marli and I are going to the fair. I'm taking Samson," she said as she put on an earring.

Teo nodded, his eyes glued to the TV, where Tom was chasing Jerry.

"Do I look nice?"

He realized she was wearing makeup. "Have you found yourself a secret admirer at the fair? Eh, Patricia? Confess!"

"No admirers for the time being. But you never know—I might be crippled, but I'm not dead!"

Teo hated the word *crippled*. In an attempt to make light of her condition, Patricia used it frequently. It was sad, he understood. Ever since the accident, they'd avoided the subject. The wheelchair had become a part of everyday life, and at the end of the day, he thought they didn't really need to talk about it.

Patricia came back from the kitchen with Samson on his leash. The golden retriever was wagging his furry tail. He had joined the family nine years earlier, when they still lived in the penthouse overlooking Copacabana Beach. Now it was an inconvenience to have the dog in a two-bedroom flat. Teo would have preferred to hand him over to a shelter. Samson had beautiful fur and a pedigree; he'd find a new home quickly. Teo had never said this to his mother, as he knew the dog was like a child to her. Although perfectly reasonable, any suggestion that she get rid of him would have been dismissed out of hand.

The bell rang. Patricia went to answer the door.

"Marli, darling!"

It was the neighbor, Patricia's best friend and lover of all things esoteric. A confirmed spinster, moderately stupid, she stood in as a nurse for Patricia, helping her to shower and to walk Samson. They played cards together on Wednesdays. Teo didn't know who was more dependent on whom in that relationship. It amused him when he saw Marli reading his mother's fortune in the cards—her predictions typically bore no relationship to reality.

He had once allowed Marli to read his fortune too. "You are

going to be very wealthy and happy," she had said. "And you are going to marry a very beautiful young woman."

He hadn't believed her. He couldn't see himself being happy. He felt fated to limbo, to monotonous routine, devoid of happy and sad moments. His life was just a void filled with timid emotions. He was fine like that.

"We'll be back in an hour," said Patricia. "The barbecue's later this afternoon. Don't forget."

"What barbecue?"

"Érica's daughter's. Her birthday."

"I don't want to go. I hardly know the girl."

"There'll be people your age there."

"I'm a vegetarian, Mother."

"My friends always ask about you. And I'm sure there'll be garlic bread."

Teo sometimes felt like a trophy that his mother showed off to others. It was her way of making up for her own deficiencies physical and intellectual.

"I'm not asking you, I'm telling you. You're going with me." Patricia slammed the door.

The only sound left in the flat was the music from the cartoon.

There was no garlic bread. Blood and fat dripped from the meat on the grill onto the charcoal underneath. Young people were dancing to the deafening sound of funk music. Patricia was enjoying herself with a group of friends. Teo barely knew those people and regretted not having stayed at home with Tom and Jerry.

Among the bottles of vodka in the cooler, he found one of water. He wouldn't stay long. He'd get a taxi home, and Patricia would get a lift later with a friend. His discomfort aside, he had to admit that the place was beautiful. Set into a rocky hillside, the mansion was divided into large living areas connected by stone stairways winding through the natural vegetation that climbed the slope. Farther down the stairs was a kind of bungalow where the party was taking place, with a swimming pool, barbecue, and wooden tables bolted to the ground. Winding paths led to a colorful, well-tended garden, separated from the forest by a white fence.

"Are you trying to escape the music or the people?" asked a female voice behind him. It was hoarse, a little tipsy.

Teo turned to look at her. It was a young woman, possibly younger than him, and very short—four foot nine at the most. Her brown eyes surveyed the flowers calmly.

"The music," he said.

A long silence put a distance between them.

She was well dressed in a blouse patterned with bright diamond shapes and a black skirt, but she wasn't exactly beautiful. Exotic, perhaps. Her light brown hair was pulled back in a messy bun, with a few strands sticking to her sweaty forehead.

"Were you dancing?" Teo asked.

"I was. But I got tired."

She smiled, and he noticed that her top front teeth were slightly misaligned. He found it charming.

"What's your name?"

"Teo. Teodoro, actually. And you are?"

"Clarice."

"That's a pretty name."

"For God's sake, don't talk to me about Clarice Lispector, because I've never read anything by her! That woman haunts me."

He was amused by the girl's spontaneity but remained serious. He wasn't comfortable around women who were so sure of themselves: he saw them as superior, almost unattainable.

Clarice walked over to him and set the plate of sausages and

pieces of meat she was carrying on the guardrail. She took a sip
from her glass. He glimpsed part of a colorful tattoo through the
sleeve of her blouse but couldn't make out what it was.

"Aren't you eating anything?"

"I'm a vegetarian."

"Don't you drink either? That's water, isn't it?"

"I don't drink much. I don't handle alcohol well."

"Well . . ." she said, lips touching the edge of her glass, "at least
you drink. They say people who don't drink are dangerous. . . .
It's a sign you aren't dangerous."

Teo thought he should laugh, so he did.

Clarice took another piece of meat from the plate.

"What about you? What are you drinking?" he asked.

"It's gummy. Some crap made with vodka and powdered
lemon juice. It tastes like bleach."

"How do you know what bleach tastes like?"

"I don't need to taste things to know what they taste like." She
said it with conviction, as if her words made absolute sense.

Teo felt a little uncomfortable. At the same time, he felt com-
pelled to continue the conversation. He glanced down at her white
legs and ballerina feet in purple strappy sandals. Her toenails
were all painted different colors.

"Why are your toenails like that?"

"My fingernails are too." She held them out for him to see.
Her fingers were long and slender, the most fragile hands he had
ever seen. Her nails, cut short, were painted in an array of random colors.

"I see. Why?"

She answered without thinking, "To be different," and raised
her right index finger to her mouth.

Teo noticed that Clarice chewed her cuticles. He assumed this
explained the misalignment of her front teeth, which projected

slightly outward. Although he hadn't studied dentistry, he'd researched the subject a lot in order to get to know Gertrude.

"And why be different?"

She raised her eyebrows. "The world's pretty dull. My parents are living proof of it. Take my dad, for example. Engineer, always out of town. São Paulo, Houston, London. My mother's a lawyer. Bureaucracy runs in the blood. That's why it's nice to be different. Not have a set routine. Get drunk and not care. Do stupid things and not remember afterward. Paint each nail a different color. Live life before it's too late, right?"

Clarice opened her little woven bag, took out a packet of Vogue menthol cigarettes, and pulled one out. "Got a light?"

"I don't smoke."

She tsked and rummaged around in her bag. The sun was setting behind the hill. Teo watched the drunken shadows moving down below. Clarice found her lighter and lit her cigarette, protecting the flame from the breeze with her hand. She took a drag and exhaled in his direction.

"You don't eat, don't smoke, and don't drink much. . . . Teo, do you fuck?"

He stepped back a little, a few inches, also avoiding the mint-flavored smoke. What was he retreating from? Why did that oddball make him feel so self-conscious? He didn't feel the need to put on an act for her. He liked the blasé way she held the cigarette and said whatever she thought.

"I'm just joking. Relax," she said, with a little punch to his shoulder.

It was their first physical contact. Teo smiled, his shoulder tingling where she'd touched him. He needed to say something.

"So what do you do?"

"What do I do?" She popped another piece of meat into her mouth and chewed on it. "I drink a lot, eat everything, and I've smoked everything too, but now all I smoke are Vogue menthols, girlie cigarettes. I fuck every now and then. I'm studying art history at the university. But I'm not sure if it's what I want to do. I'm really interested in screenwriting."

"Screenwriting?"

"Yeah, screenplays. I'm working on one at the moment. I'm not sure if it's going to be feature length. The argument is ready. And I've written about thirty pages of the screenplay so far. I've still got a long way to go."

"I'd like to read it," he said, without thinking. He was curious to see the result of so much irreverence. He wanted to know what she wrote about and how. Fiction writers put a lot of themselves in their texts.

"I don't know if you'll like it," she said. "It's a story for women. Three single girlfriends in a car driving around looking for adventure. It's a road movie of sorts."

"I can only like it if I read it."

"Okay then, I'll show you." She put out the cigarette butt with the bottom of her sandal and ate another two pieces of meat. "What about you? What do you do?"

"Medicine."

"Wow, supersquare. My mother would love that. She says art history doesn't get you anywhere. As if poring through penal codes and lugging around piles of legal documents did."

"It's not as square as you think. There's art in medicine."

"Where?"

"Well, first we'd have to define art. For example, I want to be a pathologist."

"I don't see any art in that."

"It's complicated. We can talk about it later," he said. He was trying to create another invisible link between them.

"Okay. I've got to go."

He didn't like the fact that she wanted to leave so quickly. He felt as if she were avoiding him for some reason.

"I was just going to get a taxi. Want a lift?" he said.

"No, I live nearby."

"Could I borrow your cell for a minute? I left mine at home, and I need to call a taxi. I promise to be quick."

She reached into her bag. "Here."

As Teo made the call, he watched Clarice. She had let her hair out, and it came down below her waist. The contrast between her long hair and tiny body pleased him.

Two floodlights came on automatically.

"No one's answering. I'll get one on the street." He handed her back the cell.

They walked along the stone path together until it forked into two. "That's the way out," he said, pointing.

"I'm going to get a beer and say good-bye to some people. Aren't you going to say good-bye to anyone?"

He should have made up an excuse, but he wanted to tell the truth. "I'd rather not."

She nodded, then leaned over and gave him a peck on his tense lips. Then she turned and headed up the steps two at a time, the glass of green liquid sloshing about in her left hand.

When Teo got home, he felt giddy. He ran to get his cell from the bedside table and sent a text message to his mother. Then he checked his missed calls, savoring the numbers of the last one. He lay on the sofa for a long while, staring at the ceiling, reliving the images. Something had exploded inside him. Something he couldn't explain, nor did he even want to. Although he didn't know Clarice's surname, where she lived, or where she studied art history, he had her cell number, and that made them intimate.

3

Teo wanted to call her the minute he woke up. He punched in her number, which he already knew by heart, but he didn't have the courage to complete the call. How would he explain that he had her number? It would sound pathetic, childish even, if he told her what he'd done.

He now realized how distant she still was. If he did nothing and just deleted her contact from his phone, they might never see each other again. How often in life do we cross paths with such a special person?

Samson came over, frolicking around his legs. Teo stroked his thick fur and let him lick his hands. Then he pushed him away. He didn't want to be consoled.

He dressed for church.

"We're running late!" shouted his mother from the elevator.

He took a deep breath. He didn't have to go everywhere with her, pushing her wheelchair over the sidewalks of Copacabana like a long-suffering nurse.

He suppressed the thought. "Coming, Mother."

He got his wallet and cell from the bedside table before leaving.

*M*ay *the Lord accept the sacrifice at your hands, for the praise and glory of his name, for our good and the good of all His Holy Church.*

Teo found Sunday mass an interesting ritual. The piety of some members of the congregation made him want to laugh: watery-eyed, lips murmuring in prayer, as if God could hear them.

He is among us.

There was also something surreal about it: those same people lived such debauched lives, wallowing in worldly pleasures, and then at the first sign of a problem raced off to pray for a redemption they didn't deserve.

It is our duty and our salvation.

Sunday mass used to be torture for him. He'd attended catechism class as a child and had been confirmed—Patricia was very religious. For as long as he could remember, he'd resented the fact that you couldn't question the dogmas of faith.

May your Son remain among us!

But he'd quickly realized that it wasn't a Catholic's duty to debate; rather, it was to accept and memorize, as children learn their times tables, and he'd learned to put those sixty minutes to better use.

Send your Holy Spirit!

He knew every line in the prayer book by heart. The congregation didn't even pay attention to what they were saying. They chanted in unison.

Save us, savior of the world, for by your cross and resurrection you have set us free.

He chanted along with them, smiling at his mother from time

to time, while his imagination roamed far from the noisy church. Mass and anatomy class were the moments when he felt most relaxed.

Receive, o Lord, our offerings!

That Sunday, however, his thoughts alighted on Clarice and refused to rise to loftier heights. During the homily, he remembered the previous day, the forward way she had approached him, the plate of sausages and meat, her provocative question: *Teo, do you fuck?*

May Your Spirit unite us as one body!

Memories depleted, he was beginning to imagine new conversations, scents, flavors. His time with Clarice would be much more special than that he'd shared with Gertrude.

Let us walk in love and joy!

He had an idea. It would have to be thought out carefully if it were to work. Nevertheless, it was already enough to lift his spirits.

Grant us, o Lord, eternal light!

By the end of mass, he had run through it three times in his mind and had it all worked out. Flawless. He knew how to get to Clarice.

Thanks be to God.

When they left the church, Patricia saw a friend she hadn't seen in weeks. Teo excused himself, saying he had to study. He bought a phone card at a newsstand and found a phone booth in a square that wasn't very busy. The inside of the booth was plastered with ads for prostitutes. Black stripes covering their eyes and nothing over their private parts. Velvet mouths and hot vaginas. Those were dirty women. Clarice was different: forward but sweet.

He dialed her number. She answered on the second ring.

Teo hung up. He had to breathe deeply before calling again. She picked up quickly again.

"Good afternoon. May I speak to Clarice, please?" he said, faking a São Paulo accent.

"Speaking. Who is it?"

"Good afternoon, Clarice. I'm from the Brazilian Institute of Geography and Statistics. Your name is in our system. Could you confirm your surname, please?"

"Manhães."

"Great, thank you. How old are you?"

"Twenty-four."

He was surprised that she was two years older than him.

"Please hold while I update our records."

A bus sped down the street, honking at a car pulling out of a parking spot. He covered the mouthpiece.

"Thank you for waiting. We're conducting a survey of university students. You attend a university, don't you?"

"Yes." There was a hint of impatience in her reply.

"Could you tell me what you study and where?"

"Art history, at RJSU."

"Is that Rio de Janeiro State University, ma'am?"

"As far as I know, that's RJSU."

"What time of day do your classes start?"

"Seven a.m."

"And are you satisfied with your program?"

"They'll sue me if I say what I really think of that hellhole."

"What year are you in?"

"Hey, do you want to know my birth date, mother's maiden name, and the color of my panties too?"

Teo began to feel pins and needles in his hands. "Of course not, this is the last question. What year are you in?"

"Third."

"The institute thanks you for taking part in our survey."

She hung up without answering.

Teo put the phone back on the hook and turned over the information in his mind. A smile spread across his face.

Sunday dragged on. Teo didn't like Sundays. He wasn't tired, so he researched Clarice on the Internet for hours. He discovered that she'd placed first in the art history entrance exam, with a high enough score to get into the most competitive courses. He also saw that she'd placed well in other entrance exams, always appearing at the top of the lists. He found a blog on astrology where she'd left some comments. On the social networks, the name Clarice Manhães brought up a hideous-looking woman who obviously wasn't her.

Before going to bed, Teo set his alarm for early the next day. At seven a.m., he'd be at the School of Art History.

The black Vectra was a remnant of the Avelar family's former prestige, from the days when they'd lived in the penthouse in Copacabana. Despite all her cuts in spending, Patricia had gone out of her way to keep the car.

Teo arrived at the university at six-thirty. The art history department was deserted. He pulled the hood of his jacket over his head. Although it was spring, there was an icy draft running through the silent corridors.

"Where can I find the third-year students?" he asked a cleaner. The man didn't know.

He sat on a bench in the foyer, watching the students come and go. He'd brought a book by Dürrenmatt but was so nervous he couldn't find any meaning in the words. He read and reread the first page, but it was useless. Pretty girls went past, exotic hair, fair skin, holding laptops, but there was no sign of Clarice.

At nine, Teo went to the office to ask for information. The ill-tempered woman at the desk snapped that it was the end of the semester, they might already be on vacation, and she had no way of knowing.

He returned to the foyer, clinging to the railing of the hazy staircase that connected him to Clarice. He couldn't see the steps in front of him; the climb was treacherous. It occurred to him to give up and go back to his books and bodies. If Clarice had wanted him around, she'd have found a way to make it happen. She was the kind of girl who always got what she wanted.

His defeat was confirmed by a girl with bulging eyes. "The third-years are finished for the semester. I'm a fourth-year, but I have some classes with them. The fourth-years are finished too. I just came to get my results. I have no idea who Clarice is."

Teo thanked her impatiently. The idiot didn't know who Clarice was. How absurd. He headed down the ramp in front of the university thinking that people were unaware of the best things around them.

He was already halfway back to the parking lot when he saw Clarice walk past, talking to a friend. Once the surprise passed, he followed her. He took the coincidence as a sign that he was on the right path, which made him feel strong and powerful. Clarice and her friend went into the office.

Outside, gray clouds were competing with the sun for the sky. Clarice left the office quickly, laughing at something her friend had said. Teo envied the other girl for whatever she had said that was so funny. He didn't know what made Clarice laugh. Maybe he was better off with Gertrude and her silence.

The girls walked down the ramp. Clarice was wearing a moss-green cardigan over a colorfully striped blouse, and she lit up a menthol cigarette, which she smoked until she got to the metro. She already had a ticket. Teo bought one for himself just in time to find them on the platform. He entered the same carriage, the next door down. A multitude of faces got on and off at each station, but Clarice was indifferent to everyone else, with eyes and smiles only for her friend.

They got off in Botafogo and took a bus toward Jardim Botânico.

Teo hailed a taxi and, enjoying the feeling of being in a film, said, "Follow that bus."

The journey continued as far as Lage Park, where the girls got off, still engaged in lively conversation. Teo paid the taxi driver and didn't wait for the change.

O blivious to the rain that was threatening to fall, dirty children raced through the park. Uniformed nannies sat on benches gossiping and flirting with the men who jogged past. Elderly couples strolled along hand in hand. A group of young people sitting in a circle were improvising a picnic. Clarice and her friend were graciously included in the scene. They pulled semiprofessional cameras out of their backpacks and began to photograph blue flowers and imperial palms. They took photos of each other taking photos.

Clarice put away her camera and put on some pearl earrings. She smiled at the lens, a nineteenth-century lady, struck poses in the garden and beside the pond, bent to smell flowers, and swanned up and down the stairs in front of the old manor in the middle of the park. She had the eyes of a lioness.

Lit by the sun, Clarice examined the photos with her friend. She hooted with laughter at some and asked her friend to delete others.

Teo wanted to see them, to have them for himself, including those that had been summarily deleted. From a distant tree, he also photographed Clarice, but with his eyes, saving the images in his memory between one click and another.

The two friends ate an apple at dusk. Ten hours had passed without him noticing: he hadn't even had lunch! Clarice said good-bye to her friend and lit a menthol cigarette. She climbed steep streets, turned corners, and crossed intersections. She walked lightly, a petite girl swallowed by the crowd. She turned onto a short street, took a key out of her bag, and opened the door of a house surrounded by a high stone wall. Teo waited a few more minutes and wrote down the address.

H e caught a taxi to the university to get the car from the parking lot. At home, he greeted his mother with an agitated kiss. He showered, shaved, dabbed on some cologne, and put on the best item in his wardrobe: a green polo shirt that sat well on his broad shoulders.

"You look nice. Where are you off to?" asked Patricia, returning to reality in the commercial break of her soap opera. She was stroking Samson, whose head was on her lap.

"To meet a girl. I'm taking the car."

It was wonderful not to have to lie. He often made up promising stories about the girls he hooked up with in the back row of the cinema. How to explain that he hadn't brought home a single girlfriend since his adolescence? How to explain that he preferred to watch European films alone? If he didn't say he went out with girls, his mother might think something absurd, perhaps even going as far as to assume he was a homosexual. He didn't relate to homosexuals. They were impure, motivated by sex. He'd rather be a hermit than gay.

Now he could tell the truth. There was no reason to lie to

Patricia. Or even to himself. He wanted to be in the back row of the cinema with Clarice. She had kissed him at the barbecue. Why stop? He had become a hostage of that sneaky, stolen kiss. He wasn't the invader but the invaded, and he didn't want just to discover but to be discovered. He loved Clarice, he admitted to himself. He needed to be loved.

Teo was annoyed at the thought that he wasn't going to see her that night. He'd been in the car for over two hours, watching the lights in the bedrooms, shadows moving back and forth behind the curtains.

A red Corsa pulled up in front of the house and honked twice. Clarice appeared at the door, enchanting in a black dress. The driver got out to greet her. He looked to be in his late twenties, almost thirty. His large rectangular glasses and formal black clothes made him look older. Clarice gave him a peck on the cheek and got into the car.

A few minutes later they were in the district of Lapa. The man got out of the car with a large backpack and walked into the Cecília Meireles Concert Hall holding Clarice's hand. A flyer on the door announced that night's program: Young Brazilian Symphony Orchestra—Concerts of Youth. That night they were going to play Antonín Dvořák's Symphony no. 9.

Teo didn't want to stay for the performance. The image of the orchestra with their serious faces, violins and cellos poised and ready, irritated him. Nor did he want to see Clarice kissing another man. The hand-holding had already been offensive enough.

He ended up buying a ticket. Among the heads of women's hair, he managed to identify her, sitting next to the girlfriend she'd been with earlier. The man was nowhere to be seen. When the concert began, Teo spotted him in the middle of the orchestra, with his rectangular glasses, playing a reddish-colored violin. Overwhelmed by a strong feeling of antagonism, Teo barely paid attention to the music. An ant wandered over the back of the seat in front of him before his thumb crushed it.

Afterward the three young people went to a nearby bar, where they ordered pizza and beer. Fueled by the bottles on the table, they seemed to have no end of things to talk about. Clarice drank excessively for a woman. The clock showed three a.m. when the man left the table. He walked over to his car, tensely polishing his glasses on his shirt, then slammed the door and drove off. Teo craned his neck to try to see what was going on. The girlfriend was still sitting at the table, drinking and talking to herself. Clarice had gone outside, where she lit a cigarette and stood, arms folded, smoking with brutish movements.

Teo wanted to approach her, but it didn't seem like the right moment.

Clarice flicked her cigarette butt into the gutter and went back inside. She ordered shots of tequila, which were quickly downed with lime and salt. A few hours later she and her friend paid the bill.

They left the bar with their arms draped around each other's shoulders, tripping along the irregular sidewalks of Lapa. Clarice hooted with laughter, leaning on her friend, who looked a little more sober. They talked loudly, unafraid of the poorly lit streets. He followed them in the car with the headlights off. Two empty taxis went past, but they didn't try to flag one.

On a deserted street corner, Clarice and her friend exchanged caresses, which led to breathless kisses, mussed-up hair, and shoes kicked off. They kissed and laughed, mouths thirsty for pleasure. The friend ran her tongue across Clarice's skin, tasting her fair skin and discreet freckles. Clarice opened her mouth and dug her colorful fingernails into the friend's thighs as the friend nibbled her neck.

Teo's first reaction was to close his eyes. How could she? He wanted to jump out of the car, stop them somehow. Didn't she know when enough was enough?

When a couple turned the corner, Clarice pulled back but continued to stroke her friend's hair. A taxi drove past, and the *friend*—now Teo found it hard to call her that—signaled for it to stop. She gave Clarice a noisy smack on the lips and waved at her through the window before the taxi drove off.

Clarice couldn't even walk in a straight line. A car sped past honking as she was crossing a street, and she came to her senses just in time to throw herself onto the sidewalk, cursing at the driver. She picked herself up with difficulty, blood trickling from a grazed knee. She took another few steps and fell again. She found a dark corner, the doorstep of an old house, and fell asleep right there and then.

Teo approached her in silence, not wanting to scare her. He took her arm and stroked her hair to wake her up.

Clarice half opened her eyes. "What?"

"Let's go. Come with me."

"What?"

"You're sleeping in the street. Come with me—I'll take you home."

She accepted, allowing him to support her full weight. He helped her into the Vectra and she leaned her head back. The smell of alcohol flooded the car.

"What're you doing here?" she asked, her words all scrambled.

Teo thought of an answer, but Clarice went back to sleep, eyes moving rapidly as if in a nightmare. Who was she dreaming about?

. . .

He parked in front of her house. A few people were already waking up for work that Tuesday morning. The light was tenuous and fresh. The clock on the dashboard read five-thirty a.m. He found a bunch of keys in her bag and woke her up.

"Which one is the right key?"

"That one."

"Let's go. I'll help you."

He got out of the car.

"Watch your step." He held her by the forearm and caught a whiff of her perfume suffocated by the alcohol. There was some barking on the other side of the stone wall, but the fact that it didn't come any nearer made Teo conclude that the dogs were locked up. He turned the key and walked in.

Clarice was incapable of walking without falling. She moaned when he turned on the light. Her hair was disheveled, her dress, rumpled. Teo helped her lie down on the sofa in the living room. The room was enormous, with a wooden dining table and furniture, shelves and shelves of legal books and a very large TV.

"Where's the kitchen?"

Clarice closed her eyes, wrapped in the throw blanket on the sofa.

"Who are you? What are you doing here?"

The woman who had just walked into the room was tall, slim, and somewhat desperate looking. She was wearing a burgundy robe.

"I'm just trying to help . . ." said Teo. "She isn't well."

The woman sat down on the sofa. She stroked Clarice's forehead, feeling her temperature. "Well, she's drunk, that's for sure. What've you done with my daughter?"

"I didn't do anything. I didn't even drink. I found her in the street, by chance. Where's the kitchen?"

"Why do you want to know?"

"We should give her something sweet."

Clarice's mother eyed him suspiciously. She patted her daughter's cheeks, but she was unresponsive. "She's in a terrible state. It might be an alcoholic coma."

"It'll help if she ingests some glucose."

"Are you a doctor, by any chance?"

"Medical student."

"What's your name?"

"Teo."

"I'm Helena, her mother. You can go now. I'll take care of this."

Helena took Clarice by the arm, lifting her up.

"If you need it, I can help."

"That won't be necessary. Thank you."

"I know Clarice."

Helena stopped and stared at him. "Oh, so you two are friends?"

"We're . . ." He struggled to find the right word.

"He's my boyfriend, Mum," slurred Clarice.

Teo doubted his ears, and Helena repeated, "Boyfriend?"

"My new boyfriend. Talk tomorrow, Teo," she said, and he was pleased that she knew his name. "Thanks for everything."

Helena and Clarice disappeared down the corridor.

Later, lying in bed, Teo couldn't sleep. *He's my boyfriend, Mum . . .*

What did she mean by that? Clarice was fragile. She drank too much and did things she shouldn't. How else to explain the scene with her friend? Did she know he'd seen it all?

Now that he thought about it, he was certain it was the friend who had taken the initiative: she'd taken advantage of Clarice's state to force herself on her, to steal kisses and embraces. He would never do such a thing. He preferred to win her over discreetly, with small gestures, showing her how they could be happy together.

Talk tomorrow, Teo . . .

4

Teo awoke to the sound of his cell ringing, but the line went dead when he answered it. He didn't recognize the number and decided to wait for the person to call back. It was two o'clock in the afternoon, and he was in a good mood. There was a certain beauty in the colors of his bedroom. He found a note from his mother on the living room table. She asked why he had come home so late and said she was going to spend the day in Paquetá with Marli. If Teo got hungry, there was some ricotta lasagna in the fridge. He wasn't hungry or thirsty or sleepy. The only thing he wanted was to see Clarice again.

He showered and left. There was no reason to worry about whether they were going to see each other: she'd said herself that they'd talk the next day. He thought the polite thing to do would be to buy her a gift, so he stopped off at a bookshop on the way there. The perfect book was in the window: a beautifully bound collection of short stories by Clarice Lispector. A

five-hundred-page hardback edition. He paid and asked the at-
tendant to gift-wrap it. Colorful wrapping paper, a nice bow, and
a card.

He rang the doorbell. After checking his cologne and patting
his wet hair, he put his hands behind his back, hiding the present.

It was Clarice who opened the door, looking fascinating in a
billowy, comfortable nightgown. She didn't seem at all displeased
to see him. "Hi, Teo. Come in."

Lying around the living room were piles of clothes. Two pink
Samsonite suitcases with wheels were open on the coffee table.
Clarice moved some underwear off the sofa so he could sit down.

"How are you?"

"I'm fine. Thanks for the help," she said. She was taking
clothes out of the smaller suitcase and putting them into the big-
ger one, folding them at a leisurely pace.

"I was in the area and decided to stop by to say hi."

"I'm glad you did. I wanted to thank you for yesterday."

"It was nothing. I'm glad you're okay."

"With a massive headache, you mean."

"Or that. It'll be gone soon."

Clarice bent down to pick up a coat, and Teo caught sight of
the bandage on her grazed knee.

"Are you going away?" he asked.

"Today," she said. "To focus on my screenplay. Me and my laptop. I want to finish it."

"Where are you going?"

"Teresópolis. It's my spiritual retreat, my place for introspec-
tion. In Rio we spend too much time, money, and energy on useless things."

"When do you get back?"

"I don't know. I think I'm going to stay for a while. Dad's away
on business, and my mother doesn't have anyone else to nag. She

won't get off my case. I need some time away from people sometimes. And I'm on vacation from university. I'll probably stay
about three months."

"What about Christmas?"

"I don't know if I'll be back for Christmas."

"I thought we could go out for dinner tonight."

"I'm going to take off as soon as I finish packing. Maybe
when I get back."

Clarice was slipping through his fingers.

"Will I also have to wait to read your screenplay?"

"My screenplay?" she smiled. "Do you really want to read it?"

"Of course." She said she'd be back in a minute and headed
down the corridor.

Teo didn't know what to do. The disarray of the living room
perturbed and interested him at the same time. He wanted to see
Clarice's room, to know everything about her life right away.
Three months was too long.

"I haven't finished yet. I got nothing done the last few days.
But there's enough there for you to get an idea," she said when
she returned, handing him a sheaf of pages stapled together.

"'Perfect Days,'" he read.

"That's the best I've been able to come up with so far. The argument is at the beginning, but I still haven't written the synop-
sis. I have serious problems with synopses."

"Want to improvise one for me?"

She narrowed her eyes and thought for a moment. She was
beautiful.

"I already told you it's a road movie, right? Amanda, Priscilla,
and Carol. Three friends. Amanda's just broken up with her
boyfriend. Not the other two—they've always been single. They
go on a trip to Teresópolis together. To the same hotel I'm going
to write at. Dwarf Lake Farm Hotel. Heated chalets, fondue,

and a lake with pedal boats. No cellphone reception. It's wonderful there."

"It sounds like it," he said. "Go on."

"Well, at the hotel they meet a foreigner, a Frenchman, and decide to travel with him to an island. They stop at different places along the way. And they have a few adventures, some romantic, some tragic. Anyway, you're going to read it."

"It sounds good."

"I hope it is. I'm open to comments and suggestions. All criticism must be moderate," she said with a laugh.

"I'll read it and let you know what I think," he said. Then, plucking up his courage, he asked, "Can I have your number?"

Clarice stopped packing. She sat on the coffee table, elbows resting on her knees, and looked at him.

"I thought you already had it."

"Nope."

"Are you sure you didn't get it on Saturday?"

"I wouldn't be asking for it if I had," he said, trying not to sound gruff.

"You called me on Sunday. From the Institute of Geography and Statistics."

All the beautiful things he wanted to say to her evaporated that very instant.

"I don't know what you're talking about."

"I wasn't born yesterday," she said slowly, certain of what she was saying. "I got a weird phone call on Sunday. The man said he was from the institute. His voice and way of speaking were a lot like yours, and he asked me all kinds of questions. But you see, I called the number back later in the day, and an old man told me it was a phone booth in Copacabana."

"I didn't—"

"Interestingly enough, the institute had my phone number but didn't have me in their system. They didn't know my surname or my date of birth, because the guy asked how old I was. Besides which, I seriously doubt they conduct random surveys on Sundays. Someone tried to trick me and called just to get information about me. So my question is, what do you really want?"

"Clarice, I . . . swear I don't know what you're talking about. You must be confusing me with—"

"No, I'm not. You found me in Lapa in the middle of the night. Do you mean to say you just happened to be passing by there too?"

"It was a coincidence!"

"And without asking where I lived, you brought me home. You knew where I lived."

"You told me your address when you got in the car. You were drunk! Do you think I guessed it?"

He didn't know what else to say. Was it shame or self-loathing that he felt?

"You've been following me. You got my phone number at the barbecue. You called yourself from my cell." She picked up her phone from the tangle of clothes. "Here it is. Ninety-eight, three, three, two, ninety, ninety. That's your number. Want me to call it to be sure?"

"You wouldn't do that—"

"I already did. I called you earlier today. You sounded sleepy. I recognized your voice right away. On Sunday, you called me with that cock-and-bull story and found out where I studied. On Monday you started following me and discovered where I lived. You followed me to Lapa last night. Look, I'm grateful to you for helping me. But don't you think all this stalking's a bit creepy?"

"I'm not stalking you. And I don't know what phone call you're talking about."

She smiled, shaking her head. She seemed so calm as she

revealed how she'd caught him out. Clarice was the kind of woman who acted calm even when she was nervous.

"I'll give you a kiss if you know my surname," she said.

"Come again?"

"I said I'll give you a kiss if you know my surname," she repeated slyly. "And you have to agree, I never told you my surname. But you're such a lucky guy, you might just get it right, hey?"

"You'd give someone a kiss just to prove you're right?"

"I don't want to prove anything. I just want to show you that the things you've done are a little insane. We barely know each other, Teo."

He moistened his lips. Apologizing would be pathetic. Clarice despised him.

"You don't have to explain," she said. "I know sometimes people do things that don't make much sense. But now you need to keep a distance. It isn't cool. I understand you like me. If you must know, I like you too. You seem like a nice guy. But that's not the way to get close to me. That's what crazy people do. Mental institutions, and so on."

"You're right, Clarice. I'm really sorry."

He stood, not knowing why. He didn't want to leave.

"You're really very smart," he said. "Maybe that's what drew me to you. In the state you were in, it's amazing how much you remember."

She went back to her packing, as if the matter were resolved. "I've got an excellent memory."

"Then you remember what you told your mother. When she asked who I was, do you remember what you said?"

"I said you were my boyfriend."

Teo got goose pimples when he heard her say it again. It felt real.

"So why did you say it?"

"For the hell of it. My mother's a pain in the ass. She always complains about my boyfriends. That one smokes pot, that one doesn't have any money, and that one smokes pot and doesn't have any money. And I noticed she liked you: you have neat hair, you don't stink or smoke. You study medicine, you're polite, and you brought her drunk daughter home without her getting raped along the way. She liked you. So why not make the old girl happy?"

"People *do* do things that don't make sense. I don't know why I'm here, Clarice. All I know is that I want to be here, you know? I liked it when you said that yesterday. But I don't really know why. I just did, I just do. I like you. And I wish that what you told you mother were true, and not just to 'make the old girl happy.'"

He turned to face her, thinking he'd just given a beautiful speech.

She laughed. "Been there myself. It happens to everyone. Too much anxiety, not enough sleep. And even though it was pretty bizarre, I thought it was pretty clever, getting my cell and calling yours."

"Will you give me a chance?"

She shook her head almost imperceptibly. She finished packing her suitcase and closed the smaller one, which was now empty. She stretched her arms and torso, relaxing her neck.

"That's not how it works," she said. "We'd never work out. We can be friends. You're not my type: a bit too clean-cut, too traditional. I like adventures. The wild side, you know? You'd get sick of me. And I'd get sick of you too."

Clarice seemed like one of those women who were never going to get married: single and self-sufficient.

"There's no harm in trying," he said. He took a step forward and held out the present. "Look, I bought this for you."

She unwrapped it.

"You told me you'd never read anything by her. I thought you'd like it."

"Thanks. I'll give it a go." She left the book on top of the suitcase.

"Why don't you think a bit about what I said?"

"I already told you. We can be friends." She sounded like she was growing irritated.

"I don't want to be your friend. I can't—"

"Oh, for fuck's sake! I'm trying not to be a bitch, but you just don't let up!"

"You don't understand that—"

"Take your book and forget me. Seriously, pretend we never met. Forget what I said yesterday, okay? I was drunk. I didn't mean it. Don't bother me anymore. I don't want you to call me, follow me, or buy me presents."

"Clarice, I—" The feeling of shame came back full force. "I don't like it when you talk to me like that." He moved forward, touched her arm.

Clarice pulled away. "I don't give a shit if you like it or not. Fuck off! I tried to be nice, but you don't get it! If you've got problems with women, go pay a prostitute or something."

The insults kept coming. The sweet, hoarse voice was the same, the gestures too, but she was another woman. That wasn't his Clarice.

He took another step forward, needing to shut her up. He picked up the book and slammed it down violently on her head. Clarice against Clarice. He hit her a few more times until she was quiet.

Her slender body slumped over the coffee table. Blood trickled from the back of her neck, dripping onto some shirts on the ground. The cover of the book, previously an amorphous design in pastel colors, also turned dark red. Clarice didn't move. He took her pulse: she was still alive.

His relief wasn't enough to stop his legs from shaking. He glanced at the door, sensing that someone was about to arrive. Footsteps on the floor. His imagination prevented him from moving. Nobody appeared. He was coherent, rational, unflinching; he'd work out what to do. Clarice's unmoving peacefulness pricked his nerves.

He opened the two Samsonites and transferred the clothes from the larger one into the smaller one. He smashed them in and zipped it up with some difficulty. Then he placed Clarice in the large suitcase, leaving it open a crack so she could breathe. He tidied up the clothes that were left on the sofa and put her cell in his pocket.

He stood the two suitcases on end at the door and peeked through the crack in the larger one to make sure Clarice looked comfortable. Then he dragged the coffee table to one side and rolled up the bloodstained rug. He took a look outside: a few passersby, all distracted. He put the rug and suitcases in the trunk of the car and checked again to make sure Clarice seemed okay. He returned the coffee table to its place, locked the door of the house, and drove off.

5

As he tried to calm his nerves, Teo reflected that luck was on his side. His mother's day trip to Paquetá would allow him to hide Clarice at his place until he decided what to do. And Clarice's trip to the farm hotel in Teresópolis meant that it would take her parents a while to work out she was missing.

Teo took the service elevator up. Samson came to the door, sniffing the suitcases. He wagged his tail and barked loudly. Teo ordered him to be quiet. He laid Clarice on his bed—she looked like a crumpled angel.

The larger of the two pink suitcases, an Aeris Spinner, didn't fit under his bed, and he had to empty out the top compartment of his wardrobe in order to put it away. He went to the bathroom to get gauze and antiseptic to treat the wounds on Clarice's head: there was a small cut on the back of her neck that perplexed him. He didn't really know where it had come from. Furtively, he took the opportunity to stroke her brown hair. It was so soft!

He slipped off her ballet flats, which struck him as terribly uncomfortable. He remembered her taking photographs at Lage

Park: she had walked around indifferently in those same heelless shoes, which set her apart from other women, who were always wearing too much makeup and platforms.

He listened to her breathing, synchronizing his own with hers, and sat on the edge of the bed, watching her closely, but still at a respectful distance. He didn't want to come across as sick or a psycho. With time, he'd prove to Clarice that she was wrong. He was incapable of abusing her: he lacked the animal instinct that men received at birth. This was just one of his qualities. If there were more people like him, the world would be a better place.

Clarice would wake up soon and ask to leave. She'd stomp down the stairs, indignant, left hand pressing on her wound, nervously puffing on a Vogue menthol cigarette in her right hand. She'd swear at him, wary of any new attack. He'd be arrested, execrated publically. In enormous print, the newspapers would call him a kidnapper.

He felt bad: it was the first time he had thought of himself as a villain. By stuffing Clarice in a suitcase and bringing her home, had he become a criminal? It hadn't been premeditated, nor was he interested in a ransom. He just wanted what was best for Clarice. The blow to her head had been an absurd, impromptu gesture. He was genuinely sorry. Perhaps he should tell her that. Say he was sorry.

But what if she didn't forgive him?

He couldn't let her go. He couldn't let her leave until he knew how she'd react. Even if she didn't go to the police, she'd avoid him—and that would be unbearable too. The idea of killing her wafted past, but he immediately dismissed it.

He whistled a melody out of impatience or nervousness. Samson wouldn't stop barking, his long paws scratching at the bedroom door. Teo didn't want the dog to sniff Clarice or her suitcases. He left the room, locked the door from the outside, and shut Samson in the laundry room.

He washed his face in the bathroom and felt his stress drain away with the water. Looking in the mirror, he found himself unexpectedly good-looking, as if Clarice's grace had rubbed off on him: his pale face had a distinct handsomeness, in harmony with the smile at the corner of his mouth. He rummaged through the medicine in the cupboard until he found the box of Hypnolid, the tranquilizer his mother took to sleep.

When she got home, Patricia would suspect something if she found Samson barking. Better to sedate the dog so he'd wake up the next morning, by which time Teo would have worked out what to do with Clarice. He opened the dog's mouth and shoved a pill down his throat. Ten minutes later Samson was quiet.

Teo went back to his room but opened the door slowly, considering the possibility that Clarice was now awake and waiting for him, ready to attack. He immediately chided himself for the violence of the idea. As his eyes slid down her neck in a delightful game of counting freckles, she moved a little. She half opened her eyes woozily, and he didn't know what to do. Should he apologize or act unflappable? Sympathetic or dictatorial?

She frowned, brushed her hair off her face with slow movements, and scanned the furniture. She moaned with pain. Teo raced to the bathroom and tapped two pills into his hand. He crushed them up and dissolved them in a glass of water.

"Drink this."

Her face clouded over, still groggy. She seemed frightened too.

"It's for your headache. It'll make it better." He avoided long sentences, because he didn't like lying to her.

Clarice drank it. She placed the glass on the bedside table and moved her lips, lisping a question. Her voice faltered and she tried again.

"What are you doing with me?"

Her tone made him sad. He left the room, saying he wouldn't

be long. In the living room, he paced back and forth. Five, ten, fifteen, twenty minutes. When he went back, she was asleep again.

The sex shop was three blocks from his building, on the corner of Hilário de Gouveia and Avenida Nossa Senhora. Teo had always been curious about it. He thought it funny that the place—with posters promising stripteases and erotic films free of charge—was right next to the church he attended with his mother on Sundays. Sin and redemption side by side.

He knew he was going to regret it the minute he walked in. He could imagine what they sold there—and his imagination alone was already making him queasy. That's why he had always put off going there, and he'd have done so forever if it weren't necessary.

He avoided looking at the wall of vibrators and plastic penises in a range of sizes, colors, and thicknesses—all terrifying—and walked down the aisle, surrounded by leather strap-ons, whips, and skimpy costumes. A skinny shop assistant asked if she could help, and he feigned indecision. He let the woman show him around the shop: penis rings, lubricants, fruit-flavored condoms.

"We also have chocolate, sir." She squeezed two drops of the edible gel onto the back of Teo's hand and told him to try it.

"Do you mean lick it?"

"Yeah."

The woman listed off the qualities of the product as if she were selling a household appliance. He didn't want to touch that goo with his tongue. What if it made him sick? He tasted it, watched closely by the shop assistant, and asked to see handcuffs. He looked at a number of different models and chose the most resistant, with an extra key and no safety catch. The shop assistant didn't care that he seemed like a sadomasochist.

He asked if they sold gags.

"We have several. There's a ball gag, there's one with a wooden bite. We have one with an O-ring to hold the mouth open, you know? For oral . . ."

He was shocked at the creativity that went into the things.

"We've also got a face harness with a gag," the shop assistant went on. "You adjust it at the back of the neck with a buckle. And we've got a padded gag too, of course. Here it is. To make her really submissive, you see? The padded bit goes in the mouth, as far as the throat. She'll be quiet and all yours."

"Right."

"There's also the collar. It's a thick collar with a gag. The women love it. I'll get it from the stockroom."

"Don't worry about it."

"Which one do you want then?"

"I'll take the last two. The one with the harness and the padded one."

"Handcuffs?"

"Six."

He noticed that the quantity impressed the shop assistant.

"What about the gel?"

He bought one, to change her focus. When he was at the cash register, he noticed a contraption with two rods covered in leather, with cuffs at the extremities.

"What's that?"

"An arm and leg spreader," she said, "with hand and ankle cuffs." She handed it to Teo. It was pretty heavy. "There are padlocks, which you adjust with buckles. Each of these rods is thirty inches long. And it's very versatile. You can use it as an arm and leg spreader, but the hand and ankle cuffs can also be used separately. See, you clip them on with these snap hooks. A kind of X with two rods."

"I'll take that too."

He put the face harness with the gag on Clarice. He laid her out on a gym mat, as he didn't want her to have a lot of aches and pains afterward, and pushed her under the bed, cuffing her ankles to its legs. He changed the sheets and arranged the bedspread so that the handcuffs couldn't be seen. Then he wrote his mother a note.

He drove to the university pathology lab. He got his cage of lab mice from the animal house and headed for the research room, where there were other students. In the refrigerator, he found three ampoules of Thyolax, an anesthetic used for intraperitoneal injections in mice, much more efficient than Hypnolid. He hid the ampoules in the sawdust of the cage and, for twenty minutes, pretended to be recording results. When he left, he made sure no one was in the corridor and hid the ampoules in the pocket of his lab coat.

A short while later he was home. Patricia had arrived and was watching TV. She told him her day had been tiring and that she needed to go to bed.

"Do you know where I left the Hypnolid, darling?"

He chided himself for having forgotten to return the box to the cupboard. In his haste to tend to Clarice, he had left it on his bedside table. He imagined what might have happened if his mother had decided to look for it on her own: she could have gone into his room, maybe even looked under the bed. He was lucky she was confined to that wheelchair.

He told her he didn't know anything about the Hypnolid.

Patricia turned off the TV and said she was going back to Paquetá the next day with Marli—their neighbor was exhibiting her paintings at an arts and crafts fair. He locked the bedroom door and lifted Clarice back onto the bed.

It was four a.m. by the time she looked like she was going to open her eyes. Teo approached her with the syringe. He found a vein in her right arm and injected the Thyolax solution. Clarice became inert almost that instant: sleeping beauty. Until he worked out what to do, he'd have to keep her sedated.

6

Teo awoke with a fright. He'd had a nightmare in which he was chasing Clarice through a dark forest, and the images were still very vivid in his mind. He looked at her on the bed and took her pulse. Clarice was still asleep, indifferent to chases in unfriendly settings. The sheets were laced with her scent. It was delicious, magical. They had spent their first night together.

Patricia turned the door handle and, finding it locked, knocked. "Open the door, Teo."

She sounded hurried and weary. He hid the Hypnolid in the cupboard with the suitcases and returned Clarice to the gym mat under the bed. He decided not to put the cuffs on her; it was highly unlikely that she'd wake up now. He opened the door a crack with a sleepy face and kissed his mother on the forehead.

She was wearing a purple dress and gold hoop earrings. "Why did you take so long?"

"I was asleep, Mother."

She craned her neck to see into his room. "You never lock the door. What's going on?"

"I must have woken up during the night and gone to the bathroom or something. I guess I accidentally locked it when I came back."

"Accidentally locked it? How strange."

"Strange?" He took two steps out of the room, forcing Patricia to wheel back toward the living room.

"You're acting weird," she said. "And Samson is so slow today. I've never seen him like this. I offered him some dog biscuits, but he barely got up. He just lay there staring at me with watery eyes."

"Do you think he might be sick?"

"I don't know, but I wonder if he got hold of my Hypnolid."

Samson had a whole history of such incidents weighing against him: he had already chewed up correspondence and destroyed sandals.

"Don't exaggerate, Mother! Where did you last leave it?"

"In the bathroom cupboard, I think. Now I'm not sure."

"I'll help you look for it."

"I had a bad dream last night. I dreamed that something awful was happening to you. Something really bad, darling. I couldn't get back to sleep afterward."

"What was it?"

"I don't remember."

Teo stroked his mother's dyed hair and told her to not to worry. "I had a bad dream too. But it wasn't about me," he said. "In fact, it was no big deal. Most dreams are nothing."

"I know, but . . . I feel empty. This huge emptiness, darling. I don't know how to explain it. All I know is that it's inside here. And I feel it." She was looking at him in a very unpleasant way. "Don't do anything foolish, Teo. For your mother, who loves you."

"I love you too," he said because he had no choice.

Samson came into the hallway, still a little groggy. He curled up by Patricia's legs and licked her calves.

"Okay, okay, I've got Samson too." She smiled, drying the tears from her eyes. "But the worst he can do is eat things around the house."

"I'm not going to do anything, Mother."

Samson went to the door of his room and gave a little yelp, then another and another. He growled and bared his teeth.

"Are you hiding something in there?"

"It's nothing."

"I want to go in."

"Trust me."

"I want to go in your room. Can you step aside?"

He shook his head.

"Get out of the way. I want to see what's in there."

"No, Mother."

"Teo, I don't have all day. What are you hiding from me?"

"Okay, you win. I'm with a girl. She spent the night here."

"A girl?"

His mother had expected anything but that.

"Her name's Clarice. We're kind of seeing each other. Sorry I didn't say anything."

"I want to see her."

"She's sleeping."

"That's okay, I'll can see her asleep."

"She hasn't got any clothes on, Mother."

"You go in and cover her so she's decent. I think you're lying to me. You haven't got a girl in there."

Teo sighed. "Wait a minute."

He lifted Clarice off the gym mat, trying not to make any noise. She had a hospital smell about her. He laid her on the bed, positioned her head to one side on the pillow, hiding the wound on her neck, and covered her with the quilt. Then he put the cuffs and gags away in the wardrobe and opened the door.

"Be quick. I don't want her to wake up and see you in my room."

His mother nodded, eyes bulging. She rolled closer to the bed. "Your girlfriend's pretty," she said with a smile.

He was pleased. Clarice deserved all the praise in the world. Samson came into the room and was kicked out.

Patricia left. "I'm sorry I didn't believe you. I'm glad you're seeing someone. She looks like a nice girl."

The doorbell rang, and he ran to open it. It was Marli in an overly sparkly dress. She called to Patricia and said they were late. Teo kissed his mother good-bye, wished Marli good sales at the fair in Paquetá, and was finally alone. Samson started barking again. He couldn't keep on sedating the dog forever. Nor did he want to do the same to Clarice. Now that Patricia knew she existed, he couldn't say she was still asleep when she got back. He felt a tightness in his throat. Time was running out.

H e put two Hypnolid pills in the dog's food, which was devoured as soon as he set down the bowl. A few minutes later the flat was silent and peaceful. He took the opportunity to relax.

Close to midday, a noise surprised him. Clarice's cell was vibrating in the wardrobe. Her ring tone was an instrumental version of AC/DC's "Highway to Hell." On the screen it said HELENA. Teo turned it off, feeling bad. In such a short space of time, he had made some serious mistakes: he'd forgotten to put away the Hypnolid, he'd left Clarice's cell on, and worst of all, now his mother was going to inquire about his girlfriend, schedule dinners, and ask to meet her family.

Trying to calm down, he organized Clarice's clothes. They were crumpled, thrown into the smaller pink Samsonite in the haste of the previous day. He found the book he'd bought her and, beside it, the screenplay for *Perfect Days*. He put the book in the drawer of his bedside table. The blood on the cover was a wound: the stain had crept over the author's name, and now all that could be seen was "ice Lispector" under the title. He wanted Clarice to read it, as he knew she'd like it, but he had the feeling she'd despised the present.

He saw Clarice as a diamond in the rough. Every relationship presupposes some give-and-take, an exchange of favors, so that the two poles are mutually seduced, subject to their own surprises. Teo had been surprised by Clarice: drawn in by her beauty, snared by her spontaneity, and condemned by her lemon-gummy-flavored kiss. He also knew that he could surprise her. He was a man of many qualities: well educated, with a future. He'd be a good father (truth be told, he'd never thought about having children, but now the idea didn't seem so bad) and a good husband (he knew how women deserved to be treated). He wasn't handsome, nor was he ugly.

At any rate, aesthetics excited, but they didn't sustain a relationship. The connecting force was in the give-and-take, in the surrender and discovery. The term *symbiosis* seemed appropriate. He looked up the exact definition in the dictionary. "A relationship between two beings that live in community, in which both are benefited although in varying proportion, such that they are unable to live without each other."

Leaning back in his swiveling chair, Teo leafed through the screenplay. *Perfect Days* was the doorway to many insights. How many of Clarice's nuances would be revealed? Like a child saving the best piece of pie for last, he put off reading the text. He preferred to come to it like good wine: first the label, then the aroma, and finally the flavor. He read random lines, without paying attention to their content. The characters in the story were pretty crass. Clarice wrote like she spoke: in short, bold sentences, with few syntactical inversions.

He set the screenplay aside. He was afraid to read it and conclude that there was nothing special there, just a falsely promising variation on all the other girls he'd met, uninteresting and talentless.

He went back to piling up clothes. In a compartment of the larger suitcase, he found the camera he'd seen Clarice use at Lage Park. He transferred the photos to his computer and examined them on the screen one by one. He smiled at the ones in which Clarice was smiling, remembering where he was at the exact instant she had struck this or that pose. He deleted the ones with her friend in them, with her greasy hair and promiscuous smile. He was doing Clarice a favor: he was sure she didn't want to remember the girl who'd forced herself on her with those lesbian kisses.

Just out of curiosity, he opened Photoshop. He selected photos of his own and, cutting and pasting, created new moments: the two of them hugging a tree, strolling through the garden, sitting on a wooden bench. In a more daring—and almost perfect—montage, he placed Clarice with her head on his lap, with the lake and the fountain in the background. She was smiling and seemed to be enjoying him playing with her hair. Teo was smiling too. The photo was as realistic as the ones that had given origin to it. He made it his new computer wallpaper.

He selected others (only the most beautiful ones, but it was so hard to choose!) and saved them to a CD: thirty-one photos: twenty-seven just of her, and the others of them together. He went out, leaving Clarice sedated under the bed without cuffs—a display of trust—and walked three blocks to get the photos printed.

The afternoon rolled past lazily. Four hours later Teo returned to the photo shop. He chose an album with a gold cover, which seemed suited to Clarice's classic style. The photos had turned out beautifully. They were a real couple, smiling out of the album's plastic sleeves. The images had gained a predictive quality, registering moments that they were going to experience together. He was moved. He wanted to show the shop assistant or the old lady who was asking if they sold USB sticks there.

As he was pulling his wallet out of his pocket, he felt his cell vibrate. It was his home phone. Was it his mother? Was she back from Paquetá already? Had she noticed something wrong?

He answered nervously. All he could think of was Clarice.

Patricia was screaming and crying, saying things he couldn't understand. He asked her to speak slowly. It was no use. It took him more than two minutes to understand. Samson was dead.

When he got home, Teo found the dog rolled up in the throw blanket. He patted him and held two fingers in front of his cold nose. Nothing. In the living room, Patricia was shaking in her wheelchair, consoled by Marli, who was spouting a bunch of nonsensical condolences. The dog had played a fundamental role in his mother's life: she needed to feel *truly* loved by someone.

Teo said he was terribly sorry. At the back of the pantry, he found the cardboard box they had used to transport the TV when they had moved there. He placed the golden retriever inside it.

"Let's give Samson the burial he deserves," said Patricia.

Teo sat in the armchair watching his mother cry, as sincerely as if she'd lost her son. He'd never be able cry like that for anyone. Maybe for Clarice. But he'd have to put some effort into it.

"Let's get him to a vet," she said. "I want to know what my baby died of."

Her grief was too much. All she had to do was buy another

dog. Sometimes she seemed to forget that they didn't lead the life they used to. Discovering the cause of death was an expense they could do without and would only bring trouble. Teo didn't believe he was responsible for the dog's death, but he was worried that the pills might show up in an examination of Samson's stomach contents.

When he had gone back to the photo shop to pick up the album, he'd left Clarice on the gym mat under his bed. He'd covered the mat with a sheet, because the floor was cold. Now an acrid smell of urine filled the room. Clarice's nightgown was wet. He was disgusted. Then he chided himself for his reaction. He couldn't be disgusted by the woman he loved. She was resting and had no way of going to the bathroom.

It was too risky to clean up Clarice with Patricia and Marli nearby. They could walk in at any moment—and in that state of nerves, his mother wouldn't tolerate a locked door. He squirted some cologne around and went back to the living room.

"I understand you want to get an autopsy done," he said. "If that's what you want, I'm right behind you."

Patricia dried her eyes and gave her son a wan smile.

"But it's expensive," he continued, "and we don't have a lot of money to throw around."

"I have some savings, Teo. I need to know what Samson died of. He was fine until just a little while ago."

"He was already ten years old, Mother! We looked after him well. We made him happy while he was here. There's no point dwelling on it now."

"I think he ate my Hypnolid," sobbed Patricia. "And I won't be able to . . . I won't be able to live with myself until I'm sure he didn't die because I made a stupid mistake. I feel so terrible."

"Don't. What's done is done. All we can do now is give him a proper burial."

"I want a necropsy. What if I was the cause of his death? It's like killing your own child."

"I don't think it was the Hypnolid. How could Samson have got into the bathroom and wolfed down a box of pills without a trace? We're going to find the damn box behind a piece of furniture any day now, and the mystery will be solved."

"Yeah, love, stay calm. He's right," said Marli, sitting on the side of the armchair. "I doubt he could've eaten the pills, plastic and everything. Do you remember how many were in it?"

"Yes, I keep tabs on them so I don't double up."

Teo knew his mother wrote down every pill taken in a little notepad, which was why he couldn't just pretend to stumble across the missing box.

"I'm going to fix myself up," said Patricia. "I want to find a vet open today."

In ten minutes, she was ready. She told Teo he didn't need to go if he had other plans. She and Marli would take a taxi.

Teo tried one last argument. "If they do a necropsy on Samson—they'll open him up, you know? He'll have to be cremated."

He knew his mother considered burials important and couldn't bear the thought of a body in flames in the crematorium. But Patricia said it was no problem: if she couldn't bury him, she'd accept a cremation.

When he finally took Clarice to have a shower, Teo was depressed to see the state she was in, stooped and soaked in urine, like a mental patient. The colors of the bathroom lost their vibrancy, and he found the steam from the hot water suffocating.

He was careful to close the bathroom window, then wet her

face. He removed the gauze covering the wound on her neck and put the tweezers and nail scissors in his pocket: he didn't want sharp objects lying around where she could see them. He sat her on the plastic stool that Patricia used for bathing, facing the water.

"Come on, you won't fall. Hold on here," he said, placing her hands on the grab bar. "Take off your dirty clothes and have a good wash. There's a clean dress on the hook there. Here's a towel. Don't take too long, okay?"

He thought about handcuffing her but didn't think it was necessary. She could barely stand. The water streamed down her face, wetting her clothes and outlining her slender body underneath. Teo slid the shower door closed so the bathmat wouldn't get wet. He left the bathroom inebriated.

From the living room, he listened to the sound of the water against the tiles, the shower being turned off, and the door sliding open. He waited another five minutes before going in. Clarice was sitting on the floor, already wearing the dress he had picked, one with yellow flowers for wearing around the house. Her warm skin smelled of a long shower. Teo dried her hair. He also noticed the tattoo on her left shoulder: three little stars— green, blue, and purple. The first time they had met, he had glimpsed part of it under her top. Now the thin straps of her dress completely revealed crooked stars that looked as if they'd been drawn by a child. He smiled and offered her his hand. She grabbed his wrist and squeezed it hard, as if trying to say something. She stared at him hard. Had she been crying?

Teo laid her down on the bed. He stroked her face and asked if she was okay.

Clarice muttered random words in the strange language that sprouted from her dry mouth.

He went to get an apple and a small knife from the kitchen. He peeled it and told her to chew slowly and be careful not to choke. She hadn't eaten since the previous day, and he didn't want to see her wither away because of him. Looking after each other's health was essential in a good relationship. He gave her half of the apple: she chewed it with her lips, as a trickle of saliva slid down her chin and neck. Teo wiped her chin and told her to eat properly. If necessary, he could serve her forever. He liked watching her eat little by little, so in need of care. He was hungry too, so he ate the other half of the apple.

His thoughts wandered back to Lage Park—the colorful vegetation, the picnics ruffled by a light breeze. He wanted that happiness to last forever. He let Clarice eat at her own pace and liked it when she opened her mouth to ask for more.

"I want to go," she said finally. Her voice was firmer.

"We need to talk."

"I want to go."

"I'm not going to keep you prisoner here. Stay calm."

Clarice wasn't calm. She thrashed about in a fury and talked in a loud voice, rudely, which repulsed him. He had to use force to control her. He cuffed her wrist to her bicep so she couldn't move her arm and then, exasperated, injected her with a new dose of Thyolax—this time in her left arm, because her right one was sporting a purple blotch from the last injection.

He rested in the swiveling chair, and his annoyance slowly dissipated. He got Clarice's cell from the wardrobe and turned it on. Four messages popped onto the screen. The first was from Laura, whom he deduced was the friend who had taken advantage of Clarice. It had been sent on the Tuesday afternoon. Laura thanked her for the previous night—she used the adjectives *great* and *unforgettable* to describe it—and suggested they talk if Clarice was confused about *what had happened*. She signed off with infinite kisses, saying she was waiting *anxiously*— the insolent adverb was there—for her reply. Teo deleted the message.

The next was from the operator, with the number of missed calls. Four from Helena, three from Breno, and another three from Laura. Teo wanted to know who Breno was. Beside his name was a photo of Woody Allen as a young man. Teo went into Clarice's conversation history and saw that the third message was from Breno, sent that morning, apologizing for his jealous behavior and saying he needed to talk to her and that he still loved her. At no point did he call Clarice by her name, but "my love" at the beginning and "my sonata" at the end, before repeating "I love you."

Teo reread it: *my sonata*. The way Breno had chosen to address her—and the number of times the verb *to love* appeared—made Teo feel betrayed. The guy couldn't write and referred to Clarice with a possessive pronoun as if she belonged to him.

Teo deleted the contact, but before erasing their entire conversation history (over a year's worth of messages), he decided to reply. He was succinct, almost rude:

I DON'T WANT TO TALK. I DON'T LOVE YOU ANYMORE. WE'RE DONE. I'VE MOVED ON. FORGET ME.

It was after midnight. Teo heard the key in the door and went to greet his mother. Patricia's eyes were swollen, and a box of tissues was sitting on her lap. The guilt was weighing on her.

"The results won't be ready for twenty days," she said. "I need to sleep."

He read the last message on Clarice's cell. It was from Helena:

HONEY, I TRIED YOUR CELL BUT IT'S OUT OF RANGE. HAVE
YOU GONE TO TERESÓPOLIS? CALL ME WHEN YOU CAN TO
LET ME KNOW YOU GOT THERE OK. YOUR DAD SAYS HI.
TAKE CARE. MOM. P.S.—DO YOU KNOW WHAT HAPPENED TO
THE LIVING ROOM RUG?

Lying on the sofa, Teo stared at Clarice's cell. His mind raced,
trying to think of a way to explain the disappearance of the rug.
After rereading their previous messages several times, he noticed
that Clarice called her mother by her first name, which struck
him as overly formal. He drafted a few replies, all unsatisfactory,
then scanned the screenplay for words she used a lot. A few minutes later he looked at the result. It wasn't perfect, but he might
be able to get away with it for a while. He hit send:

HELENA, I'M IN TERESÓPOLIS WITH MY NEW BOYFRIEND.
I'VE BEEN WRITING A LOT. THERE'S NO PHONE RECEPTION
AT THE HOTEL, AS YOU KNOW. I'M IN THE TOWN CENTER
NOW. HE BROUGHT ME TO THE MOST BEAUTIFUL SPOT FOR
DINNER. IT'S A BIT LATE TO CALL. TELL DAD I SAID HI. I'VE
GOT THE RUG. LONG STORY, TELL YOU LATER. DON'T
WORRY. I'M FINE AND HAPPY. LOVE, CLARICE.

Clarice smiled at him from the passenger seat. Without Teo
having to do a thing, she leaned over to steal a kiss. Then
another and another. He couldn't return the affection, because he
was driving. The highway disappeared under the dashboard,
trees flashed past on both sides. Clarice nibbled at his cheek, and
it felt nice. Her slightly protuberant teeth grazed his skin. He
called her "little rat," an affectionate nickname that she didn't
seem to mind; in fact, she thought it was funny.

They weren't in the car anymore, but sitting at a table with friends, lots of friends (some of whom, to tell the truth, he didn't even know by name). He told everyone the story of how they'd met: the kiss at the barbecue, his ploy to get her number (now they all thought it was funny), his attempts to woo her, her resistance, the Clarice Lispector book as a present (Clarice Lispector?! They roared with laughter). Then they kissed, to show everyone that they were still in love after all they'd been through.

Teo half opened his eyes, feeling really good. He didn't want to get up because every movement distanced him from the dream. Slivers of light poked through the blinds and partially lit Clarice's face as she slept beside him. He stroked her hair and leaned close to her, studying her labored breathing and the little teeth that jutted out of her dry lips. *Little rat.* It had an intimate ring to it. He repeated it aloud a few more times. *Little rat, little rat, little rat.*

My little rat.

The idea came to him as if it had been there with them, on the double bed, all along. It was eight-thirty in the morning. Teo got up, full of energy, showered, and pulled on some comfortable clothes. He got the suitcases down from the top of the wardrobe and packed a few changes of clothes, underwear, socks, and shoes. He put some first aid supplies in a toiletry bag and picked out some of his favorite classic and contemporary films to watch with Clarice: *12 Angry Men, The Secret in Their Eyes, Little Miss Sunshine.* He thought about taking *Misery,* but then decided against it. Excessive violence tired him sometimes.

On his desk, he found the lovely black leather doctor's satchel with the combination lock that Patricia had given him when he'd been accepted into the university. He was fond of his satchel and put Clarice's screenplay in it, along with the bloodstained book, the ampoules of Thyolax. He placed Clarice back in the larger suitcase. It was amazing how flexible she was and how she folded up so easily, like a little travel toothbrush.

He took the service elevator down to the garage and put the Samsonites in the trunk. Then he headed back upstairs and went to say good morning to his mother. She was sitting up in bed, going over her credit card bills.

"Clarice called. She's going to Teresópolis today, and she invited me to go with her. For a few days, I think."

Patricia looked up at her son. Her exhaustion was evident in her hunched body.

"I don't want to leave you here alone," he continued. "Especially after what happened with Samson."

"Marli will help me if I need it. I'll be fine," said Patricia, as he knew she would. "You really like this girl, don't you?"

"Yeah."

"Then go. Just remember to call from time to time."

"There's no phone reception there. But I'll go into the town center to call, I promise. Can I take the Vectra?"

"Yes, of course. And write down the name of the hotel for me. Leave it on the fridge door."

"Thanks, Mother."

Teo gave her a tight hug. He told her he still had a little time to kill before going to pick up Clarice and sat in front of the TV. When she left the bedroom, he hunted through the chest of drawers for his father's old revolver and stowed it in a compartment of the toiletry bag. He was confident: he would travel with Clarice to Teresópolis, slowly win her over, and—he laughed at the pun—together they would spend *perfect days*.

PERFECT DAYS

A *Screenplay by*
Clarice Manhães

ARGUMENT

Research name

The film starts with a ~~car~~ (posh, old-fashioned, roundish
hood and trunk) on a highway. It is night, and thick smoke
is wafting out the open windows, as if people were smoking
inside. We soon see three friends, all a bit high, laughing
so hard they're crying. Amanda (redhead, skinny, freckled
~ Rita face) is driving. She looks a bit sad, but tries to have
~ uni fun with her friends. From the dialogue, we discover that
Amanda has just broken up with her boyfriend of many
years. Priscilla (brunette, chubby, short hair, wears
Julie thick-rimmed glasses, looks kind of square), sitting in the
front passenger seat, says she'll be fine and that she'll
forget the dickhead. The friend in the backseat, Carol
(brunette, tall, very tall, like a volleyball player, short
hair), is smoking a joint and looks ~~really~~ drunk. They arrive at the Dwarf Lake Farm Hotel. *See if it's OK to use the real name in*

Carol has a serious illness (leukemia) and knows *the film*
she's going to die soon (viewers find out later). The first
night, they talk by the side of the lake. Carol gives her
friends a letter, saying that they'll know when it's time
to open it (in the letter, Carol tells them to continue
traveling if she dies). Then Carol goes to bed. Alone with
Amanda, Priscilla takes the opportunity to confess her
biggest secret: that she's in love with her. Amanda doesn't
know what to say and goes for a walk in the woods on the
hotel grounds to unwind. Priscilla is confused and looks
as if she's going to go after her, but ends up falling in
the lake (the scene is supposed to be ambiguous: viewers

don't know if she fell in the lake by accident or if she tried to kill herself).

Amanda comes across a man sitting at the foot of a tree, thinking. She strikes up a conversation with him and *Vincent* finds out that he is French. The scene has a romantic atmosphere, and they talk a lot (the Frenchman has a thick accent).

The next morning at breakfast, Amanda introduces the Frenchman to her friends. It quickly becomes obvious that Priscilla doesn't like him. There is a sequence of short scenes: the girls on the lake in pedal boats, playing football in a field and cards at night. The Frenchman is always present.

One night the Frenchman tells Amanda that he's going to *I need to go* visit the island of Ilha Grande and invites her to go with *back to* him. Amanda likes the idea and invites her friends. They set *make the* out the next day. On the way there, they get a flat. In the *details of the* scene, the Frenchman changes the tire without a shirt on *scene better* (I'm thinking blond and muscular, a kind of James Dean who says *au revoir*). There won't be a lot of dialogue in this scene. Everything will be written on the actor's faces: Carol looking sad, knowing she's going to die. Priscilla looking jealous. Amanda looking like she's in love. And the mysterious Frenchman (I won't reveal much about who he is or what he wants. I want viewers to share the discomfort of traveling with a stranger).

They end up sleeping in a motel. Carol and Priscilla in one room. Amanda and the Frenchman in another. The screen is divided in two: in Carol and Priscilla's room, the atmosphere is heavy. At the same time, in the other room, we see Amanda and the Frenchman kissing (it's the first time they kiss) and then going to bed together.

They continue on to Ilha Grande. They rent a tent and decide to camp on a deserted beach. The days pass. Priscilla still doesn't like the Frenchman. In one scene, she tries to investigate the guy (she looks for documents and information in his suitcase) while he is swimming in the sea with *Priscilla* Amanda. The Frenchman catches ~~Carol~~ rummaging through his things and is pissed off. He says he's going to leave, and Amanda decides to go with him to Paraty. *Actually, they run away together*

Night falls. On Ilha Grande, we see Carol and Priscilla talking about the fact that Amanda has left. The next morning Priscilla realizes that Carol is dead. She remembers the letter and opens it. Renewed by what Carol wrote, Priscilla *This shit* throws Carol's body into the sea (Carol asks for it in her *has to be* letter) and starts to see life differently. It becomes clear *beautiful* to viewers that Priscilla is okay in spite of everything. *and poetic.*
It's going
Cut to Amanda ~~and the Frenchman in Para~~ty. They wander *to be a* the streets, visit charming shops and famous tourist attrac- *pain in.* tions. At lunch, Amanda asks more about his life, and he *the ass to* changes the subject. He says he wants to take her out for a *write* special dinner that night, when he'll tell her everything she wants to know. Amanda accepts. At dinner, Amanda arrives at the restaurant, but the Frenchman doesn't show. She waits all night until the restaurant closes. When she gets back to *Definitely a* the hotel, she sees that the Frenchman has packed his bags *Scorpio!* and left. Amanda is sad and returns to Ilha Grande to try to find her friends. They aren't there anymore (Amanda doesn't know Carol is dead). She stays there alone, crying, staring out to sea. She realizes how badly she screwed up with her friends and decides never to see them again (she's embarrassed). We see Priscilla again, looking happy, with a pretty girlfriend. Then we see Amanda looking the worse for wear.

Cut. We see a woman lying under a sheet, sleeping. As the camera draws closer, we see that it is Carol. She wakes up with a start to the sound of an alarm clock, as if waking from a dream. Next to the bed are her packed bags. The idea is that viewers should wonder: "Will they really enjoy such perfect days on this trip?"

8

Teo was in a good mood, almost merry in fact. He had put a Caetano Veloso CD on to play. He admired Clarice sleeping—there was a trickle of saliva running from her mouth to her chin, which he wiped off affectionately. Back in the garage of his building, taking advantage of the fact that there was no one around, he had put Clarice in the front passenger seat, cuffed in such a way that she couldn't lash out with her hands or feet. He had checked to see if the cuffs were visible from outside, but the tinted glass made it almost impossible to see anything. Someone would have to look very hard to notice them.

He drove down the highway at fifty-five miles an hour but slowed down when he began the ascent of the Serra dos Órgãos Range. Teresópolis was over a half mile above sea level, surrounded by forests and mountains. On the horizon, Teo could see the Dedo de Deus, a rocky outcrop that looked like an index finger pointing at the sky. He had looked up the Dwarf Lake Farm Hotel on the Internet. The site showed photographs of the rooms, leisure areas, and lush vegetation. It was great that the place was isolated, a few miles before the main turnoff into the city. He really wanted to be alone with Clarice.

Clarice was breathing heavily, as if she had a cold. She was still unconscious. Her brown hair had fallen over her shoulders, covering her face and chest. She woke up slowly. Caetano was singing "Sonhos" to the sound of a solo guitar. Teo loved that song. *It was all a game, it grew and grew, absorbing me and suddenly, I belonged to you.* He smiled at Clarice. She looked serious and woozy, gazing out the window at the cars flashing past, the steep road flanked by green. A sign pointed the way to Inferno Cave.

Her silence lasted a few more minutes. When she turned her head, and he could see her in profile, her eyes were open, but she didn't look scared.

"I need a cigarette," she said. Her voice was raspy.

Teo liked her good manners and agreed. He had brought her menthol cigarettes. He reached out and opened the glove compartment, seeing as how Clarice's hands were cuffed behind her, around the seat. He put the cigarette in her mouth and lit it. He opened the window a crack to let the smoke out.

She closed her eyes, puffing out smoke. She couldn't hold the cigarette between her lips, and he had to help her: he held it to her mouth and took it away again, without taking his eyes off the road.

"You really shouldn't smoke right now. Your lungs are congested."

She didn't care. Coughing and clearing her throat, she kept puffing. Teo wished she didn't smoke. But Clarice was satisfied with her cigarette.

"Aren't you going to say anything else?" he asked.

The CD returned to the start. Clarice finished the cigarette, and Teo threw the butt out the window. She was still coughing.

"Why are you doing this to me?" she asked finally.

Teo pointed at a sign on the side of the road: Serra dos Órgãos National Park. They were only a few miles away. "Can't you tell where we're going?"

"Why are you doing this to me?"

"We're going to Teresópolis. Don't worry, I brought your laptop."

"My laptop?"

"Yep, and everything else you need to write. You won't want for anything."

"What are you going to do with me? I'm handcuffed to the seat. Dizzy . . . I don't know . . . what day it is . . ."

"You don't need to be afraid. Sorry about the dizziness. Maybe I went a little overboard."

"A little? Do you have any idea what—?"

"Don't shout, please," he said calmly, turning off the stereo.

Clarice resumed the conversation. "This is a kidnapping. You saw my place, thought I was rich, and decided—"

"Nothing of the sort."

He thought about saying he'd never do anything so petty but decided to stay quiet. She was just trying to get a rise out of him. Even feeling queasy, Clarice was provocative.

"Then what?" she insisted.

"There's nothing to tell. You said you were going to spend some time in Teresópolis. And that's where I'm taking you. We're going to spend some time together."

"I don't want to go anywhere with you."

"Oh, come on, Clarice. It can't be that bad. I'll be good company, I promise."

She winced, as if she felt a sharp pain in her head. "What do you want?"

"For you to get to know me. I'm doing my part for the two of us, you know." He turned the music back on. Caetano Veloso's voice in the background was appropriate for what he wanted to say next. "If I hadn't come looking for you, everything would have ended at that barbecue. We'd never have seen each other again. It would've been a waste."

"I—"

"I started reading your screenplay. I'm going to finish at the hotel. Meanwhile you can write. It'll be amazing!"

"I want to be alone."

"Oh, come on, Clarice, be reasonable!"

"I want to be alone!"

"You're too old to get everything your own way. Don't worry— you'll have your space," he said. "And we can talk about art, litera- ture, and everything."

"I'm afraid, Teo."

"We're both adults. Two people with common interests who are going to spend some time together. What's the problem?"

Signs of urban life were beginning to appear in the landscape: parked cars, florists, delicatessens.

They turned onto a dirt road.

"We're almost there. I need you to behave."

Clarice nodded, but Teo wasn't convinced. She squirmed when she saw him get the syringe from the glove compartment. She tried to free her arms, but her movements were limited. He had to pull over onto the side of the road to control her. He found a vein and injected the sedative. "Queixa" was playing. *A love so delicate, you take it and cast it away. I shouldn't have woken up, you kneel and don't even pray.* He was frustrated because the conversation, the music, everything was so pleasant that he didn't want it to end.

A s soon as they arrived, Teo sensed that their stay was going to be great. Surrounded by all kinds of trees and flowers (in exotic blue, yellow, and violet hues that Clarice would love), the gravel driveway led from the gate to a little wooden house with a sign saying RECEPTION.

Behind the counter, two dwarfs were playing chess. They stopped playing when Teo walked in, making a metal decoration on the door jingle. It was an unusual scene, and he had to suppress a chuckle when the older-looking of the pair got up to greet him. He'd never have guessed that the Dwarf Lake Farm Hotel was indeed run by a family of dwarfs.

He told them that he had a booking under the name Clarice Manhães.

"Today's Thursday. She was supposed to check in on Tuesday," said the dwarf, lowering his glasses on his nose and staring at Teo. He hadn't even needed to look at the computer.

"I know, we had a few setbacks and couldn't come until today. Don't tell me you're fully booked!" He put on a worried voice.

"She comes here a lot," said the other dwarf. "Alone, normally."

"I'm her boyfriend. She's asleep in the car. She was a bit carsick on the way here. What documents do you need to see?"

Teo pretended to look for his credit card, opening his wallet in such a way that the dwarf would see the photograph of him and Clarice at Lage Park.

"That won't be necessary right now. The chalet is the one by the lake."

"Right."

"There's a desk there for her to write at," he said proudly. "It's the most isolated of all the chalets. Clarice likes to work in silence."

Teo didn't like the affected way he referred to her and was already eager to get out of there.

The dwarf placed the key on the counter. "Our chalets aren't numbered. Each one has a different name. Clarice's is Sleepy. She knows where it is."

Teo nodded. He took the key and went back to the car feeling as if he were in a fairy tale.

He parked the car next to the chalet. A fine, almost invisible rain was falling. There was a gnome statue with a red cap pointing at the door. Sleepy Chalet was spacious, with two windows overlooking the lake. Three empty yellow pedal boats were floating on the calm water. The chalet was set back from the others, almost hidden by the vegetation. Teo carried Clarice in, taking care not to bump her head on the doorjamb. As he laid her down, he noticed that the legs of the double bed were bolted to the floor, which struck him as appropriate. He took sheets and a blanket out of the cupboard, which smelled of varnished wood, and put them on the bed.

The chalet was rustic, painted in dark colors and decorated with paintings of country landscapes. Against the wall by the bathroom door was the desk that the dwarf had mentioned. Teo put Clarice's laptop on the desk and confirmed that there was no Wi-Fi signal. He also remembered to remove the telephone plug, which he hid at the top of the cupboard, along with the key to the bathroom door.

He carried the suitcases into the chalet but left the rug in the trunk. He showered and put on a light-colored shirt so his and

Clarice's clothes would be matching. He got comfortable in the armchair in front of the desk and continued reading *Perfect Days*. With a pen, he made notes on the printed text. He thought the argument was poorly written, almost sloppy. The screenplay itself was better, but he was going to make a few suggestions.

He went back to reception and asked if he could get something to eat. Clarice still wasn't feeling well, but he was starving. He returned with a tray of biscuits and homemade strawberry and apricot jam, as well as some potato soup with croutons. He put the screenplay aside and went back to the detective novel he was reading—the classic *Tropical Crimes* by Amália Castelar.

He didn't stop reading when Clarice woke up.

"Stop knocking me out," she said in a hoarse voice. "Please."

Teo nodded in silence. He put down the book and pointed at the tray on the bedside table.

"You must be hungry. I don't want you to get weak."

He had placed the plain biscuits on a plastic plate and replaced the little jam spatulas with teaspoons.

She sat up in bed, her legs hidden under the blanket. She picked up the bowl of soup and held it out to Teo. "I want you to try it first."

"Thanks, but I'm not hungry."

"Just a spoonful."

"I don't know what you think of me, Clarice. I swear I didn't put anything in your soup."

"I don't trust you."

"It's going to be really hard if you keep this up," he said, pulling the armchair up to the bed. "I don't want to fight. I swear there's nothing in your soup."

She lifted the spoon to her lips, then pulled it away. "I don't trust you! I don't trust you!" She hurled the bowl against the wall.

"Don't shout," he said, impatient about having to repeat

himself. "No one can hear you from here. What have you got to gain by doing it?"

He got up and went to get some toilet paper from the bathroom. He picked up the pieces of the shattered bowl and the croutons and mopped up the thick beige liquid that was spreading across the floor.

"I'm surprised you refused your food. I didn't expect that from you. What I do expect is common sense and politeness. It seems I can't trust you."

He pretended to be angry, even though he was finding it all a lot of fun. It was normal for couples to fight, after all. Soon they'd be okay again.

"I don't want you to trust me," she said.

"That's a shame."

Teo went back to the armchair. He pushed her laptop aside and placed the smaller pink Samsonite on the desk.

"If you shout again, I'll have to use the gags I bought."

He took the gags out of the suitcase. Right next to them, hidden under some clothes, was the arm and leg spreader, but he kept it hidden so as not to frighten her.

"I'll avoid using the sedative as much as possible. But I need you to trust me. Eat the biscuits."

He hoped she'd weigh the situation and decide that it was best to comply with him, rather than disobey.

Clarice reached for the biscuits and spread apricot jam on them. "You said you want me to get to know you better," she said as she chewed. "What for? We're not in a relationship."

"No, we're not, but we could be. You didn't have to kiss me at that barbecue if you didn't feel anything for me. There's no point denying it now. You're in no condition to judge for yourself. You need to understand that, Clarice. Think of this trip as an opportunity for us."

"Do you really think that keeping me locked up and jabbing me with a needle every five minutes is going to make me like you?"

"You left me no choice. It was that or nothing."

"As long as I'm here, drugged and handcuffed, all I feel is afraid. Really fucking afraid of what you're capable of."

Her eyes began to water, but he knew she was just acting.

Clarice returned the biscuits to the plate. "If you want me to trust you, then you have to trust me too," she said. "I can promise you one thing. I get what you did, and I'm not going to tell anyone. Not the police, not my parents, no one."

"Don't talk like that. You're offending me."

"You can trust me. Nothing would happen. And we'd be friends. We'd get to know each other gradually. I could help you. We could arrange to go out together, to talk. And I'd introduce you to some of my girlfriends. It'd be great!" She seemed nervous but convinced.

"I think this trip might make you change your mind about the two of us," he said. "Just don't be so insolent."

"But what if it doesn't work out? Are you going to kill me?"

"I'm not a murderer."

"What are you, then?"

"In the end, if you don't feel the same way I do, I'll let you go. I just need you to give me a chance to show you that we could be happy together. The chance you refused me when I tried to get to know you. . . . I'd never do you any harm, Clarice."

"You already have! My family must be worried sick!"

"Your mother knows you're with me. She sent you a text message, and I took the liberty of answering. I told her we were in Teresópolis together and that you're working on your screenplay."

"I—"

"It shows that my intentions are good. I'm not going to hurt you. If you were to die, I'd be held responsible." He was proud to have such irrefutable answers to her questions. Proof that he was right.

"I want to see what you sent my mother."

He got her cell from the suitcase and let her read the message.

"So I'm fine and happy, am I?" she snorted.

"Don't take it so seriously, *my little rat*. It was just to make the old girl happy."

C larice asked questions all afternoon. She wanted to know how many days had passed and how they'd got there. She remembered showering and asked if it had been at his place. She also asked about the rug her mother had mentioned in her message. Teo answered everything.

They came to an agreement about the handcuffs: if she behaved, she'd only have to wear them when she was alone or when it was time to sleep. They would sleep together in the double bed. She would wear the gag with the harness when showering and in exceptional circumstances, when he had to go out. He agreed that it was humiliating, but he didn't see any alternative. He still didn't trust her enough to leave her ungagged in the bathroom: directly above the toilet was a small window facing the back of the chalet.

It was already dark when he told Clarice to get dressed to go out. She chose a lovely gold dress and put a denim jacket over the top. While she was in the bathroom, Teo tucked the revolver into his waistband, hidden under his shirt. He took the doctor's satchel with the syringe and ampoules of Thyolax with him.

They drove to the outskirts of the city, where Teo parked on a dark, steep street and made sure there was cell phone reception there. He dialed his home number. Because no one answered, he tried Marli's number. Patricia's friend took a while to pick up and said they were watching a film. He asked to speak to his mother.

It was a short call and Clarice stayed quiet during their conversation, her head leaning against the headrest, eyes closed. Before hanging up, he explained again that there was no cell reception at the hotel and that he didn't know when he'd be back. He said good-bye to his mother with a "love you too." He wanted to show Clarice that he was from a good family.

Then he handed her the phone and told her to call home.

"My home?"

"Yes. A text message isn't enough to stop a mother from worrying. Do what I did. Say you're with me, the trip is great, and there's no phone reception at the hotel. You can also say that you're going to communicate via text messages, as you want to limit your contact with the outside world in order to work. And leave the speaker on."

She agreed and dialed the number.

"Don't do anything silly, please. I don't want the night to end badly," he said, pulling the revolver out of his waistband and placing it on his lap. She turned her face, pretending not to have seen it. Her hands shook.

Helena answered quickly. Clarice balked when her mother said, "Hello, who is it?" on the other end of the line.

Teo took the phone from her and hung up. "What's going on?"

"I—"Her eyes were red, and he found the detail beautiful: different from the crocodile tears she had almost shed earlier. These genuine tears made her a real person. A certain amount of intimacy is required in order to cry in front of someone. He had never cried in front of anyone himself.

"Stay calm, my little rat. It's important that you make the call."

Clarice wiped her face with a tissue.

"Come on, try again. I need you to make an effort."

She took a deep breath, staring at the revolver.

"I'm not going to use it. If you obey me, I won't use it."

He handed the cell back to her, and the sound of the speaker-phone invaded the car.

Helena was quick to pick up again.

"It's Clarice," she said. "How are you?"

"Hi, honey! What miracle is this?"

"Teo just called his mum and insisted I call you too."

"Wow, so someone's finally putting you on the straight and narrow! How are things in Teresópolis?"

"Fine. Teo's here with me, and . . . he sends his regards."

"Send mine to him. I like this guy, you know. Much better than the last one."

"The trip is . . . different. How's Dad?"

"Still away, as usual. Invite Teo over for dinner when you get back. I'd like to get to know him better."

"I don't have a date yet, but we won't be too long," she said. Her eyes filled with water again but no tears spilled over.

"Be back by Christmas."

Teo tried to reassure Clarice. With gestures, he reminded her to mention the lack of cellphone reception at the hotel.

"It might be a while before I call again," she said. "If I need to, I'll text you."

"Okay. Now tell me, what did you do with the living room rug?"

Clarice looked at Teo. She was chewing on her nails and cuticles.

"It's no big deal . . . I . . ." She spat a piece of cuticle through the window. "I spilled something on it as I was leaving, and Teo thought we should take it to a dry cleaner."

"I hope this Teo is the right one. To put some sense into you. The last one would've left the dirty rug right where it was."

They said good-bye without much enthusiasm.

A fifteen-minute drive, and they were back at the hotel. Teo got out of the car to open the gate. He especially liked the smell of wet grass and the sound of the crickets at night. When they got to the chalet, he opened the passenger door for Clarice, and they walked inside together.

In the bathroom, she quickly pulled on her orange pajamas. She lay on her side on the bed, eyes closed, pretending to be asleep. Teo turned on the heater. When they had passed reception, he had noticed a single light on. The flickering light projected onto the curtain the shadow of a tiny body typing at the computer on the counter. He was pleased that the dwarf family was discreet.

He cuffed Clarice's arms and legs and studied her closely in the lamplight. She was pale, snow white.

9

The hotel served a hearty breakfast. There was a spread of juices, yogurt, coffee, fruit, cereals, and cakes arranged on a table, buffet style. The room smelled of freshly baked bread and had large windows overlooking the lake. A dwarf in an apron was serving the hot dishes: scrambled eggs and sliced sausage. Teo got a cappuccino and some toasted whole-grain bread with oats and chose a corner table facing the trees.

If Clarice were able to scream, it would be impossible to hear her from there.

Teo ate his toast quickly. Even though the chalet was farther up the slope, he didn't like to leave her alone. He returned to the chalet with croissants and hot chocolate. He reconnected the telephone and told her to call reception before she ate. If Clarice was a regular at the hotel, and it would be strange if she didn't at least say hi.

She chatted for more than ten minutes with the head dwarf, whose name was Gulliver, and explained that she was writing a screenplay and didn't want to be bothered during her stay. Teo was pleased. Clarice had done very well, and he hadn't even needed to show her the revolver. He praised her for her composure and let her eat in silence.

He was reading his detective novel when she said she felt nauseated.

"Lean back, and don't put your head down. It'll pass."

Clarice nodded. She raised the mug of hot chocolate to her mouth and managed to take two sips, then choked. She bent over, coughed, and vomited onto the sheet. Chocolate, croissants. She started to cry again, paralyzed by the filth on her pajamas.

He took her by the arm, told her to wash her face in the bathroom sink, and handcuffed her to the pipe behind the toilet. The smell was unbearable. He left the chalet and headed down the stone path until he found a dwarf who looked like a chambermaid: she was carrying a pile of pillowcases in her little arms.

"I'm staying in the Sleepy Chalet," he said. He felt pathetic having to refer to his accommodation like that. "I need a change of bedding and towels."

"I'm just finishing cleaning Happy Chalet and I'll be right there, okay?"

"That won't be necessary. My girlfriend—"

"Clarice."

"Yes, Clarice. She's putting the finishing touches on her screenplay. And artists—you know how it is. She's on a kind of retreat for a few days. To write. She asked me to come get a change of sheets and tidy up the room myself. . . . It's tough being a writer's boyfriend!"

The dwarf didn't seem to mind. She asked Teo to follow her to the little linen room behind reception lined with shelves and baskets of clothes. The place smelled of lavender. A washing machine was purring in a corner.

"When you come to get fresh towels, don't forget to bring back the used ones," she said. She climbed up a little ladder to get some towels and sheets for him. "Here you go."

He thanked her and helped her get a black plastic bag down from the top shelf.

"I need to collect the rubbish," she said. "If you can't find me, you can leave whatever's dirty in the basket and get fresh towels from the shelf. This room is never locked."

"I don't want to be a bother."

"It's no problem at all."

They took the path back together, making small talk. He secretly had fun trying to synchronize his footsteps with the dwarf's. They stopped at the place where the path forked off to the Happy and Sleepy Chalets.

"Thanks again," he said.

"Tell Clarice I said hi. And good luck with her screenplay—I love that girl."

O ver the next few days, Teo and Clarice fell into a routine. He would wake up before her and go for a run around the lake while there was still no one around. The Dwarf Lake Farm Hotel came to life at around eight o'clock, with children churning up piles of earth and couples lining up to ride in the pedal boats. He'd head back to the chalet with Clarice's breakfast. He tried to vary the menu so she wouldn't get sick of the same food all the time: milk pudding, cheeses, rye bread, homemade papaya and pumpkin compote.

While she ate, he changed the bedclothes and towels. Clarice was in charge of cleaning the room. Teo didn't want her to think she was going to live like a princess, as he knew that women were better suited to domestic chores.

They'd talk until lunchtime. Those were the most pleasurable

hours of the day and, unfortunately, the ones that passed the
quickest. Little by little they got to know each other. He loved
passion fruit mousse; she loved chocolate fudge. He wasn't interested in politics; she was left wing. He liked the Coen brothers; she
preferred Michael Haneke and Woody Allen. He listened only to
Brazilian music, especially Wilson Simonal, Filipe Catto, Caetano
Veloso and Jorge Ben Jor. She liked everything but preferred
American pop and English rock. They were both only children.

Other traits of Clarice's gradually came to the fore. When discussing her favorite subjects, she was as precise as a historian; she
knew dates, times, names, and surnames. When talking about
the future, she would narrow her eyes as if she were projecting
projects and dreams onto a big screen. He liked seeing her do it
and would encourage her to keep talking.

Clarice also wanted to know about him, and Teo felt very
comfortable talking about himself: he told her about medical
school and his plans for the future.

He even mentioned Gertrude. "She's my best friend."

"Where did you meet?"

"In a pretty unusual place. Anatomy class."

He told her a serious of funny anecdotes about things he'd
done with Gertrude. Clarice found it interesting that he was
friends with a much older woman and said she wanted to meet
her. Teo agreed and smiled. He said his friend would love to meet
her too. It made him a little ill at ease, as he didn't want to spoil
things by telling her that Gertrude was a corpse.

There were days when time would get away from them and
they wouldn't eat lunch until three in the afternoon. Teo
would come back from the dining room with plates of food, and
they'd eat together at the desk. She preferred red meat—which

Teo brought already cut up—and had a penchant for pasta and cheesy sauces. He ate lots of salad and had the best eggplant lasagna of his life. He made a point of going to see the cook—invariably, another dwarf—to congratulate her on the dish.

In the afternoons, Clarice would work on her screenplay. Her fingers raced across the keyboard as if she were afraid she might forget something. Pretending to read, Teo would sit on the bed watching her write. He enjoyed observing those moments. A whole other world was being created, with characters, actions, endings. He liked this idea of multiple possibilities.

Once or twice she asked him to leave the room, because she wanted to read the text out loud. Teo understood that artists had their eccentricities and superstitions. He wandered through the small wood watching the parrots and chatted with the dwarfs at reception. To avoid raising any suspicion about Clarice's habits, he was always armed with news ("She said she's never felt so at home writing and is thinking about putting the hotel in the acknowledgments of the screenplay") and feigned specific interests: he now knew that the hotel had seven chalets, as well as smaller rooms. He also knew that the lake was natural, that the water wasn't good for bathing, and that it was more than fifty feet deep. A child had almost drowned in it.

Teo never let Clarice read the newspaper or watch TV. He had taken the batteries out of the remote, as he thought it better for her not to know what was going on in the outside world: complete isolation would help her finish the screenplay. Besides, it was important that she distance herself a little from reality so she could think about him. Without the distraction of soap operas or the violence of the news, she'd have more time to better consider the relationship they were building.

In the evenings they ate soup and watched the films he had brought. Clarice loved *Little Miss Sunshine* and, full of praise for

Teo, said it had given her ideas for how to improve her own screenplay.

Before going to bed, she'd revise the pages she had written that day, while Teo read in bed. When he finished the detective novel, he had a go at the collection of stories by Clarice Lispector. The bloodstain on the cover had been impossible to remove, so he'd covered it with some craft paper and sticky tape he'd got from reception.

After a shower, Clarice would lie down next to him. They'd talk a little more, drowsily now. Then he'd cuff her to the bed and get up to turn off the light—the switch was by the door. Teo had moved the bedside table away ever since he'd had a nightmare in which Clarice had woken up in the middle of the night and started beating him over the head with the lamp.

I brought you a present," he said. He showed her the bag.

He'd gone into town to buy personal hygiene products— they were almost out of toothpaste. He'd taken the opportunity to call Patricia and Helena. From what he could tell, Clarice's communication with her mother was punctuated by long periods with no contact. It was the only explanation for Helena's enthusiasm when he called.

He helped Clarice sit up, removed the cuffs and gag, and handed her the dress. He'd seen it in a shop window: vibrant colors, soft material. It was expensive, but he'd wanted to see her in it. He asked her to put it on.

It was a Tuesday. They'd been together a week. It was raining hard outside. She came back from the bathroom looking beautiful, and he knew she liked it, even if she looked exhausted. All women liked presents. Clarice mumbled a lackluster thank-you that irritated him.

"You don't understand that I feel really happy with you, do you?"

She didn't say anything.

"I don't like seeing you like this, my little rat." He took her hands. "I know all this might seem a bit absurd, but you have to understand. The last few days haven't been that bad, have they?"

She started to speak, and each word appeared to require great effort.

"The problem isn't you."

She pulled away from him and half closed the bathroom door to change back into her pajamas. He wanted to ask questions, but the urge died in his throat.

Clarice climbed back into bed. With a cotton pad, she removed her black eyeliner. (Even though she never left the chalet, she made herself up discreetly every morning.) Then she folded the pad and, with a sigh, turned to face Teo.

"This place is my getaway. The hideout where I come to get a distance on things and live in my own little world, you know? Nothing against you, honestly. But I don't think it's a good idea that you stay here with me anymore."

Breno had cast his long shadow over the conversation. Teo was disgusted by her ex-boyfriend. It was obvious that he was still in Clarice's thoughts. He didn't need her to confirm it in order to be sure.

"It's been a great week, Teo, but I need to be alone. I need to finish the screenplay."

"Please, don't insist." He hated having to have the same old conversation. "You can ask for whatever you want. But you know that's off the table."

They sat there in silence. She began to cry.

"In exchange for the present, I want to make a request," he

went on. "Leave things as they are for a few more days. You keep writing, here with me; without thinking about it, without judging. Just live. I promise it'll be great."

She closed her eyes and dried her tears on the cotton pad. Then she went back to the bathroom to remove her lipstick and touch up her dignity.

O n the Saturday afternoon, Clarice committed a faux pas, and Teo saw her embarrassed for the first time. They were in the chalet watching *12 Angry Men*. She said her mother would love the film and asked Teo when he had seen it for the first time.

"It was my dad's favorite."

Clarice smiled, getting up to go to the bathroom.

"You don't talk much about your dad, do you?" she said, then immediately realized that the question had been inappropriate. "I'm sorry, I . . ."

He shook his head. Seeing Clarice standing in the bathroom doorway like that—sleepy, wearing a large T-shirt with a black and white photo of John Lennon on it, holding her toothbrush— he knew it was time to let down his guard and talk about it with her.

"My father's dead. He died in the car accident that left my mother paraplegic."

In another conversation, he had talked about Patricia's condition, but then they'd skipped on to a different subject.

"It happened six years ago. My father was a supreme court judge. We lived in a penthouse in Copacabana, overlooking the sea. He and my mother had a busy social life and were always invited to posh parties and outings on yachts. My surname's Avelar Guimarães. I don't know if that rings a bell for you." She didn't react, so he added, "It was in all the newspapers. My parents were coming back from a trip down south in my father's Pajero. The Vectra I drive used to be my mother's."

"Were you with them?"

"No, I'd stayed at home because I had school."

He hesitated. He'd never talked to anyone about it. Not Patricia, or even Gertrude.

"At the time, the police were investigating corruption and organized crime with connections in the judiciary. There were lots of people involved: lawyers, judges, public prosecutors—"

"And supreme court judges, of course."

"A public prosecutor is supposed to have called my father. He said their scheme had been uncovered. A lot of people had been arrested. They were all in a panic, and he was one of the bigwigs. No one knows exactly what happened. My father was driving when he received the call, somewhere near Santos. My mother was in the passenger seat. According to the newspapers, he was so thrown by the call that he lost control of the car. He hit a retaining wall, the car flipped and rolled down the hill, and he was killed instantly."

"Gee, I—I'm really sorry. Didn't your mother ever tell you what happened?"

"I've never asked. She's suffered enough. At any rate, I've got my version of the facts," he said. "I knew my father well. He was a cold man, very proud and rational. I'm not saying I knew he was corrupt. But I know how he would have reacted in a situation like that. I know what he felt when he was accused, about to be arrested . . ."

Teo considered himself to be like his father in many aspects.

"When a man is ashamed of himself and finds himself unmasked, there aren't too many choices, Clarice. Suicide is the only way out."

10

What did you think of the screenplay?"

They were in bed, ready to sleep. Teo had finished reading the unfinished text on the Sunday but hadn't said anything. He was waiting for Clarice to ask his opinion. He'd noticed that she was easily shaken by what other people thought and said. It was an interesting chink in the self-sufficient image that she had projected in the beginning.

Faced with telling the blunt truth or a lie couched in praise, he resorted to euphemism.

"I like it, but I see certain problems. I don't think the argument is well written. In the screenplay itself, I can see that you write well and think you could have put together a better argument."

She wanted more details. Teo mentioned problems with continuity and small logical incongruities. He praised the dramatic tone of the tire-changing scene.

"What did you think of the end? I still haven't written it, but it's going to be what's in the argument."

"It's all a dream, right?"

"I don't come out and say it, but it's implied. Carol doesn't die. And the suitcases suggest that she's going somewhere. Viewers have to deduce the rest."

"I like open endings," he said. "But I'm not sure it works in this case."

"The question isn't the open ending but playing with the medium. Cinema represents reality, but it *isn't* reality. I want to explore the nuances, you know? In one scene, the character dies. In another, we find out that none of it took place, it was just a wish, an impression—"

"Okay, but I don't think it works in your story."

"You're too rational. There's a film by Michael Haneke where the character winds back the actual film so that things go the way he wants them to. He controls the story. It's fucking amazing."

"Fine. So you want to use metalanguage in the film."

"I'll write it, and then you'll agree with me," she said. She gave him a kiss on the cheek and curled up under the blanket. "Good night."

He smiled, happy that Clarice was determined to convince him. The screenplay itself hardly mattered.

On the Wednesday, before she even said good morning, Clarice asked for a cigarette. Teo was relaxing in the armchair, reading Sobotta's *Atlas of Human Anatomy*. It was an ugly, rainy morning—perfect weather for a lazy day in the chalet. He hadn't gone for his daily run and was waiting for breakfast time. Clarice asked for a cigarette again.

"That was the last one yesterday," he said.

"I get irritable when I don't smoke."

"Vogue menthols. I'll try to get some for you when I go into town, my little rat."

He focused on the book again, as he didn't want her to feel like she was in charge of the situation. He'd read a study on relationships according to which women weren't attracted to men who were too available or submissive. They preferred the mysterious, self-sufficient ones. He went to lengths not to sound groveling.

"Why do you call me 'little rat'?" she asked after a few minutes.

"It's just a nickname. Because of your teeth."

"My teeth?"

"I like them," he said. "I hope it's not a problem."

"It isn't."

He knew she wouldn't mind. He wanted to come out and ask her a direct question but decided to be subtle.

"Have you had any other nicknames?"

Clarice closed her eyes, as if she were going to go back to sleep. He had hoped she'd explain the "my sonata" in the messages from her ex-boyfriend. It was inevitable that they'd end up talking about Breno. They'd been together for more than two weeks, and his name hadn't come up.

The day before, Teo had gone into town. He'd talked for almost half an hour with Patricia, who was depressed and anxious to get Samson's necropsy results back. His call to Helena had been shorter. She thanked him for the call but said she wanted to speak to her daughter the next time.

Teo felt pressured. Breno's repeated attempts to get back together with her (the guy was being downright inconvenient and had sent her more than eight text messages), Laura's messages . . . he wasn't sure if Clarice was into men or women. It was all very confusing.

Clarice seemed more at home with him by the day. She'd

make silly remarks, tell him her thoughts on things and her ideas for screenplays. He especially liked her expansive gestures, the way she could tie her hair up in a few seconds, her inexorable air of superiority, and her characteristic laugh, with her tongue touching her teeth.

Nevertheless something was still niggling him. And this discomfort made him even keener to broach certain topics. He went as far as to rehearse the question *So where did the nickname* sonata *come from?* But he knew the answer wouldn't come easily.

"Have you had any other nicknames?" he repeated.

"Yeah." She got up and went to wash her face in the sink.

"What were they?"

"They used to call me Button Nose at kindergarten, after the Monteiro Lobato character. And Magali, from the *Turma da Mônica* comic strips, because I love watermelon. I think that's it."

The pealing of a bell announced breakfast. Teo pulled on a jacket, unable to continue the conversation. He said he'd be back soon.

He put the cuffs on Clarice and asked her to put on the gag. "You can choose between the one with the harness and the padded one."

She argued that it wasn't necessary, that she wouldn't scream. She was cuffed to the bed and couldn't do a thing. Teo insisted. Before putting it on and padlocking the harness, he asked what she wanted to eat. She wasn't in a friendly mood.

"I want cigarettes."

The rain had stopped, which made Teo less keen to hurry back to the chalet. He strolled around the property, since the benches were all wet. On days when Clarice was in a bad mood, he avoided being around her. He suspected she might have some sort of bipolar disorder, that it was pathological.

Nevertheless he was satisfied. From a tender age, he'd felt out of place, an uncomfortable creature among people to whom laughter came easily, people with nothing there, no intellectual ambitions, no loftier thoughts. It had been a shock to realize that it was normal to be moved by Christmas, to call up old friends on their birthdays, and to show the neighbors that your eight-month-old has finally learned to say "da da."

He was repulsed by the notions of normality exemplified in the evening soaps. It had been difficult to adapt. Reality didn't make concessions. And then, just when he finally felt sure of himself, Clarice had come along to bring some sense to it all—or to break the sense he'd created for himself. She had repositioned him in the world. Teo still looked down on the human race, but at least now what he felt for it was a kind of disinterested pity. Finally, he was in *love*.

Moved by gratitude, Teo drove back into Teresópolis on the Thursday. He bought some moisturizer for Clarice's wrists, which were irritated by the handcuffs, and tampons, as her period had started. He phoned Patricia, who merely repeated the gripes of their last conversation. She was so caught up in her own misery that she didn't ask about Clarice. He didn't bring up the subject either, as he was in a hurry to hang up.

When he turned on Clarice's cell, he found two more messages from Breno. The desperate tone of the last one, sent only a few hours earlier, was funny:

I CAN'T BEAR THIS ANYMORE. I MISS YOU. YOUR COLDNESS HURTS. WHY CAN'T YOU TELL ME WHAT'S GOING ON? WHY WON'T YOU TALK TO ME? LET'S GIVE OURSELVES ANOTHER

CHANCE AND START ALL OVER AGAIN. YOU'LL ALWAYS BE
MY SONATA. FROM YOUR WOODY WHO LOVES YOU.

He wanted to delete the message, but it was all so outrageous
that he had to reply:

FORGET ME. I DON'T WANT TO BE WITH YOU ANYMORE.

He should have followed up with a FUCK OFF, BRENO! but
sending another message would have shown more interest than
he wanted to. All this harassment from the ex-boyfriend had
exhausted him. He didn't call Helena that day.

At the shopping center, he had a pistachio ice cream. Seduced
by chokers and rings, he walked into a jeweler's. He wanted to
get Clarice something special. A pearl necklace in the window
had caught his eye, but it was too expensive. He asked the saleswoman to show him other items.

It's funny how one idea leads to another. He had entered the
shop determined to buy something meaningful but simple. As
the saleswoman was showing him other, cheaper options, he had
another idea.

"Do you have engagement rings?"

Night fell. The cicadas were screeching in the dark. The
smell of wet earth wafted through the half-open windows,
and a breeze ruffled the curtains. As soon as Clarice came out of
the bathroom, she asked if he'd bought cigarettes.

"They didn't have any," he lied.

He'd found Vogue menthols at a delicatessen in town and had
bought two packs, but on his way back to the hotel, he had decided
to make Clarice stop smoking. Without her noticing, he would

cut the cigarettes out of her routine. A gradual process. In the beginning he'd have to invent excuses and put up with the abuse that came with abstinence, but he'd be successful in the end.

She didn't complain and just shook her head. The previous day's irascibility had been replaced by melancholy resignation.

Teo suggested they go for a walk. The night was beautiful, in spite of the cold. It was one o'clock in the morning, and the other guests were asleep. She put a jacket over her black dress and wrapped a scarf around her neck. They held hands as they walked. With slow steps, they headed down the slope, following the curve of the lake. She walked with her head down, but she didn't look sad, just distracted. She barely seemed to care about the revolver in his waistband.

They sat on a metal bench. During the day, the children ran riot there, feeding the geese and sliding down the slope. Under the white floodlight, their shadows were projected onto the black surface of the lake. They breathed in the fresh air for a few minutes.

Clarice smiled at him and rested her head on his shoulder. "Sorry about the way I treated you yesterday," she said. "I've been feeling weird."

"Weird?"

"I thought I'd be in a state, but I feel inexplicably good."

Teo couldn't see her face, but he knew the expression on it: eyes closed, lips tight, hesitant. He could tell just from her tone of voice.

"That's nice to hear."

"It doesn't make any sense. I should be scared, shouldn't I?" She lifted up her head, hands clasped to his. "I'm not sure why . . . I feel safe with you. I know you wouldn't do anything to hurt me."

During that whole time, he had been very reasonable with her. Who has never experienced unrequited love? Who wouldn't have liked to show the other person that their love could be different, that things could work out between them? He had merely done what everyone had wanted to do at one time or another. He'd created a chance for himself to be near Clarice, to allow her to get to know him better before uttering a definitive no. He'd been bold and courageous. Now he was reaping the rewards for his efforts.

He showed Clarice the rings. Solid gold, gleaming in the little box.

"Will you marry me?"

She raised her hands to her mouth.

"I love you, Clarice."

He immediately regretted having said it. It wasn't good to tell a woman you were in love with her. It frightened them off. He'd kept his feelings for Clarice under control this whole time, using a rational or ironic tone of voice when speaking to her. But now he'd been disconcertingly sincere and had blurted out his feelings.

"Please give it some thought."

She looked stunned.

Teo understood that it was a very important moment in a woman's life.

"Yes," she said finally.

Delicately, she leaned over, and their lips touched in a tender kiss. He stroked her hair and hugged her tightly, and nothing more needed to be said. Their mouths understood each other in silence.

They went back to the chalet an hour later. As he walked through the door, Teo was still inebriated by the exchange of caresses. He locked the door and returned the key to his pocket. Clarice had headed straight to the bathroom.

"Wait there," she said. She was removing her makeup at the sink, her hair pulled back in a shower cap.

He sat on the bed, feeling nervous about what was to come. He took off his shoes and put the revolver in the drawer of the table on his side of the bed. He didn't think it was appropriate to put on his pajamas. He would wait for Clarice to take the initiative and invite him over to her.

"Oh, Teo, my ring!" she said, lifting up her wet face with a start. "The water—it fell in!"

He raced to the bathroom and tried to spot the ring through the drain hole, then squatted down to examine the pipe underneath. The sound of footsteps startled him. Clarice had dashed to the front door and was rattling the knob in desperation. He walked toward her.

"Get back!" she shouted, leaning against the door. She pointed the revolver at him. "Where's the key?"

Teo took a step back. The drawer of the bedside table was open.

"Don't do anything silly, Clarice. Put it down."

"I'm going to kill you, you fucking bastard! If you don't give me the key, I'll kill you!"

Teo was disappointed. He never could have imagined there was room for so much rancor and falseness in that tiny body.

"Is this really called for, Clarice? The last few weeks have been so good! We've talked about your screenplay, watched films . . . It's been—"

"It's been fucking awful! I don't need your advice for my screenplay! You're disgusting! Give me the damned key!"

Her eyes were wide open, her legs slightly bent, hands shaking. The shower cap made her look a little macabre. There was hatred on her face. Fear too.

"I'm not going to give you the key, Clarice."

"Take another step, and I shoot. Get back. Over there, go."

"You can't be talking seriously. We've shared such beautiful moments!"

"Stick this ring up your ass!" She took the ring out of her jacket pocket and threw it at his face. "I want the key!"

"I told you I'm not giving it to you. Shoot me if you want."

"I will. I will, you fucking prick!"

Even holding the revolver, she looked petrified. "This is your last chance."

"Shoot me. If that's what I deserve after everything I've done, shoot me."

"Don't make me—"

"It's just a phase, Clarice. It'll pass," he said. He held his hands out to her.

"Shut the fuck up! Get back."

"I need you to trust me."

"I don't!"

"I'd never hurt you."

"Fuck you! I want the key! I want to leave this place. I want to go home."

He smiled at her. "That's not how it works."

"Give me the key—or I'll blow your face off."

"You wouldn't have the guts." Teo moved closer with calculated footsteps, hands raised.

Clarice pulled the trigger. One, two, three, four, five times. The cylinder of the gun did a full 360 degrees, indifferently.

Teo walked forward, feeling a mixture of anxiety and anger. He slapped her.

"I told you I'd never do you any harm! Do you really think I'd go around with a loaded gun?"

He slapped her again.

Clarice fell onto the bed, shut her eyes, and tried to hide under the covers. A purple mark was beginning to appear next to her mouth. Teo thought about sedating her again. It was what she deserved. He went as far as to get the syringe but changed his mind. He got the arm and leg spreader out of the Samsonite. She whimpered, begging for forgiveness as he put the gag on her, but he had nothing more to say. He pulled her by the hair and cuffed her arms and legs to the ends of the contraption. He closed pad-locks, buckles, and Velcro and dragged her in it all onto the cold bathroom floor. He left the light on. Clarice would spend the night there, crucified, thinking about how badly she'd fucked up.

11

As soon as it was light outside, Teo went to get Clarice from the bathroom. He walked arm in arm with her to the bed, as she was stiff all over. He suggested a massage, but her reply was silence. He had left a plate of watermelon slices on the desk.

"Don't you want to eat?" he asked.

She turned her head away, pressing her lips together like an ornery child.

Teo slipped off her shoes and massaged her dry feet. Whenever he touched Clarice, his hands tingled. He was surprised by the sensations that she caused in him. He tried to smile but was still indignant. If the gun had been loaded, he'd be dead. She was clearly not in her right mind. He felt let down, as well as a certain contempt for her weakness.

"Aren't you going to talk to me?" he asked.

Over the next few days, Clarice refused to eat or to communicate. She accepted only water but didn't thank him. She spent the afternoons at the laptop, working on her screenplay.

Teo tried to give her space. He knew she wouldn't hold out for long. Couples always made up.

Lying on the bed, he watched her in the armchair: her hunched shoulders, her skeletal arms, her apathetic, almost dead stare. The situation was becoming unbearable. He tried to be nice, but she remained aloof. No matter what topic he brought up, she gave him no more than a disdainful look. All affection was refused. The fact that she wasn't eating also concerned him.

On the Sunday evening, she broke the silence. She was under the covers, ready to sleep, when she said, "I feel really sorry for you, Teo."

Her words really hurt him. Couldn't she see he was right? He made an effort to keep the conversation going.

"I feel really sorry for you too, Clarice."

She pretended to be sleeping, but her eyelids quivered.

"I feel sorry for you because you have someone who loves you and you couldn't give a damn," he said.

She opened her eyes and glared at him. "Do you really think you love me?"

"Yes."

"What you feel is infatuation. It's an illness, an obsession. It's anything but love."

"I don't believe in the taxonomical classification of emotions, Clarice."

She shook her head and retreated back into silence.

G o into town and bring back whatever fucking cigarette you can find," she said from the armchair.

It was Thursday. Clarice hadn't smoked for a week and was

getting ruder by the day. Teo sought to ignore her. He knew abstinence was painful and had tried to solve the problem some days earlier: he had brought some toothpicks from reception.

"Most former smokers chew on toothpicks the first few days. It's important to substitute what you put in your mouth," he had explained.

She had thrown the toothpicks onto the floor, but later she'd taken his advice. Little by little her addiction was passing.

"Go into town and bring back whatever fucking cigarette you can find," she repeated.

"I'm not going into town today."

He was folding clothes and organizing them in the suitcases. He picked up her cell.

"Has anyone else sent me a message?"

"No."

"I'd like to see my cell."

"No one's sent any messages."

"I want to see my cell. You said you'd do anything I asked."

"Please don't be impudent. I said there were no messages. Therefore it's the truth: there are no messages! Now stop badgering me!"

"You treat me like a prisoner," she said. "You pretend you're being nice, but you treat me like an animal."

"You're not seeing things clearly."

"Breno," she said. The name came as a blow, like a buzzard that had been circling a dead body for some time and decided to attack. "You know who I'm talking about. My boyfriend."

"Ex-boyfriend."

"He's my boyfriend. And I miss him."

"You had a fight, from what I understand."

"It doesn't matter. We always fight, and then we make up."

"That doesn't seem to be the case this time." He made a vague gesture with his hands. "Breno sent you a message. He said he didn't want anything more to do with you."

"Don't lie, Teo."

"I'm not lying. I remember what it said very well. Sorry I didn't mention it before. I deleted the message because I didn't want you to be upset."

"I don't believe you."

"We've been here for three weeks, and he hasn't come after you, Clarice. Isn't it obvious he doesn't want anything to do with you?"

The question threw her.

"Besides, he was very offensive in his message. I was shocked." Teo squinted, as if retrieving information from memory. "He said he wasn't happy with the relationship. And he called you a slut."

"Liar!"

Her voice faltered, and he knew she wasn't so sure.

"The *slut* made an impression on me. He repeated it three or four times."

Clarice burst into tears. Teo was proud. Before he had deleted the conversation history, he had noticed that Breno didn't deal well with her extroverted ways.

"Liar! All you've done is lie from the start!" she said, hunched over in the armchair. Her head was between her knees, bobbing up and down with her sobs. Her spinal vertebrae moved under her skin like a snake. Clarice had lost around nine pounds over the last few days. She was skeletal but still beautiful. If he could paint, he'd have painted a portrait of that moment. He considered going to get his camera but thought it might be offensive.

Suddenly, Clarice jumped at Teo. She scratched him and tried to bite him. She hit him in the face with the pillow. Teo held her wrists and managed to handcuff her. He was most annoyed at her actions. She was proving to be quite uncouth. He got the Thyolax from the minibar and injected her amid her breathless protests.

T eo lost track of time as he tended to Clarice's arms. He massaged her sores with moisturizer. Her ashen skin was marked with purple blotches and scratches. She was deep in a restful sleep, her body a territory to be discovered. Her arms handcuffed over her head made her look sensual, and her white thighs poked out of her pajamas. He knew those thoughts were inevitable and went to have a shower.

It was already after midnight when someone knocked at the door. Three quick raps. He got out of bed and glanced at Clarice, who was still asleep. He pulled back the curtains of the side window. The sky was black, with dark clouds slicing up the moon. The light from the lamppost by the lake was weak, showing only the silhouette of the visitor. It wasn't a dwarf.

Teo got the revolver from the suitcase, kicking himself for not having bought any ammunition. There was more knocking.

"Who is it?"

No answer came.

"Who is it?"

With the revolver in his waistband, he opened the door. It didn't take him long to recognize the tall young man from the Cecília Meireles Concert Hall, dressed in jeans, a green polo shirt, a leather jacket, and rectangular-rimmed glasses.

"What do you want?"

Breno looked him up and down with an idiotic expression. "Who are you?"

"You knocked on my door in the middle of the night."

"Look, I just want to talk to Clarice. Is she here?"

"Do you have any idea what time it is?"

"I need to talk to her. She always stays in this chalet."

Teo thought about saying he didn't know what he was talking about but didn't want to come across as cowardly or submissive. "She's asleep. How did you get here?"

"It doesn't matter."

"I'm her boyfriend," said Teo, noticing that Breno's breath reeked of alcohol. He was shaking his head, and his eyes looked as if they were going to pop out of their orbits. "I'm not going to let you bother her anymore. We're together now. Get lost."

"I don't want to make a scene. I just want to talk to her. I'm begging you."

"You've already talked more than enough with those ridiculous messages!"

"You saw them?"

"Clarice showed me. She didn't know what else to do to get you to understand that it's over."

"Please, I don't know what's going on. She won't answer me properly. I'm desperate," said Breno with the ruefulness of a drunk. "I need to hear from her mouth that it's over. That's all, and then I'll go."

Teo looked at Clarice's bedraggled ex and found him pathetic. How could she have liked someone like that?

"I know you're her new boyfriend and—"

"I told you, she's asleep."

"She never goes to bed early. She can't have changed that much."

Breno was calmer now. His gaze came to rest on the long scratch Clarice had made earlier on Teo's neck.

"I'm not leaving here without seeing Clarice."

"Get out!" said Teo, closing the door.

Breno stopped him, pushing his way in. In the semidarkness, he saw Clarice lying on the bed and ran to her. He went as far as to say "I'm sorry, my love" before he noticed the handcuffs. He turned to Teo, confused. The first blow with the butt of the gun sent his glasses skidding under the bed. Teo continued to beat him about the head and neck.

Breno reeled back and lost his footing but managed to strike back. He knocked Teo to the ground. Clarice continued sleeping, oblivious to the scene.

Teo kicked his legs, trying to dodge the punches to his face. He managed to grab Breno's hair and smash his head against the corner of the bed. The impact made a cut, and blood ran through his hair down to his ear. Breno writhed; he was losing consciousness. Teo repeated the movement over and over, making a deep indentation in Breno's head. His body went limp and flopped to the ground. His bloody head met the floor with a thud.

Teo felt weary to the bone. He looked at Breno's large unmoving body. He examined his glassy eyes, wide open, directly beneath his shattered forehead. Was he really dead?

He hesitated, then got the syringe and an ampoule of Thyolax. He was afraid to touch him and get a nasty surprise. He kicked the body lightly. No reaction. With the speed of a busy nurse, he injected a dose of Thyolax into Breno's inert arm. Then another. And another. And then one more.

Four doses—there was no way he could still be alive.

Teo paced back and forth. He had killed a person. The body was lying there, horrendous and red. What did he know about Breno? That he was Clarice's jealous ex-boyfriend and played the violin. He riffled through his pockets. An old cell phone, turned off. A key ring with three keys on it. In the jacket pocket, a wallet. One hundred and ten *reais* in cash. Two credit cards. An expired driver's licence, which showed that he was twenty-six.

Together with the licence was a used bus ticket from Rio de Janeiro to Teresópolis. Did anyone know he had come after Clarice? Had a guest seen him arriving? There was no time to speculate. He needed to get rid of the body. The pool of blood was spreading, threatening to reach a corner of the sheet. He hoped Clarice didn't wake up for another few hours.

He opened the door of the chalet and went to the car. He was wearing only a T-shirt, but the cold didn't bother him. He got the rug from the trunk and rolled it out on the floor of the chalet. He laid Breno's body on it and cleaned up the blood. He thought about rolling him up in the rug and throwing it into the lake. He had read a few detective novels in which the criminals had done that. But in the real world, the gases released during the process of putrefaction could cause the corpse to work its way loose and float up to the surface. Perhaps a few rocks would help keep him at the bottom. Still too risky. It also occurred to him to dig a hole in the forest, but he discarded the idea: he wasn't used to digging in the earth and might wake someone up.

He made up his mind. He left the chalet and headed for the linen room. His feet moved quickly through the night. In silence, he turned the door handle and groped in the dark for the light switch. He reached for the pile of black plastic bags on the top shelf. Then he went to the kitchen, which was next to the dining room, praying it wasn't locked. It wasn't. He found a long serrated knife. On the way back, he saw a pair of pruning shears lying forgotten near a flowerbed outside Bashful Chalet. He took them with him too.

G loves on, he began to work. He cut off Breno's clothes, leaving him naked on the rug. It was ironic that Clarice had been satisfied with so little. He put the crumpled clothes in a plastic bag and hastily stuffed Breno's glasses and belongings into a compartment of the doctor's satchel. He was anxious; it was his first time exploring a fresh corpse.

Breno's body shook when the knife sank into the skin of his neck. With a vertical stroke, the skin—still warm—parted softly, leaving an open groove behind the knife. Teo was transported to the anatomy lab, to his moments with Gertrude, to the pleasures of dissection. As he visited each part of the corpse, he saw the books he had studied in his mind's eye. Illustrations became reality.

He had to squat to work on the thoracic cavity. He found the costal cartilages of the ribs and began to cut them with the shears. When he was finished, he lifted up the sternum, gaining a view of the organs inside the box of bone. The heart was still contracting weakly.

Teo slowly calmed down. He found the rusty smell of blood pleasant. He acted with calculated movements, like a dancer rehearsing steps around the body. He was sweating profusely, and when he wiped his forehead on his forearm, he glanced at Clarice. If she woke up, would she be able to see her ex-boyfriend in the corpse laid out there? He knew she wouldn't. The love she felt for Breno was physical. Faced with that sight, there could be no love or pain. Just disgust.

He squatted down to cut the edges of the diaphragm and pull out the viscera, immersed in yellow fat. The blade slipped, pierced the glove, and nicked his right thumb. Shit! Fluids oozed from the cut intestines. After washing his hands, he quickly bandaged up his finger.

He went over to Clarice and stroked her face, excited by the situation. He wanted her to wake up. He wanted her to see Breno like that, just a carcass. "Wake up, Clarice," he whispered. He wanted to nibble her earlobe but resisted the urge. No matter how positive the shock might be, he didn't want to take any risks.

He put on new gloves and began to dismember the body. He cut joints, chuckling to himself when he heard the peculiar sound of the legs being detached at the groin. *Pok*. It reminded him of a jar of olives being opened. He divided the legs into two segments, at the knees. He did the same with the arms, at the elbows, after cutting them off at the shoulders. *Pok. Pok*.

Two hours passed. He wasn't used to carrying out those procedures with such rudimentary instruments. His back hurt, but the worst part was still to come: separating the head from the body. He sawed at the bottom of the neck. The muscles gave way, and only a few ligaments offered some difficulty. The blade was growing blunt, making the task exhausting. With his weight on the thorax, Teo continued sawing, as he forced the head in the opposite direction until it came lose.

Breno's face was covered in blood, his mouth wide open in a black, tongueless void. His eyes were open too, but Teo closed them: he was a medical professional, not a butcher. The rug was filthy. He rolled it up and tied it with a pillowcase. He double-bagged the pieces of Breno, adding some white stones he had found in the garden.

Through a crack in the door, he stared out at the darkness. He calculated that he'd need to make two trips—about three minutes each—to dump the bags into the lake. None of the other chalets had a direct view of that area, so he allowed himself to make a little noise. He hurled the bags as far from the edge as he could, then ran back and repeated the exercise. He did the same with the rug. He washed the instruments and returned them to their places.

When he finally sat down to rest on the armchair, he needed

a shower. He stood under the jet of hot water for half an hour as it massaged his back. Looking in the mirror, he noticed a swelling on his right cheek. He sprayed cologne around the room to get rid of the acrid smell clinging to the furniture.

In a state of ecstasy, he sat on the metal bench at the side of the lake. Breno was dead. Clarice was his alone. The fact still hadn't sunk in emotionally. He had yet to absorb what it meant, but something told him it was good.

He scanned the surface of the lake, looking for anything abnormal. He sat there for hours, cracking his fingers, reflecting, smiling, until Friday began to dawn. It was time to go back to bed and try to sleep. He knew he wouldn't be able to.

12

The pedal boat splashed along noisily. Father and son were pedaling hard, laughing out loud, feeding the geese pieces of bread and dipping their hands into the water to feel the temperature. Teo watched it all.

Shortly before sunrise, he had gone to the chalet. A purple mark was beginning to appear on his right cheek next to his swollen upper lip. He had iced it with some ice cubes he'd taken from the kitchen. He had taken a painkiller and rubbed some ointment onto his lip to relieve the pain. Then he had returned to the metal bench with the book by Clarice Lispector. It sat closed on his lap.

How long would it take someone to notice Breno was missing? Would the investigation lead the police to Clarice? Had someone seen him leave home or take the bus to Teresópolis? These things were out of Teo's control, which made him uneasy. He didn't want to think about them.

He opened the last pages of the book. The short story was

called "Forgiving God." The character's initial state of mind was like his when he had first met Clarice: lighthearted and unperturbed, a tenderness and fondness he'd never before known. The story was about the character's breakdown in the face of the brutality of nature—a metaphor for God—when she came face to face with a dead russet-furred rat. The narrator responded by turning against God, who had placed a dead rat in her path.

He understood what it meant: he hadn't been responsible for Breno's death. A higher power had placed Clarice's ex in his path. Breno had been an obstacle to be overcome, a piece to be eliminated. There was nothing to be upset about. His inner state of disarray was a result not of the causes but of the consequences. His peace of mind had become frayed. What would Clarice think of him when she found out?

Teo returned to the chalet around midday. Clarice was awake.

"What happened to your face?" she asked as soon as he took off the gag.

"I hurt myself when I was out walking this morning. You were asleep."

"That's what I do most of the time these days."

He turned on her laptop and apologized for having missed breakfast. He found it odd that she'd accepted his excuse about the bruise so passively. Had she really believed him? He glanced around the room. Everything was as it had been before—or appeared to be.

"I need a date," she said. She lifted her hands to her hair and shook it in a beautiful movement.

"A date?"

"How long is this going to go on?"

"I don't know, Clarice."

"It's almost Christmas." She narrowed her eyes. "My mother's going to think it's strange if I don't show up."

"Don't ask me for a date."

"I need to be home for dinner on Christmas Eve."

"Christmas is only three weeks away."

"So, three weeks."

"You told me you didn't know if you were going home for Christmas."

She sidled over to him and slipped her arms around him. Her breasts under her blouse brushed his T-shirt.

"Please," she asked.

She climbed onto the bed behind him, massaging his shoulders. Her smell was delicious. He was almost able to forget what he'd done.

"Jesus, Teo, you're really tense," she said without stopping the circular movements over the knots in his neck. "My ex was like that too—he couldn't relax."

His shoulders stiffened.

"I thought about what you told me. I think you're right," she said. "My relationship with Breno is over. I don't love him anymore. I'm just afraid to turn the page."

"I'm glad to hear you've come to that conclusion."

"I think he was cheating on me," she said. "He had flings with some of his violin students. If our relationship meant something to him, he would have come after me. But he hasn't, has he? He hasn't come."

Clarice looked at him from only a few inches away. Was that a smile in the corner of her mouth? He was certain she knew. She knew and was playing with him. She was challenging his sanity.

"I need to go out," he said.

"What's wrong?"

Teo put the cuffs and gag back on Clarice. He had cramps in his legs. He slammed the door, saying he was going into town and wouldn't be long.

. . .

He didn't want to go out. It was Friday, and he was tired. Clarice's voice was suffocating, the hotel was suffocating, the line of couples waiting to ride the pedal boats was suffocating. The trip into town was his escape valve.

While he was there, he had lunch and did some shopping. In a café he ordered a glass of guava juice as he watched the afternoon news on the TV on the wall. He didn't see anything about Breno's disappearance, which made him calmer. Clarice was a prisoner on the bed and could never make it to the door without unlocking the cuffs. Breno was at the bottom of the lake and didn't seem to be from an influential family. When his family reported his disappearance, it would be filed away before they even made it home.

He sat down near a colorful garden and closed his eyes. He needed to talk to someone—someone who wasn't Clarice. He called his mother.

"Hang on a sec, son. I'm just taking down a recipe," she said.

In the background, a man's voice was saying . . . *two cups of apple cider vinegar, two cups of cream, two green apples, a pound and a half of* . . . Thirty seconds later the television was turned off.

"There. How are you?"

"Fine, and you?"

"Samson's necropsy results are in. They found residues of my medication in his stomach. Samson died of an overdose of Hypnolid."

"Oh . . ." he said, feeling rotten. "Don't beat yourself up over it. You had no way of knowing he was going to eat your box of medication!"

"You don't get it. Samson didn't eat my box of medication. Someone did this to him."

"Come again?"

"Someone gave Hypnolid to Samson. He didn't eat the box."

"Who would do something like that?"

"I can only think of one person."

Teo felt like hanging up but resisted the urge. He pressed the phone to his ear.

"Clarice. She's the only other person who's been over here recently."

"Clarice? She wouldn't be capable of such a thing."

"I think it's monstrous too, but there's no other explanation."

Patricia must have thought a lot about the matter over the last few days.

"What about Marli?" he said.

"Marli? Do you think she'd do something like that to Samson? She knew how much I loved that dog!"

"She has the key to the flat. And she knows you take Hypnolid."

"But why would she do it?"

"Well, Clarice doesn't have any motive either. And I was with her the whole time."

"I don't know what to think."

That was when it dawned on Teo that his mother suspected him. But she was dependent on him to look after her and couldn't just accuse him with impunity.

"It wasn't Clarice. I'm sure," he said.

"When you get back, I want to talk to her. I'm very perceptive, you know. I want to get a sense of her character."

Marli had told Patricia she was "special," and ever since his mother had used the argument to justify every harebrained notion that popped into her head.

"I don't want you to confront Clarice."

"I wouldn't. I've got more tact than that. But maybe this young lady isn't good for you."

"She's very good for me, Mother."

"Remember that nightmare I had just before you took off on your trip?" Patricia's voice grew weak. "I had it again, three times this week. The same one."

"It's just your imagination."

"I'm frightened, Teo. Someone poisoned Samson. And in these nightmares, you die of poisoning too. It's horrible!"

He said good-bye, pretending to be upset. The conversation had made him feel even worse. It wasn't Clarice's voice or the chalet. It was the world that was suffocating.

That night Teo slept soundly. He woke up early and feeling good. Before breakfast, he chatted with the dwarfs at reception: no one seemed to have seen or heard anything the night before last. He strolled around the lake. The darkness of the water attracted his gaze to the surface. He kept waiting for something to suddenly bob up—a forearm, a liver. Nothing did.

He took Clarice's breakfast to the chalet.

"You snored last night," she said, biting into a croissant.

"Sorry."

"I wasn't complaining. You seemed really tired."

"Yes, I was." He opened the suitcase to organize his shirts.

"What sign are you, Teo?"

"I'm not into that stuff."

"What sign are you?"

"My birthday's in September. On the twenty-second."

"Virgo. On the cusp. But you're a typical Virgo."

"Typical how?"

"Rational, determined, methodical. That's you."

He didn't believe that the position of the stars determined his personality traits, but he didn't say anything. He remembered the

site where he'd seen Clarice discussing astrology and deduced
that she had a bit of a soft spot for the subject.

"What time of day were you born?"

"I don't remember."

"I need to know to work out your moon and rising sign."

"What's your star sign?" he said. He didn't feel like talking
about himself.

"I'm a textbook Aries."

"How so?"

"Impulsive, independent, sincere, often too sincere. Tempera-
mental too, but I'd rather not tell you all my flaws just like that,"
she said with a generous smile. She set aside her laptop. "I need to
sleep a little more. You snored really loudly."

Teo took the opportunity to read the screenplay on her laptop. He saw how the story was progressing and identified the
changes Clarice had made. She had taken his advice on several
points, and it made him happy. He knew she'd never be able to
write again without his notes. Little by little his agitation began
to lift, and he started to feel good again. Distracted, he hummed
a song, drumming his fingers on the bed frame.

Teo was leafing through the photo album when Clarice woke
up and asked what he was doing. His reaction was to close
it. He still hadn't shown her the photos and didn't know how
she'd react. Then he decided it wouldn't be a problem to let her
see them. They weren't offensive or base. On the contrary, they
recorded beautiful feelings, such as affection, companionship,
and love.

"My mother would love that," she said. She looked at the photos as if she didn't recognize herself in the images. "She'd leave it
on the coffee table in the living room, next to her wedding album."

Clarice's tone of voice when she talked about her mother was disparaging. Teo wanted to understand their relationship, but it seemed like such a mess to him. Although he didn't love Patricia, he treated her with respect and care. Sometimes he thought about the day when he'd feel the coolness of her skin under his lips when he went to kiss her good morning and would realize she was dead. There wouldn't be anything there besides the flaccid, worn-out body that had put him in the world. He imagined what he would feel. And also what he was supposed to feel. He was supposed to cry and let people see him with his defenses down.

But deep down, in some obscure part of himself, he knew it wouldn't make much difference. He'd miss his monthly allowance . . . the cheese omelet that she used to throw together for dinner when there was nothing else to eat . . . and that was it. Omelets and money. The connection between them was basically that. But was there a problem with that? His relationship with Patricia was, beyond a doubt, better than Clarice's relationship with Helena.

"Do you like your mother, Clarice?"

"Why do you ask?" She put down the album.

"The way you talk about her."

"My mother and I used to be really close. Time pushed us apart."

"Time?"

"Time, friends, her mentality," she said. She was running her fingers over the plastic pages of the album, trying to hide her discomfort. "My mother comes from a working-class background, closed-minded. She thinks writers are lazy, people who smoke pot are criminals, and people who fall in love with people of the same sex are sick. Things I don't agree with."

The opportunity was ripe to talk about Laura but Teo didn't know how to broach the topic.

"So you grew apart?"

"She pretends to look after me, and I pretend to need her. She feels guilty—that I know."

"About what?"

"She was the one who gave up on me," said Clarice, and her words were heavy with pain. "She saw that I wasn't going to fit into the mold of a perfect daughter with a job in the public service and a nursery full of children. So she gave up. She cut me loose in the world."

Teo had been reticent about promising Helena that he'd get Clarice to call her. Now he knew that she wouldn't think anything of it if her daughter didn't contact her for several days. His main fear was that Helena might mention Breno's disappearance.

"I know it's not her fault," Clarice went on. "I'm a woman of the world. My rising's in Sagittarius. There's no point trying to control me. I belong to no one, you know? And I never will."

Teo smiled, but he had the impression she was insinuating something for his benefit. Her statement triggered a chain of thoughts in him, good and bad, that led to a harsh realization: he'd never be able to let Clarice go.

13

Tuesday began with a problem. Clarice was suffering from writer's block, and the lack of cigarettes was to blame. She said she wasn't able to write anything more. She was stuck at the part where the characters arrive at Ilha Grande.

"Bloody hell. I went there when I was five. I can't remember a fucking thing."

He knew that writers wrote about the things they knew. That's why there was no way he'd ever write fiction. He'd end up creating a character who was a doctor living happily in Copacabana with a woman who was a bit of a nutcase.

"It'll pass," he said.

Tired of staring at the computer screen, Clarice lay down next to him on the bed. She was wearing the nightgown she'd worn the day he'd picked her up at her place. She was sloppier now: hair uncared for, nails chipped and chewed, no makeup on her face, and circles under her eyes. Her eyebrows had grown in, and her legs were a little hairy. Nevertheless, she was still beautiful. There was nothing in the world capable of making her ugly.

"Why don't we play cards?" she suggested. "I need to think about something else."

Teo agreed. He didn't want Clarice to feel like a prisoner. The day before he had suggested they watch *Little Miss Sunshine* again, and that night she had asked him to teach her how to play backgammon. It was a lovely, fun day, set against the bucolic backdrop of Teresópolis.

He gagged and handcuffed her and went to reception to get some cards. Gulliver, the oldest dwarf, was on the phone and signaled for him to wait. Teo liked Gulliver: he was a quiet chap, a little serious but level-headed. He avoided looking at him for too long, as he would invariably stare at his tiny fingers, which were like worms.

Teo was surprised when Gulliver said into the phone, "I understand, Helena. You must come stay again, okay? Lately only Clarice's come to visit us!" He let out a chuckle. "I don't know why I wasn't able to call their chalet. But you're in luck. Her boyfriend's standing right here in front of me. Hold on a sec."

Gulliver covered the mouthpiece with his left hand and turned to Teo.

"Clarice's mother wants to talk to her. I was trying to transfer the call to your chalet, but I keep getting a busy signal. I was going down there now to let Clarice know her mother's on the line."

"Let me speak to her."

Teo went over to the private phone booth in the corner.

"She'd rather talk to her daughter," said the dwarf, but he ignored him. He closed the folding door, sat on the stool, and picked up the phone.

"Could you get Clarice?" Helena's voice was agitated but firm.

"She's in the chalet writing. How are you?"

"A little upset. Could you get her please?"

"You know what Clarice's like. She asked not to be disturbed. I've been kicked out of the room myself," he said, and laughed, trying to be pleasant.

"I need to talk to her. Is she okay?"

"Today she woke up in a crisis because she's stuck in one part of the screenplay. Besides that, we're having a really good time."

"Something horrible has happened."

Teo flinched and gripped the phone tightly.

"Breno's disappeared," she said.

"Breno?"

"Clarice's ex-boyfriend. She must have mentioned him."

"Oh yes, the violinist."

"He's been missing since Thursday."

"What do you mean?"

"The police have just left. They wanted to talk to Clarice."

"To Clarice?"

"I think they're talking to everyone who was close to him."

Helena's voice was empty and bitter, marked by the tension of a visit from the police.

Teo tried not to sound defensive or afraid. "Clarice broke up with him almost a month ago. It's awful that he's missing. But I don't think you should tell her right now. She's finishing *Perfect Days*." He clenched his left hand and began to beat it softly on the shelf in the booth. "Something like this could affect our relationship. I don't want Clarice to start thinking about the guy again."

"The police want to talk to her. They insisted."

"She can talk to the police after the holidays," he said. "We might not be back until the new year."

"Come back before Christmas. I want to go to Teresópolis to talk to the two of you."

"You don't need to. Everything's fine. I'm just not going to bother Clarice with a thing like this. I'm sure they'll find the guy."

"The police are going to call her on her cell. Or they might call yours. I gave them your number."

He thought about saying *You shouldn't have done that* but ended up saying, "Okay. It's fine if they call."

"Do either of you have any idea what might have happened?"

"We're not aware of anything."

"It's just that . . ." She was crying on the other end of the line. "I think I was the last person to see Breno before he disappeared."

Teo felt his legs growing weak. If he hadn't already been sitting, he would have fallen to the floor. He looked at Gulliver through the glass. The dwarf was typing on the computer keyboard and didn't seem to be able to hear the conversation.

"Breno came over here on Thursday afternoon," she said. "He wanted to talk to Clarice. He kept saying it over and over. He seemed really distraught. I said she wasn't here and that she'd gone to Teresópolis with you. He left here like a madman, saying he had to talk to her no matter what. Right after that, he disappeared. And, well, I thought . . ." Her voice petered out. "I thought you two might have had something to do with it."

"We don't."

"Are you sure?"

The question offended Teo. "What do you think? That Breno came to Teresópolis that night and we killed him?"

"I'd never think something like that!" she said. "Maybe he showed up there, and you kicked him out," she said. "I think it's possible he killed himself. He was really beside himself when he came to talk to me."

"Helena, as I said, I've been with Clarice the whole time, and

I can assure you that he didn't show up here on Thursday or Friday or any other day. I don't even know what he looks like."

"Do you think he might have committed suicide?"

"You never really know what a person's capable of, do you?"

"I never liked him. But I'm scared, Teo."

"The most important thing right now is to protect Clarice," he said. "I'd rather not tell her that this is going on. She's so excited about the screenplay. Let's give it some time. Breno might be hiding somewhere. He might have gone somewhere to think, taken some time out to get over it all."

"You're right."

"I'm being rational. There's nothing Clarice could say that would be of any help. And she'd end up feeling shaken and unable to continue writing. It'd be a lose-lose situation all around."

He hesitated but had to ask, "Did you tell the police that Breno had come looking for Clarice?"

"No. I didn't want to say anything until I knew what was going on. I don't like dealing with the police."

"I hope you're okay," said Teo politely, "and that this is all sorted out quickly." There was a heavy silence, then he said, "I'm very happy with your daughter. Her bubbly personality is contagious. She's so focused on her screenplay that she's even eased up on the cigarettes."

"She's stopped smoking?"

"Let's just say she's avoiding it," he said, as if letting her in on a secret. "I'm putting a little pressure on her, of course."

"That's great."

"Clarice doesn't want to leave until she's finished the screenplay. She spends all day writing."

"I understand," she said in her slow, serious way. "Maybe I'll come and visit you."

They hung up after a tepid good-bye.

. . .

As he walked, Teo went over the conversation with Helena in his mind. He tried to interpret things she'd said, think through nuances. Before hanging up, she had sounded convinced and agreeable. Almost too acquiescent. But the possibility of Helena showing up at the hotel at any moment flooded him with fear. If that happened, he wouldn't have an excuse not to let her talk to her daughter personally. And then what would he do?

When he walked into the chalet, he left the decks of cards on the bed and removed Clarice's gag. He said he needed a shower to cool off.

"What took you so long?" she asked.

"Your mother called."

"My mother? Why?"

"She wanted to know how you were. And when we'd be back. I told her we weren't sure yet."

He closed the bathroom door. Facing the mirror, he trimmed his beard and changed the bandage on his face. He had let his beard grow to cover the scratch on his neck. Now all that was left was a discreet line. The area had stopped hurting, but the bruise was still there.

He was ready to get into the shower when there was a knock at the door. He ran out wrapped in a towel and signaled for Clarice to stay quiet. He was completely panicked, even though there was no logical way Helena could have got to the hotel so fast. *Unless she was already somewhere nearby,* he thought, and for a second, he was certain that it was Clarice's mother outside. He pulled the curtain aside a little.

Gulliver saw Teo looking at him and smiled. "I've come to see what's going on with the phone in your chalet," he said.

Teo nodded and went over to Clarice. He sat down next to

her on the bed, stroking her arm as he removed the cuffs, and set her laptop on her lap.

"Please don't try anything," he said. He put a dose of Thyolax in the syringe. Clarice stiffened in the bed, thinking she was about to be sedated, but he went over to the door and opened it, keeping the syringe hidden behind him.

"Be quick," he told the dwarf.

Gulliver ran his pernicious little eyes around the chalet. He smiled when he saw Clarice and went over to greet her with a peck on the cheek.

"I'm so glad to finally see the great writer!" he said. He stared at her for a moment, as if waiting for her to give him some kind of signal with her eyes.

Clarice just smiled. Teo stayed close by, ready to immobilize the little man if he or Clarice tried anything. It was obvious that the problem with the phone line had been an excuse to get into the chalet. Gulliver was suspicious.

"The plug is missing," he said when he went over to the phone. "Someone must have removed it."

Teo smiled, dying to kick the dwarf. He imagined him bouncing off into the garden among the gnome statues.

"Someone?"

"One of the chambermaids, of course." His tone of voice was ironic.

Teo scowled and asked him to leave. "You can fix the phone when we go. We're fine without it."

Gulliver left reluctantly. Teo slammed the door behind him and leaned against the wall. He clapped his hands to his head, trying to control his labored, furious breathing.

"You're really not okay, are you?" said Clarice.

"Shut up!"

The silence gave him a few seconds of respite. Then she asked, "Why don't we hit the road?"

"What did you say?"

"Seeing as how we're going to be spending the next few days together, why don't we hit the road? We can sleep in a motel, then continue on to Ilha Grande and Paraty. I think it'll be good for the screenplay if I make the same journey as the characters."

It was an excellent idea, and Teo was surprised that it had come from her. Truth be told, he really couldn't bear to stay there any longer. There was something in the air, an undefinable stuffiness. He wanted to forget the dwarfs, forget Helena, forget Breno, and think only about the two of them. Go back to being what they used to be. A perfect fit.

"So, what do you say?" she said.

"I'm not sure."

Something was keeping him in the chalet. What would Gulliver think if they left now, right after that unpleasant episode with the phone line? He should have controlled himself. But he didn't really care. Sooner or later they'd have to leave. Gulliver's suspicions were as relevant as his height.

They packed in a few hours. While Clarice was showering, Teo packed the suitcases and got the ampoules of Thyolax from the minibar. He put them in the toiletry bag this time, along with a syringe, where he'd have easy access to them. Afterward, he settled the bill and accompanied Gulliver to the room to confirm that they hadn't consumed anything from the minibar. Clarice was waiting in the car, cuffed and gagged.

They set out at dusk. At around eight o'clock in the evening, she suggested they spend the night at a roadside motel with a neon sign that said WONDERLAND MOTEL.

14

The lighting was dim. Mirrors on the walls and ceiling reflected each other in an infinite sequence. The double bed was covered with a white sheet and smelled of washing powder and cigarettes. On the bedside table was a cordless phone and the remote for the twenty-five-inch television.

"It's not so bad," said Clarice, smoothing the sheet. "I hope they wash this well."

Teo followed her in with the suitcases. He left them on two chairs by the door. In the bathroom, he checked to make sure the beige-colored toilet flushed properly and tested the faucets in the shower. The plastic shower curtain was decorated with pink strawberries. He had never imagined himself in such a place.

Clarice was wearing a low-cut dress with little bows on the sleeves. She lay on the bed and smiled at him.

"There are no towels," he said, looking away.

He thought about phoning down to reception but decided to get them himself. Sharing a room with Clarice had become inexplicably uncomfortable. Was he avoiding her or himself? It wasn't time to be thinking about these things. He cuffed her and left.

"Oh my God! Oh my God! I'm going to be late!" the man at the front desk was saying on the phone when Teo walked in. The man glanced at his watch with worried eyes and hung up. "What do you need?"

"Towels."

"I'm sorry! I forgot to take them up," he said. "The person who relieves me isn't here yet."

"No problem."

Teo looked at the statue of a warrior holding a lance next to the door. When they'd arrived, he had parked in the motel garage and come up in a back elevator that led straight to reception. The walls had a medieval look, poorly painted to suggest piles of rocks. Two low towers confirmed the establishment's architectural ambition. It was supposed to look like a castle but didn't.

When the receptionist handed him the towels, he remembered to ask, "Is there Wi-Fi in the rooms?"

"No."

"Thanks."

Above each door was a red light. Teo quickly worked out the code: when the light was on, there was a couple in the room. He went up to two or three doors but didn't hear any moans.

When he arrived with the towels, he found Clarice staring at the television. Two men and a woman were having sex on a kitchen counter in a position that didn't look at all comfortable.

He took the cuffs off Clarice and put her laptop on the bed.

"Do you enjoy a bit of porn, Teo?"

He turned his face away. He didn't like to talk about intimate matters, even with her. He unzipped the suitcase and randomly chose a book.

"I do," she said. "Can you believe that most women don't masturbate? I read it the other day in a magazine. They're ashamed." She made herself comfortable on the bed and turned off the television. "Are you ashamed to have a tug every now and then too?"

"Stop it."

"It's natural."

"I—"

"The other day you were in the bathroom for half an hour. I bet I know what you were up to."

Clarice was looking him up and down invasively. Teo felt comfortable with the distance between them. He wanted to end the conversation, talk about less awkward subjects. He masturbated when he felt the need but avoided thinking about specific women. Ever since he'd met Clarice, he'd avoided thinking about her. He thought it was disrespectful. Naked, holding his stiff penis, he felt like an ogre, an animal on the loose.

"You've had girlfriends, haven't you?" she asked.

"I want to read my book."

"I'm just trying to talk. What's the problem with telling me if you've ever had a girlfriend?"

He ran his eyes over the pages. "I had a girlfriend," he said. "Once."

"Did she have a name?"

"Leticia."

"How long did you go out with her for?"

"Not long."

"How long?"

"A few months."

He wasn't lying. He had been involved with Leticia a long time ago. He was fifteen, and all his classmates were talking about girls, girls' butts, kissing. He'd wanted to be a part of the group too. Leticia lived in São Paulo and was a little chubby, a little nerdy, and a little clingy. Ideal at the time. They met on the Internet and chatted about films, music, and everyday subjects. She thought he was special, more intelligent than the rest, which was great for him.

It hadn't taken Teo long to realize that Leticia felt something more for him. He fed her illusions, not to be mean but out of the need to like someone. To *pretend* he liked someone. It was a novelty for him.

It had lasted five months. Leticia would send him daily messages on his cell, asking where he was, how he was, and what he was thinking about. Although they had no physical contact (they never actually met in person), she seemed determined to take over his life. She wanted to share secrets, give advice, get intimate. She wasn't content just being his online girlfriend. Women always wanted more. Teo's natural reaction had been to back off. Ignored messages, monosyllabic replies, excuses that he had to go to bed early. Until it completely derailed.

"Why did you break up?" Clarice insisted.

"Because it wasn't working."

"Were you two-timing her?"

"I don't do that."

"Men always do that."

He shook his head, exasperated. "I don't two-time, Clarice," he said, and went back to his book.

She came out of the bathroom and walked over to the bed, naked, a white towel wrapped around her head. Teo was distracted, and when he saw her like that, it rattled him—Clarice had always changed behind closed doors. He tried to act naturally.

She picked up the phone and handed it to him. "Why don't you order some wine for us?"

The bottle of wine was delivered a few minutes later in a bucket of ice, along with a bottle opener and two plastic glasses. She watched him serve it, smiling, hands on hips, with welcoming eyes.

"Are you a virgin?" she asked.

She clinked her glass against his and took a sip. A drop escaped her lips, ran down her chin, split into two, and continued over the curve of her breasts. Two ripe oranges.

Teo didn't answer. He could barely think. Pink nipples.

"If you're attracted to me, I want you to know that I want to go to bed with you," she said finally. She wiped up one of the drops of wine with her finger and put it in her mouth, sucking her cheeks in.

He shook his head. "It can't be like this. I don't want it to be like this."

"Don't be silly. Couples fuck."

"I—"

She shushed him with an index finger on his lips. It was still moist with saliva from her mouth. Teo blinked, trying to memorize every inch of the image. Clarice was perfect: her tongue timidly touching her teeth, the stars tattooed on her shoulder were more vivid on her naked body, so white.

"Aren't you going to drink?"

"I am," he said. He took a gulp of wine and took a deep breath, the perfumed air filling his lungs.

"I know you're a virgin," she said. She sat on his lap. The glasses clinked again. "But I'll teach you everything."

"I'm not—"

She leaned over and gave him a little kiss on the lips. It lasted a few seconds, and she nibbled at his lower lip. Teo pulled back, anesthetized, his mouth tingling. Her hipbones jutted out beneath her slender waist. For an instant, he wanted to tear off the towel, throw her onto the bed, and fuck her. He stared at the harmony of lines that converged, like streams, at her vagina.

As if reading his thoughts, Clarice let the towel slide off her hair and straddled him, pulling his pajama shirt over his head. He moaned, shuddered, panted. He placed his hands on her breasts, feeling their softness, their aroma, their shape. Clarice reached over for the handcuffs on the bedside table. She ran the cold metal over Teo's broad chest, scratching him subtly with her fingernails. She tilted her head. Moist kisses on his neck. Her tongue made circles around his nipple as she slipped the cuff onto his right wrist. Smiling, she allowed Teo to be hypnotized by her curves. She was trying to close the other cuff on his left wrist when he stopped her.

"You're not going to do that," he said.

He shoved her away violently and stood up, the handcuff dangling from one arm.

"Teo, come back here."

He got the key from the table and unlocked the handcuff.

He tossed it to Clarice. "Put it on yourself," he ordered. "Attach it to the bedpost."

"I wasn't—"

"Just do it."

He sat in an armchair studying her light, almost aerial movements. It took Clarice a few minutes to cuff herself to the bed, hands above her body. The chain between the cuffs was short and almost wasn't long enough to make it around the post.

"What are we going to do now?" she asked in a sensual voice.

He was still on fire. The contact with her skin had been indescribable. He got up and paced nervously around the room. She was saying something, but he tried not to listen. She moved her arms, spread her legs, but he refused to look. The image was inviting. Dangerous too. He needed to breathe, he needed to think, he needed to . . . He exited quickly, leaving Clarice behind in the Wonderland Motel.

15

Teo bit into a potato chip and ordered another shot of cheap whiskey. The place mirrored his state of mind: the tiny bar smelled of frying oil, and a drunk was spending his coins on shots of *cachaça* and Raimundo Fagner songs on the jukebox.

Clarice's invitation had disturbed him, confronting him with images as obscene as they were painful. Most men would have taken advantage of her there and then. He felt honorable but also like an idiot.

I know you're a virgin, she had said, as if it were blazoned across his forehead. It was an open wound. Clarice was attractive to all men. What did he have to offer her? She had made the invitation knowing he wouldn't take her up on it. She was clever, astute in a primitive way.

He was a prisoner, so close to happiness, but strong bars prevented him from reaching it. He had Clarice naked on a motel bed, but he didn't have her completely. There were parts of her to which he'd never gain access. At the end of the day, he was the one with his hands tied.

He gulped down the whiskey and ordered *cachaça*. He up-ended the little glass quickly: one, two, three shots. His cell vibrated in his pocket. On the screen it said HELENA. He put it on the table and waited for it to go to the answering service. A butter-fly fluttered quickly past. It did something pretty in the air, near the lightbulb. It flapped its little yellow wings covered in brown spots and did another somersault.

He threw down his fifth shot, feeling the alcohol slide down his throat. The frisky butterfly was beginning to make him feel queasy. He thought he might toss the potato chips back onto the greasy plate on the table. Or onto the butterfly, depriving her of all her colorful yellow and brown, making her beige. The color of vomit.

He placed his hand on the empty glass, readying himself for the attack. Then in one quick movement, he trapped the butter-fly under the glass. It thrashed about, its wings clicking against the walls of its prison. Teo pressed the mouth of the glass to the table, making it impossible to escape. That was his life. Twenty-two years old. No escape.

He ordered more whiskey. What Clarice didn't understand was that having her near him was already enough. He didn't need caresses or kisses or sex. All he wanted was that she be his, like a book of photography on a coffee table.

He liked seeing the butterfly in panic. It was comforting to share what he was feeling with someone. The butterfly couldn't accept the loss of its freedom. It hadn't expected to be incarcerated in glass to the sound of "Bubbles of Love." The rustling grew, and he took it as an answer. Clarice was under his control, but she wasn't *really* under his control. For that, handcuffs, gags, and Thyolax were useless. He needed to surprise her. Surprise her as she had surprised him with suggestive words, unexpected looks, and caresses. He needed to make a mark. Could he do it?

He lifted up the glass and let the butterfly do its acrobatics in the air. Yellow and brown. The insect was surprised by its freedom, and now it liked him. That was how it worked: surprise and gratitude went hand in hand. The butterfly liked him, and he liked it. He was filled with courage and wanted to remain so.

The butterfly fluttered away at a height that was beyond Teo's reach. He waited for it to come closer again, but it was ungrateful, flitting here and there, flapping its wings, avoiding him. Teo waited for it to land on a nearby table, then smashed it with a closed fist.

He went back to the motel room. Clarice's sylphlike silhouette was drawn in shadow: arms above her head, legs crossed, head hanging to one side. It was an uncomfortable position to sleep in, but she was asleep. He stroked her belly. Soft skin, tiny freckles. He pulled her to him. Her body flopped back; he moved forward. Her steady breathing was replaced with short gasps. He tugged on her hair and sniffed her, giving in to lust. Armpits turned him on. Hers were perfect and offering themselves up to him.

"Teo, you're drunk . . ."

He slapped her—not to hurt her but to tell her to be quiet, to swallow her words. He got the padded gag from the suitcase and put it on her. Her hands were still cuffed to the bedpost. Legs and stomach. An orchestra of clanging metals started up. He took off his shirt, stepped out of his trousers, tossed his clothes onto the floor. Human, vulgar, shameless. It felt good.

He lowered his head and ran his hot tongue around her groin, leaving a trail of saliva on her belly and thighs. He nipped at her skin as if wanting to tear off a chunk. Sex came with a dose of pain—he knew from the films he'd seen. He rubbed his nose, mouth, and eyes on her, exploring, blowing, inhaling, probing. Hands on her waist, nipples, lips. Everything about her was small and slender, his Lolita.

Dizzy from the alcohol, he pulled off his underwear. His erect penis stood in a nest of hair. He was sorry he hadn't groomed it, but what the hell. He mounted Clarice, holding her legs apart forcefully. She retreated in spasms, skin flushed, blood vessels dilated. The handcuffs jangled against the bedpost. For the first time, it felt reciprocal.

They twisted around each other, bathed in sweat. Violent banging against the bedpost. His hairy chest against the gag in her mouth. Clarice came and went like a piston. Teo panted, choked, kept going. He dominated, ravished, surprised.

He came with muffled grunts, then lay back on the bed to rest. He took off Clarice's gag, kissed her on the lips, and unlocked the handcuffs too. She lowered her head and massaged her sore wrists, staring at the door. Then she burst into tears and began to punch the mattress, arms and legs flailing.

Teo grew alarmed. He asked her to stop, but she wouldn't listen. It was as if she were having an epileptic fit. He cleaned himself up in the bathroom and went to get a syringe.

16

The car tore up the highway. Teo drove quickly, gripped by an effusive happiness. Clarice was asleep in the passenger seat, without cuffs or the gag. Before setting out, he had stowed the suitcases in the trunk and returned the engagement ring to her finger. She was more beautiful like that, a bride-to-be.

He rubbed his eyes, trying to rid himself of the effects of the alcohol. He was still a little dizzy, but his pride trumped his queasiness. His shame at having undressed in front of her had morphed into a boldness that told him to keep going. Slowly, Clarice was opening up to him; she liked him. It was natural— she didn't have anyone else. He nourished her, gave her love and attention. The least he could expect in return was a subtle form of affection, which would soon grow stronger—he was certain. At the end of the day, even hippie feminists succumbed to real men.

Good sex was an exchange. Before having sex with Clarice (something he had imagined was unpleasant for any woman), he had gone to the trouble to satisfy her. Her expression, somewhere between fear and ecstasy, had been proof of his conquest. Clarice was another person now: she didn't drink too much, she didn't smoke, and she wrote better. They had evolved together. There was something magical about what they were doing: packing bags, following an itinerary laid out in a screenplay. They were probing fiction and building a new reality, their own reality.

He took Clarice's hands and kissed them. Her pale fingers were cold and deserved some new shine. He decided to buy her some nail polish along the way. Dark colors to pay homage to Caetano Veloso, who was singing "Tigresa" on the radio as if he'd composed the song for Clarice.

The traffic was flowing smoothly against the landscape of mountains and wide meadows until, near the town of Itaguaí, just past Rio, orange cones funneled traffic into a slow-moving line. Roadwork, he imagined. He was eager to get to Ilha Grande, and the delay annoyed him. A little farther along, at mile thirteen, the situation became clear: at a highway patrol post, police officers in vests were controlling the traffic.

Teo glanced at Clarice: she was wearing tight jeans and a bright yellow blouse; she was pretty but looked tired. He took her hands and shoved them brusquely between her thighs to hide the handcuff marks on her wrists. A subtle scratch near her mouth betrayed the use of the gag.

He reduced his speed and got in the line of cars in the left-hand lane to pass in front of the police barricade. There were lots of cones, lots of officers, and lots of nervous drivers on the road-side looking for their documents. For some reason, the sight reassured him. He was certain he wouldn't be stopped; he was free of the men in uniform. The next instant an officer waved him over.

Teo considered accelerating out of there. Instead, he rolled down the window.

"Where are you headed?" the officer asked.

"Ilha Grande."

There were another five cars stopped there. Some drivers were sent to the police post.

"Has something happened?" asked Teo.

"Driver's license and ownership papers, please."

He reached for his wallet, trying not to let his hands shake, and smiled.

"Are you on vacation?"

The officer's eyes invaded the car. They came to rest on Clarice before returning to his documents again.

"Yes. My fiancée and I are going camping."

The passing seconds drew his nerves taut. The officer glanced back at Clarice.

"She takes medicine to sleep," said Teo. "She gets carsick."

"Can I have a look in the back?"

"No problem."

When Teo got out of the car, his legs buckled under the weight of his body. He leaned discreetly on the hood, trying to calculate how many hours earlier he'd given Clarice the Thyolax. Four, five? She could wake up anytime. Especially if she heard strange voices.

The officer had a superficial look around the trunk, which relieved Teo somewhat. He didn't have a license for the revolver; nor would he have known how to justify the products he had bought at the sex shop. He imagined the two pink Samsonites would convince the officer that they were just a couple going to Ilha Grande for a vacation.

"That's a lot of suitcases. How long are you going to stay for?"

"You know women—they always overdo it. We won't be staying long, as we have to be back for Christmas with the family."

"What's in the glove compartment?"

The officer's question, made so emphatically, made Teo feel as if he were going to faint. In the glove compartment was the toiletry bag containing the ampoules of Thyolax and the syringe. He went ahead of the officer, opened the passenger door, and leaned into the car, only inches from Clarice. He held out the toiletry bag to the officer, who gave it a perfunctory glance and then turned his attention to the doctor's satchel behind the seat.

"Can you open that, please?" he said

Teo turned the numbers on the satchel until he reached the combination and wiped his forehead on his shirt. For a second, he wanted to confess to killing Breno, tell the officer where the body was and what he'd been forced to do.

The officer poked around inside the satchel and held up Breno's glasses. "These yours?"

Teo didn't know how communication between the police worked, but it occurred to him that they might have put out a bulletin with a recent photograph of Breno. If so, the glasses would be the easiest detail to recall. Why hadn't he thrown them away?

"They're my fiancée's."

"And who's this?" asked the officer. Luckily, Breno wasn't wearing glasses in the photo on the licence in his wallet.

"A friend."

"'Breno Santana Cavalcante,'" the officer read. Hearing the name come out of the officer's mouth made Teo see himself in prison. He saw Clarice in a rage, shaking her finger at him in court, repeating *Now who's wearing the cuffs?*

"He left his wallet at our place. We're going to meet him on Ilha Grande," explained Teo. Was this the moment when he'd be told he was under arrest? Or was it still too early to confirm his involvement in the disappearance?

"Come with me, please," said the officer, pointing to the patrol post. "She can stay in the car."

As he followed the officer, Teo felt like a man on death row.

Although the December sun was shining in the sky, he felt the day grow gray and dark. He tried to record every detail of those minutes. They were his last as a free man. The future held nothing but concrete and bars. Even if he told the truth—that he'd acted in self-defense—he'd be found guilty by a jury of idiots. It wasn't always easy to sidestep the dead rats in one's path.

Teo squirmed in his chair. He was perspiring heavily, like a criminal. The officer had asked him to wait. Teo knew what he'd gone to do: at that exact moment, he was checking to see if the glasses in the satchel were the same as those in the civil police bulletin and confirming that the name of the missing man was indeed Breno Santana Cavalcante. There was no way out. Clarice would be taken away from him. She might testify in his favor in court. *He treated me very well*, she would say.

The officer returned to the room. He was holding an object that Teo was unable to identify. He sat down in front of him and gave him a long look, as if thinking about where to start.

"I feel quite awkward asking this next question," he said. "Believe me." He sighed and smiled. "Everything's okay with your documents, Mr. Avelar Guimarães. But I couldn't help but notice that you've had a drink recently, right?"

"Yes."

"I brought the breathalyzer." The officer showed him the object, which looked like a pacemaker. "By law, I have to ask you to take the test, but to be honest, it seems a bit irrelevant now." He smiled even more, a broad grin showing most of his teeth. "I think you know where I'm going with this. We're looking for drug smugglers who travel along this highway, not law-abiding citizens who have the odd beer here and there."

He handed Teo his documents.

"But in order to forget it all, to get around the bureaucracy, I need to know if you can help out. In whatever way you can."

"I have some money here," Teo said, unable to believe his luck. He had stopped at an ATM as they were leaving Teresópolis and was prepared to pay whatever he had to. His self-confidence was back, in full.

"How much?"

"About three hundred."

"Okay."

The money was passed from hand to hand with the discretion of children exchanging notes in the classroom.

"Can I go now?"

"It's all forgotten," said the officer.

Teo shut the car door. He heard a "drive safely" through the glass but didn't turn to answer. He hoped the officer really had forgotten everything, including Breno's name, the glasses, and the photo he'd found in the satchel.

He left the Vectra in a covered parking lot near Mangaratiba Quay and paid for a month's parking. The prospect of leaving his problems behind for thirty days quickly relieved him of the stress brought on by the encounter with the highway patrol officer.

He asked the parking lot employee about passenger ferries to Ilha Grande. There were no more that day, but a schooner was leaving in an hour. He used the time to withdraw money from an ATM and buy some nail polish for Clarice. He chose the most expensive one, as it was probably better quality. At a newsstand, he bought several different newspapers, from the most traditional ones to tabloids, and scoured them for anything about Breno. There was nothing. He asked the newsstand owner if he still had the previous day's papers, but he didn't. He returned to the car ten minutes before the schooner was to leave.

The day was still cloudless, with the sun high in the sky scorching heads. Without any difficulty, Teo opened the Samsonite on the backseat and stowed Clarice away. He had become skilled at doing it. He paid a boy with a trolley to take their luggage to the port.

The boy was talkative and curious. "Pink suitcases, mister? They the wife's?"

"She's not coming until tomorrow, but I came ahead to bring everything," he said, a little annoyed.

On the schooner, he looked for a spot that was out of the way. Noisy children were playing tag, and there were a lot of tourists. The town slowly became a row of shiny little dots, while the blue of the sky merged with the blue of the waves. The schooner lurched up and down, churning stomachs.

Lost in thought, Teo barely noticed his surroundings. Worried that Clarice might be woken up by the tossing of the boat, he opened the zipper of the Samsonite a little more. He kept the syringe handy, in case there was any movement in the suitcase, and turned on Clarice's cell. The battery was running out, but the screen indicated new messages. Breno had called more times and sent more messages. In the last one, sent on the Thursday night, he had told her he was going to find her in Teresópolis.

Three messages were from Helena asking her daughter to contact her urgently. The number of missed calls was also worrying: since their last conversation, Helena had called twenty-two times. There were eleven missed calls from another unidentified number. Teo checked his own cell: twelve calls from Helena, ten from the same unknown number. A feeling of happiness spread through his body.

On an impulse, he opened the satchel and tossed Breno's cell into the ocean. He watched it disappear and felt relieved. Then he took the driver's licence and credit cards and threw them into the water too. He waited for them to sink before throwing the empty wallet in after them. It was like leaving a heavy weight behind.

Teo took Breno's glasses and was about to throw them, then hesitated. He stared at them solemnly: they were the last piece of evidence that connected him to the dismembered body. At the same time, they were a kind of trophy of his victory. He returned them to the satchel.

17

When they landed on Abraão Beach, a local woman, old and wrinkled by the sun, offered to carry Teo's bags, recommend hotels, and take him on guided boat tours. "I can take you to have the best seafood *moqueca* in the region," she added in her shrill voice.

All Teo wanted was to rent a tent.

"Where are you going to stay?"

"I don't know. I'm finishing writing a book. I need to concentrate."

"I can take you to a campground."

"Are there any deserted beaches?"

The old woman studied him, a serious expression on her face. She smelled of salt and eau de cologne. "Camping in the wild is illegal," she said as if reading a script.

"I can pay well," said Teo. He remembered the highway patrol officer and decided to call that day "Bribe Wednesday," then chuckled to himself.

The woman glanced around to see if anyone was listening.

"I have a cottage on Never-Never Beach. It's out of the way. It isn't all that comfortable, but it's okay."

"I don't need comfort. It is really out of the way?"

"There's nothing else there, believe me. Just sand and clear water. Forest and mountains behind you. Hardly anyone goes that way, only avid hikers."

"I want to stay a month. How much will it set me back?"

The woman mumbled an outrageous price, then smiled. "Half of that goes to the wildlife rangers. To make sure no one bothers you."

He'd have to withdraw a good chunk of his savings and watch his spending over the next few months. But Clarice was worth it.

"You'd best go to the supermarket and get some supplies before you go."

"Okay."

"And you'll need to stop by an ATM too," she said, flushing. "Payment is up front."

In little over an hour, Teo withdrew money, bought groceries, and went to a drugstore. He bought a necklace of precious stones at a crafts shop to give Clarice for Christmas. At a newsstand, he tried once again to get the previous day's newspapers, without success. He sat in a café with background music and ordered some passion fruit juice, which was said to soothe the nerves, even though he didn't feel nervous or agitated. The other customers shot him curious looks, possibly because he was carrying the large pink Samsonite.

He had arranged to meet the woman at the quay in half an hour. He thought about sending postcards to his mother and

Helena but decided to phone them instead. He dialed his home number.

"I'm on Ilha Grande," he told his mother.

Patricia was surprised. She asked when he'd be back.

"We've rented a room for a month. Clarice is writing her screenplay, and part of it is set here." He didn't mention that they were going to Paraty afterward. "We'll be back in early January."

"Next year?"

"Yes."

"It'll be the first Christmas we've spent apart."

"I'm a grown man, Mother."

"And I'm getting old."

"Don't say that."

"I put up our Christmas tree. I managed not to break too many balls this year," she said nostalgically. She gave a forced laugh. Teo didn't say anything. "I want to apologize for what I said the last time you called. I shouldn't have suspected your girlfriend. Is everything okay with the two of you?"

"Yes."

"Doesn't her family mind her being away for so long?"

"Her mother also complained about her not being back for Christmas. But I think this time together will be good for our relationship," he said—and speaking in the plural made him feel sensible.

"Will you call me again?"

"I might not be able to. We're going to stay on a beach where there's no cell reception."

"I'll miss you, son."

She said it in a funereal tone that bothered him. Nevertheless he said he'd miss her too. They wished each other Merry Christmas and a Happy New Year before hanging up.

The fluidity of his conversation with his mother—and the

fact that she hadn't brought up Samson—encouraged him to phone Helena.

"Hello." The gruff way she answered frustrated Teo. He drank the rest of his juice and motioned for the waiter to bring him another.

"It's Teo."

"I've been trying to reach you since yesterday."

"Yes, we only just saw the missed calls, and—"

"You lied to me," she interrupted him.

"What?" He decided to play dumb at any cost.

"You lied to me. Breno was there on Thursday. I'm no fool."

How could she say something like that so categorically? The new glass of juice arrived, but he didn't notice.

"Gulliver called me as soon as you left the hotel. The police are looking for you, and you go and make a run for it?"

"We're not running from anything."

"Gulliver told me everything."

"Everything what?"

He was already thinking about what to say if she told him that the dwarf had seen Breno arrive at the hotel that night.

"He told me how he was treated when he went to your room to fix the phone. And he told me about the sudden way you took off."

"I don't owe you any explanations," he said, matching her rudeness. "Clarice didn't want to call you. She said you're always on her case. . . . Because she's not here at the moment, I can tell you whatever you want to know."

"Tell me the truth."

"The truth is that Breno didn't come to the hotel. Did Gulliver say he saw him there?"

"No, he didn't," she replied with a dry gulp.

Teo wondered if Helena was bluffing just to see how far he'd go. "Then how can you accuse me of lying?"

"I . . ." She was so tense that she sounded hysterically funny. "Tell me what's going on. Why did you run away from the hotel?"

"We didn't run away. Clarice is taking her screenplay very seriously. You don't know how important it is to her."

"I do know. She's my daughter."

"Part of the story takes place on Ilha Grande. She said she'd only been here as a child and could barely remember a thing."

"You're on Ilha Grande?"

"Yep, we just got here. We're going to stay on a beach for a month. There's nothing wrong with that."

"I want her to come home for Christmas."

Teo let out a long sigh. "That's between you and her. I insisted that she talk to you, but she doesn't want to have contact with anyone until she finishes the screenplay. She was pretty upset when Gulliver went to our room to snoop. She was the one who suggested we come here. And I can't exactly force her to talk to anyone on the phone."

"Did you tell her Breno's missing?"

"I told you I wasn't going to," he said. He couldn't see any holes in his story. "Hasn't he shown up yet?"

"No. The police called me earlier today saying they hadn't managed to talk to you two."

"There's no cell reception in Teresópolis. And there isn't on the beach we're going to now. Tell them we'll call when we get back."

"The detective has asked the phone company for Breno's call record."

"So?"

"He's going to see Breno's calls here and to Clarice's cell."

"That doesn't mean anything. If I come into town, I'll call you without Clarice knowing and let you know how we are. I understand your concern."

"Thanks, Teo." Helena really did seem grateful. "When you think the time is right, tell Clarice that Breno's missing. Don't keep it from her for too long."

"I reckon he's going to show up anytime now. Who knows? I might even be able to spare Clarice the worry."

"I hope you're right. The police have also requested his credit card records. That should help clear things up."

"Yes, it should."

They finished the call, and Teo realized he was late to meet the old woman. He paid for the two glasses of juice and left.

The red-and-blue-striped boat was bobbing up and down among others at the quay. The name *Tinkerbell* was written on the side.

"That's what they call me around here," said the old woman, ringing the bell hanging at the front of the boat. "My name's pretty weird."

The bags were placed in a deposit under the deck, but Teo kept the Samsonite with Clarice in it with him. He rested against the railing in the prow, thinking about many things and the consequences of those things.

The boat pulled away from the coast. It spluttered along, reeking of burned diesel oil and fish. Teo tried to relax with the breeze on his face, but he was gripped by a feeling of insecurity. He tried to remember what there had been in Breno's wallet: one hundred and ten *reais*, two credit cards, documents. . . . There hadn't been any credit card receipts, he was sure. It was likely that Breno had paid for his bus ticket to Teresópolis in cash. At any rate, there was still a small chance that he'd bought the ticket with a credit card. Lots of people threw out credit card receipts. He did it himself all the time.

18

Clarice had woken up early in the evening, looking confused. She had asked Teo where they were and how they'd arrived there. He had proudly recounted the last few hours in detail. He had even gone so far as to mention being pulled over, but he had omitted the conversation with Helena—he still found the whole thing terribly disturbing.

Clarice was sitting on a chair in the kitchen, legs crossed on the table, staring through the window at the silhouette of a rocky outcrop. Every now and then a boat would pass in the distance, and the light would cast ghostly tree shadows on the strip of white sand of Never-Never Beach. Teo was at the counter making a Thai dressing with nuts to put on a mixed-leaf salad. In the wood-burning oven, he was baking rolled-up crepes stuffed with ricotta—his favorite dish. He had his back to Clarice but tried to make conversation.

"So, what do you think of the place?"

He really wanted to know what she thought of the sex but

didn't have the courage to ask. He knew the night before had made conversation complicated.

"I hope the mosquitoes don't eat me alive," she said, slapping her neck. "Apart from that, I prefer the pollution and infernal noise of traffic."

They ate dinner in silence, by the light of a kerosene lamp hanging from a hook on the door. Clarice helped herself to more ricotta crepes, but made sure Teo knew she was annoyed at having to eat them with a spoon. As soon as he'd arrived, Teo had hidden the knives and forks under an old sofa.

Although the cottage had two bedrooms, he had put all their bags in the larger one. Clarice didn't complain and actually seemed happy to be sharing a bed with him again. The advantages of the place were many: they could wear what they wanted, and she hardly ever needed to be cuffed or wear a gag in the shower, which had only cold—or "freeeezing"—water, as she pointed out in a hysterical squeal.

Little by little Clarice won back a few freedoms. She'd never go back to being the breezy young woman he'd met at the barbecue. After all, you had to give up certain things to be in a relationship. They were connected to each other. He would take her with him forever: he could no longer live or even die without her.

The days passed, hot. Teo felt a kind of pleasant tiredness. He and Clarice would walk two or three miles every morning after eating some biscuits. They'd climb the rocks, which would take just over ten minutes, and sit at the top staring at the horizon and the large boulders on the slope behind them. In the distance, they could see a flat stretch of land that almost disappeared in the mist. Teo especially liked this feeling of distance and forgetting.

On cooler days, they'd take a sandy path into the forest. They never got very far, as the vegetation was thick and they were afraid of getting lost. They'd return exhausted and sweaty, go for a dip in the sea, and rest on the deck chairs. Clarice would go into the water naked from time to time, which struck him as an invitation to get intimate again. He held back, knowing that anticipation was more exciting than consummation.

Lunch consisted of cooked vegetables, rice, and beans. When Clarice asked for meat, Teo would fish—with some difficulty at first. He'd fry up the fish with herbs, and a delicious, pungent smell would waft through the cottage. It took him back to his childhood. Patricia used to say he was a gifted cook. It was true: Clarice would eat heartily and often said she'd never tasted anything better.

"The only thing missing is a cold beer," she'd joke, wolfing down her food.

Clarice missed alcohol. It was possible that she also missed her libertine lifestyle. But she'd stopped talking about cigarettes. She finally seemed to have forgotten them. Her inspiration to write had returned, and she was indignant about the lack of electricity in the cottage.

"How am I going to work on my laptop?"

"Take the opportunity and give yourself a break. You can write when we get back."

She hadn't looked terribly satisfied, but she didn't appear to be in a hurry to leave either. She didn't once ask how long they were going to be there. Teo noticed that she was making an effort to be nice, without being rude or seductive or mysterious—all the tactics she had used before.

She rarely insulted him. When she did so, it was over small things, subtly poking fun at his intelligence and rationality. Teo would merely smile. Smiles were the best defense to her attacks.

"You should lighten up," she insisted.

"You shouldn't be so sincere," he'd reply.

The on-again, off-again seduction, the superficial conversations, the attacks of fury followed by apologies—Teo had grown used to it all. At some point, he'd wondered if he still loved her. Perhaps she was right, perhaps it had only been infatuation—a fleeting flame. What did he know about love?

He'd quickly discarded the absurd idea. What was happening between them was simpler and more beautiful: they had reached a new, more mature phase in their relationship. Their love was steady now. The surprises had ceased, which didn't mean they no longer felt anything for each other. On the contrary, with every day that passed, he saw more and more of himself in Clarice: her thought process, previously chaotic and emotive, now revealed more method, more nuance. Her blind confidence as a scriptwriter had been replaced with a deeper self-awareness. It was a painful path but fairer and truly artistic. In the afternoon, they'd have long discussions about the meaning of art and its job of revealing the truth. Clarice believed that all it had to do was entertain.

They watched the sunset every day. Teo would take photographs but always felt a little frustrated, as the lens didn't capture the essence of the moment. When they got back, he wanted to put together an album of their trip. In the future they'd be able to show their children how they'd met.

When night fell, they'd sit side by side on the deck chairs staring out to sea. Teo would leave the lantern nearby. In silence, they'd gaze at the starry sky. Those were lovely moments, with the wind ruffling the sand and nature chanting its spells. Two weeks passed in this fashion, eradicating all worry. Teo had forgotten Breno, Patricia, and Helena. He felt that nothing could get to him.

"I'm really happy, Clarice," he confessed one day.

She was leaning back in the deck chair, her face turned up toward the sky, eyes closed. She was still, hands by her side, relaxed.

"Breno's dead," she said a few minutes later. She opened her eyes and turned to look at Teo.

"What?"

"I feel that Breno's dead."

With just a few words, Clarice had flooded him with terror and shame. He felt like clouting her. He went as far as to lift his arm but quickly brought it back down.

"Dead in my heart, I mean. Now I'm free to like you."

Clarice got up, kissed him on the lips, and walked gracefully toward the cottage.

Teo was very quiet that Thursday. He wanted to find out what Clarice knew. At the same time, he was afraid to accept the hypothesis that she really did know something. He tried to remember the hours directly after Breno's death, but tension had rendered the images unclear. Now he couldn't say with absolute certainty that Clarice had been asleep when he dismembered Breno's body and stuffed the pieces into plastic bags.

The thought that she might have been awake led to other more disturbing thoughts. Was he actually winning her over? Or was a profound hatred silently growing in her heart?

Clarice got out of the shower in a chatty mood. She had woken up wanting to talk about controversial subjects. She asked him what he thought about the death sentence and abortion. He didn't reply, so she asked again, and he was forced to say something.

"I don't think about them much."

"But you have an opinion, don't you?"

"I'm against the death sentence."

She smiled. "So am I. What about abortion?"

"I don't know. They're complex issues."

He didn't feel comfortable talking about subjects he barely understood. It bothered him that the human sciences were discussed by laypersons who felt they had the right to have opinions on matters of which they had no knowledge whatsoever. At home, he'd overheard Patricia and Marli debating how a corrupt politician should be punished ("By hanging!" Marli had said) or what should be done with a mother who aborts an anencephalic baby ("It's a creature of God," Patricia had argued).

"Gay marriage?" Clarice asked, sitting in front of him and placing her hands on his knees.

Teo looked at her, fearing where the conversation was headed. He didn't want to talk about Laura. Nor did he want to confess what he thought about homosexuality.

"Why don't we go for a walk?" he said, trying to change the subject.

"First tell me. It says a lot about a person. Are you in favor of gay marriage?"

"Yes. But I feel uncomfortable when I see it."

"You feel uncomfortable? Lots of men are turned on by two women kissing."

"I'm not," he said. *Have you ever kissed another woman?* he felt like asking.

"Hmm, that's a bit suspicious," she said teasingly.

Teo just smiled because he knew they'd end up fighting if he replied. He got up to go get his camera and put on some Bermuda shorts for the walk.

The day was beautiful and cool. During the entire walk, Clarice didn't return to the subject, nor did she bring up any other. She kicked an empty bottle as she walked and whistled an endless tune.

When they reached a clearing, he asked her to undress. "I want to take photos," he said, noting her surprise. "It'll be the secret part of our album."

Clarice didn't offer any resistance. She pulled her orange top over her head and stepped out of her denim shorts and lacy panties. She took off her sneakers, stepping over some ants in a deliciously feminine way.

"Do you want me to pose?"

"Just act naturally."

Clarice looked healthier now. In the first few days, her pale skin had become tanned. Her hair, previously straight, had acquired natural waves all the way down to her waist. Between smiles, she offered him her rosy cheeks in profile. Teo stopped taking photos and approached her. She was leaning against a broad tree trunk with her eyes closed.

He placed his hands on the tree, on either side of Clarice. "Kiss me," he said.

She noticed his gloomy tone of voice and smiled. "You're acting weird."

"I didn't like it when you brought up Breno yesterday."

"Oh, Teo, it wasn't anything important!"

"As long as you talk about him, it's a sign that he's important."

"I'm not interested in him anymore—I already told you. He's dead and buried."

"Stop talking like that."

Teo wanted to tell her everything. He felt vulnerable, under attack in a game of words. If he explained his discomfort, how would she react?

"What's going on? Let's start a relationship without secrets."

"I don't have any secrets. I just don't want you to talk about your ex."

"Fine, I've stopped. But I want you to know that I hate jealous men. Breno himself—" She stopped short and apologized.

Teo didn't feel like talking anymore.

"Truth is, I'm a well of emotion," she said, narrowing her eyes. "I know you're insecure. I get it."

She hugged him tight, whispering in his ear with her hoarse voice, "People float around in this deep well of mine. I don't know how to explain it. Lately, you've emerged, come to the surface. Breno has sunk. Don't worry about him. He's already hit the bottom, and you're still swimming."

She gave him another peck on the lips.

"I'm enjoying liking you, Teo. Please don't ruin it."

19

It was Saturday, Christmas Eve. Teo was swimming in the sea when he saw the boat on the horizon accelerating toward the coast. Clarice was reading Lispector on the sand. She looked up when she heard the drone of the motor. Teo swam back to land and told her to get inside. He cuffed her to the bed, put away the key, and came back in time to find the old woman climbing out of the boat.

"Good morning!" he said.

The woman was wearing too much makeup: red lipstick, powder on her brown face, eyeliner around her eyes, which stared lengthily at the two deck chairs by the water's edge.

"Is there someone with you?"

"No. What are you doing here?"

"I came to see if everything's all right." She continued to stare at the chairs.

"I put my legs up on the other chair," he said, but immediately felt ridiculous. Even from afar, the woman could easily have seen Clarice dash inside.

"Tomorrow's Christmas Eve, and I thought you might want to go into town to buy something. Or call someone."

"I appreciate it."

Teo wanted to buy a pound of filet mignon for Clarice, who'd been complaining about the lack of red meat, as well as some ingredients for Christmas dinner. He was going to make tagliarini with white sauce and Chilean olives, his specialty.

"I'm going to get dried off and change my clothes."

The woman nodded, staring at Teo with vibrant little eyes. She had a boorish face, with large cheekbones, thick eyebrows, and a nose like a fleshy strawberry. Her back was slightly curved, projecting her forward in an intimidating manner.

"I'll come with you," she said with a smile.

"That isn't necessary. I'd rather you waited for me in the boat."

The old woman's curiosity made Teo imagine her dead, in little pieces in a plastic bag.

"I won't be long," he said.

As he headed back to the cottage, he heard her shuffling along behind him and swung around. "Wait for me in the fucking boat, please!"

She took a step back, shocked, arms raised in a defensive gesture. "As you wish."

She turned and walked away, looking frail. Teo noticed her legs were shaking, due either to fear or to age.

He got dressed, on edge. Peering through the window, he made sure the woman was keeping her distance. He asked Clarice to put on the harness gag.

"It's not necessary. I won't scream."

"Please," he insisted. "Do what I'm saying."

"Trust is essential—"

"Put on the gag!"

He got his wallet and their cell phones. Had he forgotten any-thing? Under the sofa he found a medium-size knife and hid it in the waistband of his jeans.

Clarice kept talking, still handcuffed to the bed. "I could have screamed when the boat arrived. I saw the woman arrive. I could scream now. She'd definitely hear me."

"You wouldn't do that."

"I don't because I don't want to. You think you can make me happy. I want to give you a chance."

"I'm going to make you happy."

"Then no gags. We're in the middle of nowhere. And I have no reason to scream. Ever since that night—" She stopped mid-sentence, suddenly ashamed.

He was happy that Clarice had brought up *that night*. He was excited and tried not to let it show. "Okay then, no gag."

She smiled. "Thank you, my love!"

Teo froze. It was the first time she had called him "my love." He wanted to talk about *that night*, but the woman shouted for him to hurry.

As he stepped onto the sand, he felt as if he were floating. He savored Clarice's words and would have savored them all the way into town if it hadn't been for the nosy old woman's lack of tact.

"There's someone in the cottage with you, isn't there?" she asked suddenly.

They had pulled away from the coast. The woman was driv-ing the boat too fast, and Teo wondered what the hurry was.

"I don't know what you're talking about."

She didn't react and remained with her back to him, hands on the steering wheel. "I saw someone run inside when I arrived."

"You're imagining things."

"You don't need to explain anything, boy. But don't lie to me."

"Well, then, maybe you're right."

"I am," she said, shooting him a vulgar stare over her shoulder. "Don't worry, I'm not going to do anything. You've paid me well enough not to ask any questions. I just mentioned it for the sake of it."

They were only a few feet away from each other, and her stare bothered him tremendously. He fidgeted in his seat in the stern. She knew he was with someone on the beach, and it wouldn't be long before she began to wonder who the person was and how he or she had got there. What's more, curiosity would lead her to investigate why he had gone to the trouble of hiding it.

Teo clutched the knife in his shaky hand, without even realizing what he was about to do. He crept up cautiously. They were out at sea, and the coast was only a pinkish smudge, which made him feel safe and invincible. All he had to do was make a cut in the old woman's jugular, then throw her into the sea. In under a minute, the problem would be removed. He'd have a hard time handling the boat, but it wouldn't be impossible.

His weight made a board in the bottom of the boat creak. The noise startled him, but she didn't seem to have heard it, as she didn't turn around. He decided to make conversation, which would be an excuse for him to get closer. In the fraction of a second in which it occurred to him to talk to her, a series of possible questions ran through his head. The infinitude of questions was even greater than the immensity of the sea in front of him.

Nevertheless, unwittingly, Teo asked the key question. The question whose answer made him back away, drained of strength, and toss the knife into the water, before quickly returning to his place in the stern. If it had been anything else, he would have made his second kill. But something wanted things to happen as they did: he bought supplies in the town, decided not to call anyone, and went home a few hours later, still on a high from that moment in the boat.

Teo's question was "So, Tinkerbell, what's your real name?"

And the old woman's reply, with a toothless smile, was "Gertrude."

On the morning of Christmas Day, Teo woke up upset after a nightmare that, like all upsetting nightmares, had seemed all too real. Gertrude was in it. Not his Gertrude, who was very polite and incapable of disturbing his sleep, but the other one, the ghastly old woman. Clarice was in it too, cackling with laughter. He tried to recall the exact volume and timbre of her voice but realized he'd never seen Clarice laugh like that. He closed his eyes, reorganizing fragments into a logical order.

He'd been set up. It had all been a big ruse to trick him—and everyone had been in on it. The highway patrol officer had identified Breno from the photograph and alerted other units. They'd instructed the old woman—whose name wasn't really Gertrude—to meet him on Ilha Grande and rent him the cottage on the deserted beach. Helena's phone calls had been to make sure Clarice was still alive. What were they waiting for to arrest him? It all fit together so perfectly, which alarmed him greatly. The old woman showing up out of the blue would have been the perfect opportunity for the police to go to the island and reassure Clarice. He hadn't taken a long time in town, but it had been long enough for someone to pay her a visit. It also explained why Clarice had been so tolerant of late.

Teo shook his head: so many crazy ideas! Clarice was finally growing fond of him, and he had to go and think such things! It was so grotesque that he laughed out loud—the same laughter as Clarice's in the dream. He decided to go for a dip in the sea to shake off the idea. He had a long swim and spent a good deal of time underwater holding his breath, as the brief inability to breathe was soothing. He spent the afternoon thinking about setups.

The night was cold but cozy. Teo fixed his special dish—which Clarice praised for the smell alone—and opened a bottle of Italian wine. He put on a formal shirt and squirted on a bit too much cologne. Clarice was wearing a navy blue dress, which Teo thought a little old-fashioned on her, and her earrings were semicircles of pearls.

They didn't talk much and polished off the bottle of wine at the dinner table. Clarice was drinking faster than Teo was and consumed more than three-quarters of the bottle. They decided to open another one outside, in the deck chairs on the beach. Clarice had suggested they climb the rocky outcrop, but the wind was too strong. She put on a little red jacket to stay warm.

"Do you believe in God?" she asked. The wine was already taking effect: her arms were draped over the sides of the chair, the wineglass was wobbling in her right hand, and her legs were outstretched, feet playing in the wet sand.

"I don't know."

"I was hoping for a better answer."

Teo was relaxed and had even forgotten the nightmare. "I think people need to believe in a higher power for life to make sense. And to impose certain limits too."

"And what would that higher power be?"

"For me, it's science. I don't need God, but I go to church."

"I don't believe in him either."

She tossed her head as if defying the heavens, then poured herself another glass of wine before putting the bottle in a hole in the sand.

"I prefer to think we're all free and came from nothing."

"And what's above you? What gives you limits?"

"Well, my mother gives me limits. . . . And you too, now."

Teo found a certain criticism in those words. He didn't like that Clarice had mentioned her mother. He drank the rest of the wine in his glass, but when she reached for the bottle, he said he didn't want any more.

"You've been a bit sullen the last few days. I don't like it." She stroked his arm.

He wanted to get the necklace he'd bought her for Christmas, but he allowed her to continue stroking him. For an instant, the plan he'd put together for that night struck him as childish

"I want to apologize, Clarice . . . for what I've done."

"You haven't done anything."

"I did, I know I did," he said. He didn't exactly regret what he'd done, but the urge that had almost caused him to kill the old woman had changed into something positive. Maybe he had over-done it a little. "I'm sorry I didn't trust you yesterday. It was silly to ask you to put on the gag."

"It's okay."

"Sometimes I act a little crazy, but . . . it's just that you make me feel something . . . I can't lose you. You're my reason for living."

She smiled. Her inviting lips were dark from the wine. "Thanks for this Christmas," she said, and gently took his hand. "Let's go for a walk."

. . .

They headed away from the cottage. The lantern cast light only a few yards in front of them. Clarice asked how long he'd believed in Santa Claus and then launched into a description of her childhood Christmases. She got talkative when she drank.

Teo's replies were flat. He couldn't understand what was going on with himself. It was quite absurd: previously, he had desired Clarice with a force he hadn't even known was in him. Now he felt lost, despondent, foolish. He held the lantern as if it weighed a ton.

"Here, let me carry that for you," she said, transferring the lantern to her right hand and slipping her left arm around his waist.

He wondered at which moment he had ceased to be the protector and become the protected. With Breno's death? Helena's suspicions? The tree shadows became monstrous figures in his imagination, the ruffled leaves muttering indiscernible sounds. They walked for several minutes, picking their way around twisted branches and swampy ground. It was a full moon night.

The impact of the blow knocked his head back, and he fell to his knees. The bright spot swung down again, and he groaned and bit the earth. He saw the red hood, the light. Then he saw Clarice. Swinging the lantern through the air, she was beating him on the head.

He howled with pain. He tried to get up, but she hit him again. The metal tore into his face and blood ran down his cheeks. He begged her to stop, but the blows kept coming. He felt his body grow weak and darkness close in.

20

It was coming from inside. The brain-crushing thumping made all thought impossible. He couldn't speak, see, or move. His body was covered in pins and needles, which was a good sign: he still had a body. The rest was all a dark void.

Then the light. Forces clashed: the impact of immobility and the desire to escape, to get away from the thumping. The ache had been there first, shut away in the black box of his brain. The light was external. He blinked, forced his eyelids to open, but couldn't see. He felt stabbing pains in his head, which made him wince. Lines began to take shape, and colors filled the scene. He saw the curtain, open a crack, and the room lit by slivers of sunlight reflected on the white ceiling.

He was on the bed. The furniture melted like hot wax. His nose was on fire. He breathed in, feeling a jab somewhere. His cry got stuck in his larynx. Something was filling his mouth, pushing on his cheeks and throat. His tongue felt a strange, leather-flavored object. He pushed on it, tried to get it out of his mouth.

It was attached to his face, pulling open the corners of his mouth. His face stung, itched, stung, itched. It was extremely cold.

His senses tried to bargain with the pain. Metal around his wrists and ankles. A bumpy mattress under his sweaty, dirt-covered body. A recollection: the strong light of the lantern. The shadow in the dark. A woman filled with hatred. Clarice in a red jacket. Where was she? The image of Clarice merged with the movement of the door. Another Clarice appeared. Red and dark. Have mercy. She sat next to him.

Her cold hand touched his forehead, and he thought he heard the word *sweat*. He wasn't delirious. Clarice was saying something. He saw her lips moving as if he were watching a television on mute. He forced his mind to be quiet.

"Sorry, I'm not very good at this," he heard her say.

The pain came back. It was brutal. The noise shot through his brain.

He saw the needle piercing his forearm, which had a loose piece of elastic wrapped around it. Clarice pulled the syringe out roughly.

"I never find this vein on the first go," she said with a smile.

He wanted to scream. His eyes were heavy, his head spun. He saw the specter of Clarice stand and run her hands over his cheeks in a discreet caress.

"Good night, *my little rat*."

It was nighttime when Teo woke up, short of breath. He was startled, and it took him a while to recover. Breathing put pressure on his thorax, increasing the drowning sensation. A bolt of electricity ran throughout his body, causing involuntary reactions. His hips thrust forward, his legs shook, his abdomen contracted in spasms. He needed water, he needed food, he needed to go to the toilet. His bladder was swollen. It was a miracle he hadn't wet himself.

He tried to move his arms but couldn't. His wrists were still cuffed to the posts of the wooden bed frame, his hand raised above his head, putting pressure on his shoulders. His shoulder blades screamed. The handcuffs held his numb arms firmly back, with only four inches of leeway. His body had slid down the mattress so that his muscles were stretched to the maximum, tingling from the tips of his fingers to the base of his neck.

He twisted his arms to see the wounds on his elbows, covered in dried blood. The formal shirt he'd been wearing on Christmas Eve—the night before?—was torn, and his left nipple was visible. He tried to find a better position. He leaned his head against the headboard and tried to use his legs to push his body upward. Gravity got the better of him: his feet gave way, his buttocks bounced on the mattress, and his spine creaked.

The smaller bedroom was unexpectedly suffocating. The window was closed and covered by a curtain with a pattern of little blue birds. The mattress was of yellow foam, and the headboard cast a discreetly disturbing shadow across the door. The china terrier on the bedside table stared at him with an expression of pity. Beneath the windowsill was a wheelbarrow. As far as he could remember, there hadn't been a wheelbarrow there before. The observation was useless, since he hadn't noticed the tacky curtain either. Everything was very big and close now.

The doctor's satchel with Breno's glasses in it was on the chest of drawers, just slightly above his line of vision. He could see the combination lock, and it looked shiny, as if someone had polished it. The idea of Clarice polishing the digits—trying to discover the combination—produced a feeling of sheer terror in him.

He forced himself to stay calm. He knew Clarice wanted to make him suffer. Her persistent self-deception prevented her from seeing the benefits of their relationship. In a way, he understood the brief confusion, but wanted to clear things up. And forgive her.

She came into the room a short while later holding a glass of water in her right hand. She was wearing white overalls and looked unexpectedly sad. With her head hanging, eyes downcast, and mouth pressed shut in a serious expression, she seemed possessed by the devil. Standing in front of the bed, she swayed subtly forward and backward.

"Clarice, please, talk to me," he said, breaking the silence. Only then did he realize he was no longer wearing the gag. His voice was rusty but strong. "Talk to me. Is everything okay?"

"Drink." She held out the glass of water.

Teo moved his arms, but the handcuffs kept his hands at a distance. He tugged on the chains, scraping his wrists, but it wasn't enough. He swallowed, dry-mouthed. He didn't feel anything else. Just thirst.

"Please, come closer."

She looked up, smiled at Teo, but didn't move an inch.

"Don't be lazy. Come on, drink."

"I can't."

Clarice glanced down at the glass in her hand and then back at him. Her eyes looked like black holes.

"Gee, I'm really sorry!" she said. Her tone was irritatingly sweet. She tilted her head to one side, still smiling. "I'm thirsty too."

She drank the glass of water in front of him in long gulps.

"Are you trying to get revenge on me?" he asked. His face was stinging and itching again.

"Are you hungry, darling?"

Without waiting for an answer, she left the room and came back holding a bunch of bananas in one hand and a long knife in the other.

"What are you doing?"

She sat on the bed and tore a banana off the bunch. She peeled it. They were only a few inches apart: he could smell her perfume, which was now too sweet. He wanted to touch her but was afraid.

"I tidied the place up. There were dead insects and dust everywhere! All it takes is for a woman to get a little tied up, and everything becomes a mess," she said. "I found a lovely set of knives under the sofa."

She sliced the banana awkwardly, as the knife was very big and heavy. She placed a slice between Teo's lips, and he wasn't able to resist it. He was starving. He chewed slowly, thinking about what to say to her.

"Why don't you let me go?"

"It's so nice like this!"

"What are you going to do to me?"

"Oh, stop asking such difficult questions!" she screeched like a fifteen-year-old girl who'd just found a cockroach in the bathroom. She shoved another slice of banana into Teo's mouth and waited for him to chew. "Have you seen your new means of transportation?"

She pointed at the wheelbarrow. Only then did he notice that the wheels were covered in dirt.

"I needed it to bring you here. You're pretty heavy—did you know that?"

"Stop it. Let's talk seriously now."

"You need to go on a diet. How much do you weigh? Over two hundred pounds?"

"This isn't right, Clarice. Revenge—"

"Revenge?" She grinned, and her grin was so hypocritical that it rattled him. "I don't know what you mean, darling. I'm just showing you what I feel."

"Everything I did was for your own good. Thinking about your well-being."

"I thank you for it."

"Clarice, you're not a bad person." He made a point of saying her name, a psychological tactic to create a sense of intimacy between them. "Anger only leads to bad feelings."

"My feelings are good, I assure you. Cleaning the place up did me good." Her eyes flitted across the walls, and she stood up as if she'd just remembered something urgent she had to tend to. "I found lots of interesting things."

She hurried out again. Through the open door, Teo could see part of the kitchen table and the metal sink. There was a pile of dishes waiting to be washed, and he wondered how much time had passed for Clarice to have dirtied so many dishes. He also wondered if she'd been lying when she said she'd *tidied up*.

"I used this time to think," she said when she came back. She placed his toiletry bag on the bed. Teo felt nauseated. He glanced at the satchel on the chest of drawers before returning his gaze to Clarice's hands. He saw her pull the packaging off a new syringe and screw the needle into place.

"Please don't sedate me."

She nodded her head slightly, unconcerned. It was disrespectful.

"I might get contaminated!"

"It won't happen, darling."

Teo wanted to reply, but all the arguments he could think of sounded incoherent. From his point of view, lying with his arms over his head and needing to pee, Clarice seemed like an evil nurse out of a horror movie. He was scared.

"Want some more banana?" she asked. She shook an ampoule of Thyolax in front of his eyes, measuring the dose.

He was still hungry, but he said, "I'm disappointed in you. I don't believe you're going to sedate me again."

Clarice sat a few inches away and stared deep into his eyes. Her eyes made him feel something he'd never felt before. It was as if she knew about Breno's death and believed it was all his fault.

"I've thought a lot the last few days . . ." she said, plunging the needle into the ampoule and sucking the solution into the syringe. There was a tiny amount of liquid left, and if he wasn't mistaken, it was the second of the three ampoules. "I thought about the first few times we talked, your ploys to get near me . . . you holding me prisoner with handcuffs, gagging me—"

"Clarice, I'm sorry."

"Don't interrupt me." This time she sounded like she was going to cry. "I thought a lot about what happened, Teo. And I really tried to understand. I put myself in your shoes. It all sounds crazy, but you wanted me to fall in love with you. You wanted me to love you like you love me." She put the elastic on him and wiped the inside of his forearm with gauze soaked in alcohol as she felt for his veins with cold fingers. "Our story can't end like this. You don't deserve it. We don't deserve it."

He was confused.

"You had a chance to show me your side of things," she said, wiping away a tear. "You feel something for me, I get it. But now it's my turn. I feel something for you too. And I want to show it to you."

She nodded at the door, then stretched out the skin on Teo's arm and slowly pushed in the plunger of the syringe.

"Now let's sleep."

21

Teo was woken up with a bucket of cold water. The shock made him shiver, and the throbbing in his head returned full force. It was a sunny day. The closed curtain created a pleasant half-light: a few rays of sunlight came in near the ceiling over his head. He was in a cold sweat, shouting. When the pain eased off, he saw Clarice in the doorway, laughing her head off as she shook the empty bucket.

"My God, you look frightened!"

She shook her head solemnly. That movement, previously so enchanting, revealed all her perversity. Clarice was toying with him and appeared to be enjoying it. She returned to the room with the bucket full, holding it clumsily with her thin arms.

She took a wet sponge out of the bucket and rubbed Teo's legs with it. The texture was abrasive on his skin, pulling off scabs and causing open wounds to bleed. It was unbearable. He tried to move his legs, but it was useless.

"Don't be such a wimp," she said in a tone of voice that was at once scolding and maternal. "You look awful. Look."

She took the mirror down from the wall. Teo was shocked by his reflection. He was unrecognizable, covered in swellings and festering wounds filled with yellow pus. It looked as if his face had been sliced up with glass. His right cheek had become a large purple ball over which a beard was growing. He stank. How had Clarice left him in that state?

She smiled, slightly flushed.

"What's so funny?"

"I woke up in a good mood."

She put her left hand behind his head, tilting it back. With her right hand, she lifted up a razor. The blade was rusty and probably blunt. He tried to lower his head, but Clarice held him by the chin. She wet his cheeks and rubbed household detergent on his neck and around his mouth until she'd worked up a lather, then positioned the blade near his jugular and carefully scraped it off.

Teo imagined she was about to kill him. And the idea didn't sound that bad. It would be a relief from his problems, resolved by a painless cut. His mother and her disabilities, Helena and her desperation, and Clarice and her ridiculous revenge would all be left behind. It was a settling of accounts. As a martyr, he had to die so that they could miss him.

"Why don't you kill me?"

Clarice stopped for a moment. She let out a long sigh as she lightly pressed the blade to his skin.

"I'm not like you," she said, and then went back to shaving him with her previous diligence. She dried his face with the tip of the filthy sheet. It reeked of urine.

Teo felt strange; something grotesque and repugnant was now a part of him.

"Let me have a shower."

"You're much better like this."

Clarice tended to his face with some ointment and gauze that she'd found in the toiletry bag. He tried to tell her the best, least painful way to apply them, but she ignored him. She returned the mirror to the wall and dragged a chair from the kitchen into the bedroom. She sat down, put her legs up on the bed, and pulled a packet of Vogue cigarettes out of her pocket.

"I had a poke through your things and found these treasures!"

She lit the tip of the cigarette on the flame in the lantern. She took a drag, filling her cheeks with smoke and closing her eyes with pleasure.

Then she blew smoke at him like a naughty child. "I thought you wanted to talk to me."

"I want you to take these handcuffs off me."

"You know I can't do that."

"You can and will. I refuse to play this game."

"I just want to have a bit of fun."

She was very comfortable, puffing on her cigarette and chewing her nails irreverently. Teo felt the pain of betrayal for everything he'd done for her and everything he wasn't receiving in return. He rolled his eyes, and only then did he notice that the satchel wasn't on the chest of drawers anymore. Its absence was unexpectedly disturbing. The smell of mint in the smoky air transformed his impatience into fury, and he wanted to hurt Clarice too.

"Don't be insolent, you slut from hell!"

She smiled, a sarcastic idiot, and puffed hard on the cigarette. "Fuck me dead—I've missed this so much!"

"Undo these cuffs!"

"Stop annoying me, or I'll have to use the separators on you, *little rat*."

He gulped. The thought of himself on the cross terrified him. "I'm sorry . . ."

"Want a drag?"

"You know I don't smoke."

"Just one cigarette!"

"Are you really going to keep up this shit to provoke me?"

Her face darkened like the sky before a storm, then brightened. "Shit to provoke you? That's a good one, Teo. Shit to provoke you!"

Clarice crushed the cigarette in her hand, the smoke escaping through her fingers. Tears poured from her red eyes, as her slender body convulsed with laughter. She tried to control herself, eventually stifling the laughter and fixing her empty eyes on him.

"The slut from hell is going to do shit to provoke you until you cry with desperation," she said with an indescribable expression. She touched his nipple with the tip of the cigarette and let his flesh burn. He howled. "You're just lucky there's no cell reception here. When that old woman comes back, I'm going to hand you over to the police, and everyone in prison is going to do to you what they do to motherfucking rapists!"

Clarice got the harness gag from the headboard and put it on him. Teo saw the situation with a mixture of indignation and rage. Rapist? If he could, he would have killed Clarice that very second. He'd have killed her and thrown her pieces into the sea without the slightest remorse. He'd even have taken some pleasure in it.

She didn't come back to the bedroom the whole afternoon. He saw her moving back and forth with a broom and bucket. The image of Clarice-the-housewife was rather comforting, but the fact that he was cuffed to the bed with a disfigured face, a fresh wound on his chest, and the harnesses pressing on his cheeks made the situation a little sordid.

Clarice didn't let up. After the exchange of offenses, he had apologized and begged her to bring his arms down: he could no longer feel his elbows, much less his fingers.

He racked his brains for arguments to persuade her to release him, but somewhere deep down he believed she would come to the conclusion on her own and walk into the room to remove the cuffs. She'd apologize, say she didn't know what she'd been thinking. Then she'd give him a kiss on the lips and lighten the atmosphere with a funny swear word.

Teo came to the conclusion that she was treating him like that because intimacy breeds contempt. She was doing it not out of malice but to let out a buildup of anger. Anger was the worst emotion in a relationship. He needed to let her get it out of her system.

He imagined what they'd call their children. (The boy would be Dante, and the girl, Cora.) He imagined Patricia's joy when she saw her grandchildren and the career paths the children would take. (Would they be artistic like their mother or methodical like their father?)

It was strange to think about these things and, at the same time, still be hurt by Clarice's actions, but he knew how to keep his feelings separate. She was like all women: smiling one minute, only to burst into tears the next. He needed to be understanding. With Gertrude there hadn't been any clashes, but there hadn't been love either. Only Clarice had been capable of jolting him out of his university-home-laboratory routine. And he didn't want to go back. If he could, he'd stay on the road forever. He didn't need Clarice to love him back. Better to feel unrequited love than not to love at all.

Later in the afternoon, he heard Clarice typing vigorously on her laptop. Perhaps the screenplay and all his help in the creative process would make her see that her revenge was unfair. He was pleased that she was writing again, as he knew her fury would be channeled into her creative work.

It was already dark outside when the beeping of the battery indicated that the computer was going to shut down. There was no way to recharge it. Teo heard the laptop being closed, footsteps going into the bedroom next door, water running in the sink. Then silence. When Clarice appeared in the doorway, he moaned, begging her to take off the gag.

"I hope you behave," she said, unbuckling it. "Uncomfortable, isn't it?"

"I need to go to the toilet."

She was wearing a blue dress that suited her figure. Her body was beautiful, that of a grown woman. He realized he'd never told her that. Women liked to receive compliments, although she might not be too open to praise under the circumstances.

"Please, I need to go to the toilet," he repeated.

She gave him a weary look. "I can't release you before that old woman comes back. Sorry."

"Look, I think we got off to a bad start. We were getting along so well. I understand that you want revenge—"

"I already told you this isn't revenge."

"Okay, it isn't revenge. I understand you're doing what you're doing. But I need you to think a little. And to listen to me. You can't go on treating me like this. I'm human. I have needs."

A harsh expression came over Clarice's face. Her bottom lip twitched. "You talk as if I were holding you prisoner."

"I *am* a prisoner!"

"After our conversation, I came to the conclusion that maybe you were right," she said, and the accompanying smile made her look even more dangerous. "I should kill you."

Teo's Adam's apple moved up and down.

"I was tormented by the idea all afternoon. I even made a list. There are lots of places to dump a dead body around here, if you get my gist."

She retrieved a piece of paper and a pen from a drawer.

"Let's see if I've forgotten anything," she said, tapping the paper with the pen. "Number one: Kill Teo. I think you deserve a slow death. I ruled out slitting your throat with a knife. And I ruled out the gun too, since we don't have any ammunition. What do you think of drowning?"

"Don't be an idiot."

"No? Okay then." She crossed it out. "How about buried alive? That seems like a good one. It'll be a bit of work to dig a really deep hole, and I can't really be bothered today. Maybe tomorrow?"

"Are you really going to kill me?"

"Number two: Explain things to the old woman," she read. "What's she like? Is she dense? Or will I have to come up with a good excuse?"

"Stop it."

"I thought about telling her the truth, but I don't think she'd understand. Ditto for numbers three and four: Explain things to my mother and the police. Do you think anyone will come looking for you, Teo? Or will your mother be relieved to be rid of her sick son?"

"Fuck you, Clarice."

She looked up. "Seriously, you really don't think you're at all sick? That album of the two of us is totally psycho."

She waited for him to reply and shook her head.

"We've come to number five: Things to do with Teo. This was a stroke of genius." She smiled, running her tongue over her front teeth. "Let's do some things to make you see that you're a total *freak*."

"I won't do anything to you."

Her smile gave way to an expression of displeasure. She left quickly and came back carrying the album and a heavy clay pot. She set the pot on the chest of drawers and pulled the photographs out of the album, rubbing them violently in Teo's face.

"This is all a lie. The fantasy world of an asshole. What do you think we should do with it?"

Sick with panic, he looked at Clarice smiling, felt the gentleness of her gaze and their bodies occasionally coming into contact. How could such a beautiful feeling have become so base and diabolical? He wanted to cry, but he felt dry. He watched in silence as Clarice picked out the photos of the two of them together and tossed them into the pot. Then she took the lighter out of her pocket.

The flame found the photo paper, which twisted, shriveled, and darkened in a few seconds. The images disappeared in the toxic, oily smoke coming out of the pot. Clarice watched the pyrotechnical display, clapping her hands with delight, Beauty transformed into Beast. She threw the other photos into the pot as she poked and fanned the flames. She blew on sparks as if they were soap bubbles, imitating the crackling sound with her mouth. *Pop, pop, pop.* The room was awash with the smell of burned paper.

She stood holding the pot, staring into the still-bright embers. In the doorway she stopped and turned.

"Happy New Year, Teo!"

The information came as a blow. It meant that he'd been a prisoner there for seven nights. He'd been sedated most of the time and had calculated three or four nights at the most. It also meant that the old woman would be back to get them in a week. Seven days in which to try to escape. If Clarice didn't kill him first.

22

The smell masked the pain. It was strong and hot. He could feel the sticky blob under his buttocks, like a soft, slimy mattress. He was ashamed. And enraged. Through the closed door, he could hear Clarice moving about in the kitchen. It sounded like she was cooking. She hadn't shown her face since the previous night. Teo had woken up in the middle of the night and begged to go to the toilet. He had shouted for hours, but now it was done. It felt horrible.

Clarice opened the door and said good morning. She was wearing nothing but a bikini and had a dirty shovel in her right hand. She was sweating.

"How are we this first day of the new year?" she asked. She set the shovel aside and gave him a light kiss on the forehead.

Teo closed his eyes. The smell of death had invaded his nostrils.

"I made you lunch. You must be hungry, now that there's room in your stomach," she said.

She brought a plate into the room, pulled a chair up to the bed, and sat down with a straight back, like a child watched by a teacher. She rolled some spaghetti onto a fork and served him carefully, catching the sauce that dribbled from the corners of his mouth. He spat out the food.

"Eat, Teo."

"I'd rather not."

"You're in no position to be dramatic."

"If I'm going to die, I don't want to."

She raised her eyebrows slightly, and a timid smile appeared on her lips. "I'm not going to kill you, silly. You don't deserve so much peace."

"Are you serious?"

"Of course I am. Now, eat."

Teo accepted the food. He didn't know if he could believe Clarice, but the wind seemed to be blowing in his favor. His hostility slowly lifted, and he felt compassion for Clarice, an affinity of sorts. She wasn't humble enough to apologize, but deciding not to kill him and hand-feeding him spaghetti was a way of saying sorry, wasn't it?

"I'm glad you've had a change of heart," he said, and was so happy that he wanted to ask *have you ever fallen in love with someone and been certain that you'd do anything for them?*

Clarice skewered two pieces of filet mignon at the bottom of the dish and offered them to Teo on the fork.

"I don't eat meat."

"It's good for you. You will eat it, and you'll get used to it."

He closed his mouth.

"If you don't try it, I'll be offended," she said reprovingly. "I made it with love."

"I don't want it."

She returned the meat to the plate and stabbed the fork into his nipple until it bled. "I want you to eat. Don't force me to be impolite."

"That meat must be rotten. It hasn't been refrigerated for days!"

"Eat!"

He chewed against his will. It tasted rancid. The generosity that had made him buy the mignon for Clarice now seemed pathetic.

"Delicious, isn't it?"

"Yes."

"I knew you'd like it." She hand-fed him until she'd scraped the plate clean.

"Please, put my arms down, cuff them to the bed frame," he asked finally. "I can't bear it like this anymore. I can hardly feel my fingers."

She tilted her head to one side and stopped for a moment in the doorway, as if considering it. Then she left.

Clarice didn't return until late afternoon. A cold breeze was blowing through the window, and Teo had tried to wrap himself in the squalid sheet. The filth in his underwear was solid. The room stank unbearably, making his urge to vomit stronger. Vomiting would only make things worse. He made a great effort to stifle his retching.

"Take this," she said, jamming a pill down his throat.

His lips stiffened: his dry tongue tasted foul. He hadn't brushed his teeth in days.

"It's for your queasiness. We need to talk."

"Talk?"

"One hundred percent honesty. What do you say?"

"I've always been honest with you, Clarice."

She laughed and lit her Vogue cigarette. She was wearing a dress that was too short for the weather and too sparkly for the occasion. Around her neck was the necklace of precious stones he'd bought in town but hadn't had the opportunity to give to her. Clarice had found the package, which made him proud and bitter at the same time.

She crossed her legs and made herself comfortable. "You know that Woody Allen film? *Everything You Always Wanted to Know About Sex But Were Afraid to Ask*? Let's play our own version: *Everything You Always Wanted to Know About Me But Were Afraid to Ask*."

"Huh?"

"Something for something. You ask me something, I ask you something. Quid pro quo, Teo."

"I haven't got any questions."

"I said one hundred percent honesty."

"You're wrong."

"Laura and the kisses you saw," she said. "We've never talked about that."

"It's in the past. I'd rather not know."

"You sound like my mother sometimes. She'd also rather pretend that certain things never happened."

"Certain things are too painful."

"Like seeing me kiss another woman?" She blew smoke onto him.

Teo couldn't stand Laura. He could barely bring himself to think about her, and his feeling of nausea was growing.

"It's not her fault," said Clarice. "I like women."

The statement gnawed at Teo's soul. Clarice had a knack for hurting him when she wanted to.

"And what does your mother think about it?"

"It really bothers her." Now there was pain in her voice. "I don't know if I want to talk about it."

They sank into a melancholy silence. Teo didn't know if he wanted to talk about it either.

"Finding out that her precious little daughter liked someone of the same sex was just one more disappointment. The worst," she said finally. "But I don't know how to hide who I am."

Clarice's irresponsible freedom had fascinated Teo at first. It was unthinkable to someone like him, who calculated every move before he made it, weighed every word before he spoke it. She wasn't ashamed to be like that. He wanted to be like that too.

"Did your mother catch you doing something?"

"She caught me with a girl from school. We were drunk and had gone to my place to hook up. She found the girl hiding under my bed."

"That's horrible."

"Horrible is what came next." She frowned as if she were still bitter about it. "They took me to a psychologist. Can you believe it? In the twenty-first century, they thought I could be cured."

"I hope you're not a lesbian, Clarice. I still have hopes that you'll come to like me."

She tied her hair back. For the first time, he noticed some fine lines on her face. Tiny signs of age.

"Did you really think you'd manage to win me over like that?" she said. Her tone of voice was affirmative, perhaps contemplative. He realized it was all still very new for her.

"There was no other way."

"Believing in me was stupid."

"I needed to try. I couldn't hold you forever. Little by little you had to be free again. We came to this island, and I needed to see how you'd react."

"I don't think I reacted very well."

The smoke from the cigarette created a subtle fog between them. She got up and shut the window. Then she got the key to the handcuffs from the kitchen. She turned the key in the right lock, and the metallic click sounded liberating.

"Don't try anything," she said.

She slowly brought Teo's arms down and cuffed them to the bed frame.

He was in no condition to strike out. His distended muscles shook and quickly cramped up.

"I'm sorry I don't like you the way you like me," she said, and put the key on the bedside table.

Teo didn't know what to say. Saying he loved her would sound too repetitive, even to him. He wanted to say something unusual and shocking, but couldn't think of anything. Clarice left the room for a moment and returned holding the satchel.

"Now it's my turn to ask a question. What's the combination for this?"

Teo was petrified. He thought about Breno and his dratted glasses.

"Please, let's do this the easy way," she said.

"Clarice, I—"

"I was nice enough to put your arms down. Tell me the combination."

It was disconcerting not knowing what to say. She insisted in a way that he didn't have the strength to argue against.

"I've tried everything imaginable and can't crack it." She shook the satchel near her ear, trying to divine what was in it.

"Some things are just too painful, Clarice."

She put the satchel on the bed and leaned over him. She placed her hands on his wrists, squeezing them firmly. Her breath smelled good, even if there were traces of cigarette on it.

"I want you to tell me. And I want you to do it now. Or I'll put your arms up again."

Teo closed his eyes and saw himself as if in a dream. He was patiently building a house of broad red cards. There were trees around it, and the sun was shining brightly. Then he blew the house of cards down with a single puff.

"The combination is zero-seven-zero-six," he said, eyes wide open. "Please don't do anything."

23

Clarice smiled as she turned the digits, opened the satchel, and fished out Breno's glasses. Teo would never forget the image: her eyes darted about in confusion, and her mouth dropped open. Her long, slender fingers felt the glasses as if they could turn them into something else.

Suddenly she looked frantic, or wounded. The color drained from her face, her vocal cords stiffened, and an inconvenient vein bulged on her forehead. She closed her fists, almost crushing the glasses, and punched the air. The profound look of betrayal that replaced her air of superiority made Teo feel very clever.

"Explain," she begged.

The silence was absolute, and he let those minutes of peace stretch out. He didn't feel like explaining anything. And now, with his arms down by his side, he didn't feel any obligation to be nice.

"What are these glasses doing here, Teo?"

"Breno is dead," he said, and it sounded so banal, it was as if he'd borrowed the line from a novel.

Clarice blinked, as if avoiding something, and started to cry.

Teo couldn't understand how she was still able to think about Breno after everything they had been through. Her reaction damaged something special in their relationship. He wished he could say something that would put an end to her suffering, but he knew there were moments in life when it was necessary.

Besides which, he was sure she already knew. Clarice was just crying because she felt she should look upset. It was as if they were in a theater: stage, lights on, the audience waiting for a dramatic performance.

"We killed Breno," he said.

She didn't look as surprised as he thought she would. "Did we?"

"Yes. Don't you remember?"

"You're lying!"

"We did it together, Clarice. He was going to kill us."

Teo was finding it all very amusing, especially her reaction.

Clarice dropped the glasses and fell to the ground, where she curled up like a baby. She buried her face in her hands and let out a piercing scream. "I don't remember . . . I don't . . ."

She pressed her temples frighteningly. She was very red and looked as if she were going to fall apart before his eyes. Teo wished he were free of the cuffs so he could hug her, but he knew she would stop him if he tried to reach the key on the bedside table.

"It's most unfortunate, I know. But no one knows."

"Liar! Psychopath!" Clarice shouted insults without any logic. She sucked in her lips, shook her body, and sobbed pathetically like an irritating child.

"Stop crying," he said very calmly. One of them had to keep it together.

"I love Breno!" she cried.

Teo laughed. "He tried to rape you."

The lie made him feel a tad perverse, but it wasn't entirely untrue. After all, Breno had gone to Teresópolis uninvited and hadn't been in his right mind. He probably would have hurt Clarice if he hadn't been stopped.

"You helped me bury his body," said Teo finally with a thespian smirk on his face. The lights would fade, and the audience would give them a standing ovation. He tried to clap, but the chains on the handcuffs were too short: his fingers managed to touch, but it wasn't enough.

Clarice made an effort to stand—her little arms looked like twigs—and staggered toward him. Now Teo could hug her and tell her that everything was going to be okay. He reached out his hands. He wanted to feel her skin, which must have been very hot with all that excitement.

He didn't expect to be slapped hard across the face. It made him dizzy. The noise rang out again like a creaking floorboard. It was selfish of her to flog him as if she could transfer her part of the blame to him. Teo was so horrified by her attitude that he offered no resistance.

He let her beat him in silence, even though it hurt a lot. His skin tore, the scabs on his face split open again, and he had to close his left eye when a drop of blood ran into it. All that fuss over a piece of shit who played the violin and had interfered in his life in a most inopportune way.

Clarice wasn't really upset over Breno's death; she was probably even relieved. She needed to let out feelings that couldn't be explained, like when an aunt you don't like much dies, and the news makes you feel strangely emotional. She needed to take it out on someone, and she was taking it out on him.

Clarice got the revolver from the chest of drawers. She held it clumsily, with shaking hands. The barrel was pointed straight at Teo. She cocked the hammer, readying it. She didn't remember that it wasn't loaded.

The Clarice in front of him wasn't the same woman he'd met

at the barbecue. Nor was it the Clarice with whom he'd spent such happy times in Teresópolis and had shared that unforgettable night at the motel. Nor was it the Clarice who'd sought revenge by burning photos and blowing smoke in his face. It was someone else, disturbingly agitated, with wet, stony eyes. A soulless Clarice.

Then she pointed the revolver at her own head, leaning against the wall to remain standing. She was shaking a lot. The weapon seemed to weigh heavily in her hand, as if she were drained of all strength. Clarice gave Teo a diabolical look, and he returned an expression of incomprehension and regret. She pulled the trigger without hesitation.

The dry click frustrated her. She threw the revolver to the ground, stomping on it irrationally and yelling "I love you, Breno" as if the wretch's spirit could hear her hysterical bellowing. Her ribs shook, and her body looked about to explode. He was very sorry that she was going crazy.

She bumped into the kitchen table and flung open the cottage door. Teo heard her sobbing accompanying her crooked footsteps through the sand. Where was she going? The relief that ran through his body was greater than his curiosity, and he wanted to prolong the moment. He closed his eyes and rested his head on the pillow, trying not to think about anything. He barely existed as far as Clarice was concerned, which was terribly sad. Attempting suicide had been particularly offensive. He would never forget it.

The bedroom felt lighter and happier without her there. When he opened his eyes, he felt better. Out of the corner of his eye, he noticed something moving outside. Through the window he saw Clarice in the water swimming toward the horizon, as if to get away from him. Her little arms thrashed at the water with useless strokes. Then an enormous wave swallowed her. She didn't return to the surface.

24

Teo writhed on the mattress in horror. In his mind's eye, he replayed the sight of Clarice's body disappearing into the sea over and over, the water exploding in white spray and swallowing the love of his life. *The love of my life.* He tried to reach the key on the bedside table, but he wasn't close enough. He turned his body around on the bed, shimmying as near as he could to the side, straining to reach the key. His fingers touched the table but not the key, which had slid across the top. He tried even harder, allowing the cuffs to pinch his forearms, and finally managed to reach it.

He unlocked the handcuffs and raced outside. Pulling off his clothes, he waded into the sea, the salt water stinging his wounds. He swung his head from side to side, looking for the place where Clarice had disappeared. He felt impotent and a little stupid because it all looked the same and he had no reference points. It was high tide. When he thought he was near the right place, he realized he could no longer touch the sand with his toes. He stood on a rock covered in slime and slipped when a sea urchin pricked the tip of his big toe. He climbed back onto the rock and shouted for Clarice.

He thought he'd seen a human shadow in the greenish-blue water, but when he swam out there, he didn't find anything. How much time had passed? Definitely more than three minutes, maybe as much as five. His greatest fear was that Clarice had been dragged down to the bottom. He didn't consider the possibility that she might have drowned. The world wouldn't let someone so special go without the slightest ceremony. It would be unfair, criminal.

The sea was turning a bright red—the sun was yawning on the horizon, and the sky had merged with the scarlet seascape. Teo kept treading water, with greater difficulty now, as the current seemed determined to suck him down. He dove underwater with his eyes open. The splendor of nature took his breath away. He had to swim back to land. The cold wind made his bones creak. It was a strange feeling: his brain remained logical while his body succumbed to involuntary reactions.

He felt ill. All he could think of was tragedy. Then he saw Clarice's body. It was near the rocky coast, snagged in an unlikely position between two rocks. Her face was covered with her hair but appeared to be above water. Her arms were beside her, bobbing up and down grotesquely on the waves. Apart from that, she wasn't moving.

Without hesitation, Teo headed into the water, feeling jabbing pains in his chest and right arm. He kicked his legs and lifted his arms high into the air with each stroke, as he wanted to make sure Clarice remembered her rescue as something heroic. When he got to the rocks, it was hard to find a place to hold on. His vision was clouded by the cold or by tiredness. He had to hold onto Clarice's arms and clamber over her body. Her dress was torn, and when he climbed over her, he saw blood.

The bottom half of her body was covered in abrasions, mostly around her lower back. Clarice was conscious, but disoriented. She was gasping and appeared to have taken in a lot of water. Her heart was beating quickly.

"Stay calm, I'm here," he said.

He tore off her dress—she had nothing on underneath—and tried to turn her over. The waves were strong, throwing them against the rocks. Blood was gushing from a deep cut that had turned her left buttock into a jagged piece of flesh. She shook and spluttered incomprehensibly. He thought he heard her call out for Breno but tried not to take it personally.

He needed to deconstruct the image of Clarice—his Clarice— and all his remorse regarding her. He had the skills to save her and was proud of the certainty. In a quick movement, he lifted her hips and tied the dress around her buttocks. The procedure helped stanch the blood, and he was able to remove her. He held her by the armpits as he swam, but she felt heavier than ever. It required inhuman strength. He had to find another position. He put her on his shoulders and swam, although the weight on his neck and back was enormous and he went under frequently, swallowing salt water and losing his senses for a fraction of a second.

Clarice was sliding off him and he was no longer in control of the situation. He could barely manage to stay afloat himself. At that instant, as his feet felt in vain for the sand and he realized that he was still too far out, it struck him as interesting that they should die there, awash in the seductive arms of the Atlantic Ocean. *The seductive arms of the Atlantic Ocean*—he was certain a writer had already used the line in a novel. He loosened his grip on her arms a little, ready to let her go first, but then his feet touched sand, and he felt very much alive, confident and sure of himself again.

He held Clarice up above the water and, digging his toes into the sand, carried her through the backwash and surf. She was growing pale and still coughing. Her long hair clung to Teo's chest, which made him feel like Prince Charming saving the life of his beloved. By the time he had carried her into the cottage, he was already deeply moved and had given up trying to keep a professional distance from the situation.

The setting sun cast a pretty pattern on the white walls. He laid Clarice on the bed in which she had slept, as the one in the other room was disgusting. He arranged the pillows around her body. After a quick examination, he was relieved. Her injuries weren't as serious as they had seemed out in the water. She hadn't sustained any wounds to her upper body or head. Nevertheless she looked small and hurt, like a bleeding mermaid. She had deep lacerations in her back and the calf of one leg, but the most critical were in her buttocks: the abrasions on one snaked up to a place where the flesh was exposed, protruding slightly outward.

Teo leaned over her face. For an instant, he wished she wasn't breathing so he could touch her lips with the excuse of performing mouth-to-mouth resuscitation. They were very close to each other, and he gazed into her half-open eyes. They say you can see a person's soul in their eyes. In Clarice's, he saw serenity and affection, a declaration of true love that filled his heart. He covered his face with his hands, crying. For the first time, he wasn't trying, nor did he hope to gain anything with the display of emotion: the tears just came out.

He knew it was a revelation that few were lucky enough to have: love in a raw state, the essence of life. Everything was reordered and took on meaning. He had acted on an impulse, trying to control Clarice, but now he realized how insignificant his domination was. Like puzzle pieces that fit perfectly together, they had had to reach that extreme in order to understand that they loved each other. He hugged her tightly, certain that she too was moved. It was the most important moment in her life, he was sure. He held her and cried on her shoulder.

Clarice continued to cough and wheeze, but he clearly heard her say, "I love you."

"I love you too, Clarice. You're my princess."

He kissed her at length—a series of pecks and then a long final kiss that put an end to her coughing.

"I'm going to have to sedate you. It won't hurt. I know what I'm doing, and you're going to be fine."

He pulled on surgical gloves and got some gauze from the toiletry bag. He gave Clarice a serious look, trying to inspire trust in her, and injected her with the Thyolax. Her eyes quivered before they closed. Teo got a cooking knife and held it over the lantern, with the blade in the flame. Clarice would have been terrified if she'd seen it, which is why he preferred to reassure her, in case she could still hear him.

"Don't worry."

He untied the dress that was holding the main wound closed. The bleeding intensified, and he had to press gauze directly onto the small torn vein. He cleaned Clarice, taking care not to accidentally hurt her. Her hips were slight, which Teo liked. The cut in her left buttock was so deep that it had gone through the subcutaneous tissue and bared the fibers of her gluteus maximus, responsible for her perfect curves. The muscle was torn, and the skin, dilacerated. He hoped no bones were broken. He sutured the muscle and then the skin. As he closed the wounds in her feet and thighs with simple stitches, he felt an abstract anger at Clarice's irresponsibility begin to grow in him.

When she had gained the upper hand, she had switched off from reality. It was something Teo had been thinking about for weeks. The use of handcuffs sounded offensive even to him now. Throwing herself into the sea without a second thought had revealed the extent of her madness, and it was all so absurd that he could no longer ignore it.

The decision didn't require any reflection: he had thought for long enough to know that it was the right thing to do. He was confident and only slightly annoyed now. Rolling Clarice onto her side, he gave her a little kiss on the forehead. Unhurriedly, he folded her over, pushing her legs and shoulders forward until her spine was as curved as possible. He ran his fingers down her white back, covered in scratches, where her spinal column could be seen under her skin.

He picked up the knife with the hot blade and buried it in Clarice's back, between vertebrae L1 and L2. There was resistance, so he changed position to increase the pressure. The incision opened even further, gaping like a wide, smiling mouth. The blade sunk into the intervertebral disk, leaving a smell of burned flesh. There was a marked contrast between the blood coming out of Clarice's back and her unshakable sleep. Teo was vigilant. He didn't want to put her life at risk. He let go of the handle, exhausted by the effort. The knife in her flesh shuddered, and her body appeared to relax. He knelt next to the bed, looking for another optimal position, and finished slicing through Clarice's spine.

25

The night was relatively peaceful. Shortly before five o'clock, Clarice woke briefly with labored breathing and a high fever. Teo managed the situation with fever reducers, antibiotics, and Thyolax. The maneuver had been a success, he knew it, but he was so eager for Clarice to wake up that he wasn't able to sleep himself. He changed the bloodied bedclothes and cleaned up the filth in the other bedroom. He returned Breno's glasses to the satchel and had a quick shower to get rid of the horrible smell that was clinging to him. On the kitchen counter, he found the clay pot with the ashes of the photos and threw the whole lot away.

He ended up falling asleep in the armchair and dreamed he was chatting with Sobotta, the author of *Atlas of Human Anatomy,* about what he'd done to Clarice. They were in a mountainous place, Sobotta was observing him with flinty eyes, and Teo was nervous, but when he woke up, he thought it was all very funny. It was seven o'clock in the morning, and Clarice was still asleep. He checked her vital signs. Her fever had come down.

He decided to dress her, but the black dress he chose—the same one she had worn with Breno on the night of the concert—was very tight and could hurt her. He had a hard time deciding between another two and finally chose one with a pattern of wildflowers. It was good to be in control once again.

He wanted to make breakfast but was limited by the ingredients at hand. He put some water on to boil and was disappointed that he couldn't make oatmeal. Patricia loved his oatmeal, with a touch of cinnamon and cardamom, and he knew Clarice would love it too.

As he was trying to decide whether to serve biscuits or toast with coffee, a loud thud came from the bedroom. Teo ran to the door and saw Clarice on the floor, tangled in the sheet and looking terrified. Without a word, he went over to her, picked her up by the armpits, and tried to hoist her back onto the bed. It was hard, as she was howling and thrashing about.

"Stay calm," he said. He took her pulse and finally managed to get her back on the bed.

He got her some painkillers from the drawer. He preferred not to think too much about the intense pain she must have been feeling. He sat on the edge of the bed and waited for her to say something. Clarice had woken up quietly and, instead of calling for him, had tried to get up on her own. She was as pale as a corpse and looked as if she were upset for some very personal reason. Her eyes stared at the curtain that he had closed earlier to protect her from the sun.

"What's the matter?" Teo asked.

She shook and began to cry, but not in the silly way she had previously. It was intense, convulsive sobbing. When she looked up, there was a dark void in her gaze, and he knew that something primordial had died in her.

"I can't feel my legs, Teo."

He expressed the surprise that he had practiced in front of the mirror so many times.

"What do you mean?"

She lifted her torso with her arms. She wanted to sit up in bed but couldn't do it alone.

"I try to move my legs, I concentrate really hard on it, but . . . they won't *obey* me," she said.

It was horrible that she wouldn't stop crying. He stood solemnly, went to the end of the bed, and touched her feet. He took them in his hands and massaged them. They were flaccid and very hot.

"Do you feel anything?"

She took a while to answer, perhaps because she was a little groggy. When she shook her head, Teo saw a picture of sheer desperation. Clarice couldn't feel anything below her hips, and he knew it. For an instant, he imagined himself on stage again, rehearsing positions and memorizing lines. He donned the con cerned expression that he did so well—pursed lips, raised eyebrows—and said:

"I'm going to do some tests."

He bent her legs slowly, moved her feet in circles, pressed on her thighs and ankles, and asked her to look around and try to turn her body by herself. She did everything with great effort, swallowing her tears. He thought she was being a little melodramatic, but she was so upset that he couldn't smile.

"I think you really have lost the movement in your legs," he said. He knew the rhythm and timbre of his voice had to be just right in order to sound convincing. "I'm so sorry."

Clarice massaged her numb legs. Although nothing else had changed, she started to cry again. It was all so boring and repetitive that he wished he could speed up time and get to the bit where she'd resign herself to her condition and live happily in his care. But there was no way to speed anything up. That week was going to be unbearably long.

"Stop crying," he said. "Sorry, I didn't mean to be callous. I'm just thinking about what to do—"

"Help me, Teo. Please help me!" She grabbed his arms invasively, clinging to him. "I don't want to be crippled."

"Don't talk like that."

"Do something! I'm begging you! I'll stay with you forever! I'll do whatever you want. . . . Just cure me, please!"

"You threw yourself into the sea. It's a miracle you're alive."

He was nervous and preferred not to talk to her in that state. He wanted to sedate her, but didn't have an excuse.

"I can't walk anymore!"

"I look after a mother who can't walk, as you know. You might be able to recover with physical therapy," he said, knowing full well that physical therapy would get her nowhere.

"I want to walk now!"

Clarice opened her eyes very wide and stared at her legs, as if she could oblige them to do something. That same instant her torso lurched forward, her head tilted slightly, and she vomited. She pressed her hands to her stomach, howling.

Teo went to go get clean clothes and sheets. It was a relief to get out of the room, and he purposely took a long time at the clothesline, as if choosing the driest sheet—which was absurd, since there was only one. Her cries couldn't be heard outside, which also reduced his feeling of claustrophobia. Before going back to the room, he put a kitchen chair under the shower.

"You need a cold shower," he told Clarice.

She was covered in sweat and had vomited up her painkillers. Her movements were feeble, hands clasped to her lower back. Teo pulled back the sheet and tried to lift her as best he could, although there wasn't much he could do as she was as floppy as a ragdoll. He carried her to the shower and sat her down in a way that wouldn't put pressure on the bandage on her left buttock. He turned on the cold water and rinsed her forehead.

He helped her take off her dress. For the first time, her nakedness didn't inspire anything in him. He felt mediocre. He liked her—loved her—and needed to feel it at all times, even if she was sick, filthy, or whatever else. He hated the feeling—the same one he'd experienced on Christmas Eve.

Clarice was shaking a lot and asked him to stop throwing water on her. Teo made her brush her teeth, but she threw up some more and had to brush them again. He dried her carefully, and at one stage she looked as if she were about to faint, so he said silly things in an attempt to keep her awake. Clarice was at the most critical point of her weakness, but he knew she was tough and very lucky; she'd be better soon.

He'd buy her the best wheelchair there was, motorized and imported. He had already researched models for Patricia on the Internet and knew that the best one cost about eight thousand dollars. It was a kind of colorful four-wheeler and would suit Clarice's jovial personality down to the ground.

She vomited for the third time, and he began to think he'd never get out of the bathroom. He was somewhat consoled by the thought that there couldn't be much else left in her little body. As he rinsed her off again, Teo began to think about what to serve for lunch. When Clarice was finally clean, she still looked exhausted. He left her in the bathroom and changed the sheet once again. He sprayed cologne around to mask the bad smell.

"Are you okay?" he asked after returning her to the bed.

Clarice's moist eyes looked vacant. "I need to be alone."

He shrugged and got up. He didn't want to leave her side. Nevertheless, he headed for the door.

Clarice made a vague gesture to call him back. "Please tell me this has a cure."

She was desperate.

"I don't know. I'm not going to lie to you."

"What happened exactly?"

"You tried to drown yourself, and the waves must have pushed you onto the rocks," he said. "There's a deep cut in your back and another on your buttock. The fact that you can't feel anything from your hips down means you hurt your spine. The wound on your back confirms it, but I couldn't see anything. You were bleeding a lot, and all I did was stitch you up."

Clarice nodded her head as if trying to imagine the scene.

"I think the rock was pretty sharp," he added.

"How did you get the handcuffs off?"

"You had put my hands down, and the key was on the bedside table. You were really lucky, Clarice. I saved your life."

"Saved?" The expression on her face was disturbingly inexpressive. Not a single tear came out now. "I want to die. And you won't be able to stop me forever."

Teo slammed the door behind him as he left. He got into the shower and stood there with the jet of water on his face. The admiration he felt for Clarice was turning into concern. He was furious and knew that if he went back into the bedroom right then, he'd end up hurting her. His rage was just indignation, he concluded, indignation for everything. He thought about the things he'd said to her and the things she'd said to him. Clarice still had feelings for the dead guy, who was very much alive in her thoughts. Her actions had confirmed that she was not of sound mind: serving rotten meat, burning photographs, effectively torturing him. Clarice needed to be protected from her. Teo understood that she was suffering, but he didn't regret what he'd done for one second. At the end of the day, it had been for her own good.

26

Teo walked into the room with a sandwich. Clarice was asleep, but he had the impression that she'd only just shut her eyes. He decided not to force anything. The world looked very dark beyond the window. There was no moon.

He didn't think it was necessary to lock the bedroom door. He ate the sandwich even though he wasn't hungry and lay down in the other room to read for a while. As he closed his eyes, he thought that he deserved to sleep in the next day—until after nine even. He dreamed bizarre dreams, with psychedelic figures that castrated animals and chatted with inanimate objects. There was a lot of blood, as well as the colors white and gold. He awoke with the strong feeling that Clarice was dead. He imagined her body hanging over the bed, with the sheet he had fetched from the clothesline around her neck.

He wanted to race into the other room but controlled himself. Believing in dreams was absurd, and if he kept on like that, he'd end up going crazy too. He put on his flip-flops and went to brush his teeth. Looking at himself in the mirror, he saw that his face was already a lot better; his wounds were healing and might even be gone by the time the old woman came back.

He removed the razor that Clarice had discovered God knows where—possibly in the house itself—and the nail clippers. He found a new hiding place for the knives and other sharp objects, just in case: there was a thick pipe in the kitchen poking out of a hole in the wall behind a large pot. He pulled back the pot and stuffed everything that looked threatening into the pipe.

In the bedroom, Clarice was fast asleep. The sun was hot, although it was only seven in the morning. Teo closed the curtains and was certain she'd pretended to be asleep the night before so she wouldn't have to talk to him. Such rudeness, along with the image of her hanging from the sheet, frustrated him. He made some coffee, and then, not in the mood to fix anything to eat, he went back to the bedroom. He pulled back the sheet that was covering Clarice and poured the coffee on it. The other three sheets in the cottage were still waiting to be washed—one dirty with vomit and the other two with blood. There was nothing else she could use to hang herself. Despite her condition, he didn't want to underestimate her.

It was still early, so Teo decided to go for a swim. The temperature was pleasant, and he stayed underwater for a long time. The sun made his body pulsate. He wandered away from the cottage with the waves breaking against his ankles, which felt nice. Halfway down the beach, he turned around and came back.

His thoughts began to lose their vigor, and he found himself humming a sad song that he didn't even like.

His mood was up and down: he thought about wars, massacres, traffic jams, corruption, and stray bullets and felt blessed to be in that paradise, free of tragedies any greater than those of the

heart. Then he thought about Breno with his arty demeanor—
violin in hand and not a penny in his pocket—and felt deeply
despondent. Breno, like him, didn't have a friendly face. But he
had worn those rectangular glasses that had made him look older.
To be honest, Teo didn't really understand what Clarice saw
physically in Breno.

He realized it had been a mistake to keep the glasses. It was so
obvious that he was shocked he hadn't thought of it earlier, when
they arrived on Ilha Grande. The police officer had seen the
glasses, and Clarice had tried to kill herself because of them. He
ran to the cottage and took them from the satchel. All his misfortune was concentrated in that object, and if he got rid of it, things
would set themselves right. He snapped the frame in half and
stomped on the lenses until they cracked—they were very thick,
Breno had been practically blind—and that very instant he felt a
weight lifting off his shoulders. It was like floating in outer space.
He went back to the water's edge and hurled the glasses as far out
as he could. He flopped onto the sand, laughing at nothing in
particular. He swam a little more before returning to the cottage.

Clarice was awake. As he passed the half-open door, he
glanced at her and nodded, without slowing his pace. He showered and got dressed. Clarice didn't appear to be in a good mood,
nor did he feel very receptive after everything she had said.

He made potato soup for lunch. When he walked into the
bedroom, she looked down, blatantly avoiding looking at him.
He placed the dish and spoon on the bedside table and left. He
spent the afternoon in the living room, studying *Surgical Patient
Safety*. He liked to feel productive and intelligent, but he had
been much less so since he had taken off on the trip with Clarice.
He also realized she had curtailed some of his habits and knew it
meant something.

At night, Teo served Clarice the rest of the potato soup. He walked into the room casually, with no desire to talk to her. The awkwardness was uncomfortable.

"I can't remember the day we killed Breno," she said casually.

He shrugged. "I know."

"How can I not remember?"

"Breno attacked you, and you went into shock. Loss of memory after a traumatic incident is common."

"It's disturbing. As if there were a hole in my mind, a blank . . ."

"It happened here, on Ilha Grande. The first night."

"How did he find us?"

"I called your mother and told her we were on Never-Never Beach. She said Breno had been calling your place insistently. He'd call and hang up, make threats."

"He wasn't like that."

"A man blind with love is capable of many things. Breno was never a good boyfriend. He lost it when he realized you weren't his anymore. Your mother agrees with me."

"My mother didn't like him."

"Breno was a drain on your talent. Didn't you ever notice? He was mediocre, with no future."

Teo sat on the bed, close to her.

"You're going to want to know how it happened, of course. I'll tell you so we can get it over and done with. Breno showed up in the middle of the night in a rickety old boat that he must have hired somewhere. We were at the table in the kitchen, talking after dinner. I made crepes, remember?"

"I remember the crepes."

"It was a nice night. I was happy, and you looked happy too. You liked the crepes and the dressing I made for the salad."

"A Thai dressing."

"Breno came through the front door, and he was pretty worked up." He put on a tone of regret. "You fell off your chair. He had a knife. He said he was going to kill me and teach you a lesson. I think he was going to rape you, Clarice."

Teo reflected on the story he'd just made up; it was vulgar and dramatic.

"We fought. You helped me bring him down. We didn't do it on purpose. Then we realized, he was dead. You were shocked. You cried a lot, but you managed to help me bury his body. We dug the grave in the middle of the forest. I don't remember where. I was nervous too."

"I want to find where we buried Breno."

He nodded at Clarice's legs, and she got the message.

"Forget it, please."

"What about the boat?"

"I filled it with stones and sank it. I did it all on my own because you had fainted. I thought you'd remember the next morning, but you didn't say anything when you woke up. I decided not to bring it up. It was only afterward that I realized you'd forgotten everything, erased the night from memory."

"I remember putting on my pajamas that first night. And going to bed afterward."

"You must be imagining it—or confusing it with another night. After you fainted, I decided to sedate you. I had to. You were really shaken up. I bathed you and put your pajamas on you myself."

"I'd never kill Breno," she said, but she seemed to be saying it to herself, as if she needed to believe it.

"A few days later we were out on the beach looking at the sky, and you said 'I feel that Breno's dead.' Remember?"

He saw Clarice's eyes hesitate. She really had said it, and now she was wondering where the feeling had come from. She looked torn between what she thought she knew and what he'd just told her.

"I thought you'd remembered killing Breno, and I was worried."

"I was just expressing a feeling."

"I understand that you've forgotten. But your unconscious knows what happened, even if you can't access the information. Without remembering the facts, you felt that Breno was dead. It was no accident that you said that."

Teo couldn't help but laugh on the inside.

"We killed Breno, but . . . he was armed and dangerous. We acted in self-defense. I really wish you could remember."

He wanted to keep talking, but he noticed that Clarice was no longer paying attention. He touched her hands, but she recoiled as if he were an insect. Teo didn't take offense, as he was determined to make her believe him.

"I tried to talk to you. We talked about death and burials, and well, I hoped you'd remember at some point. It's normal for things to come back slowly. I didn't mean to hide anything. I kept Breno's glasses precisely for that reason, to have some kind of material proof. It's our secret, Clarice. I need you to trust me the way I trust you."

She shrugged, but it wasn't a gesture of indifference. Her slender body looked like a very taut wire. She raised her head, but instead of looking away, she stared straight at him with eyes as deep as an abyss.

"Something's bugging me, Teo. About the day before yesterday . . ."

"What do you mean?" He didn't like that she had changed the subject.

"When you pulled me out of the sea, I . . . was in a bad way."

"You couldn't even open your eyes properly."

"Yes, but I wasn't unconscious. I was awake, and I remember you carrying me out of the water in your arms. I remember *feeling* my legs."

"It's just an impression."

"I remember *feeling* chills in my feet because I was wet and shivering. Do you understand what I'm saying? I could feel, Teo. I could feel my feet."

Clarice sobbed without taking her eyes off him, and her anxiety made him anxious too.

"I just sutured your wounds," he said. "Are you insinuating that I made a mistake as I was stitching you up?"

Clarice shook her head, and with that quick movement her expression became dangerously cruel. "I'm saying that you did this to me, Teo. On purpose."

"I don't believe you could think that."

When he got up, his legs buckled slightly. He paced back and forth. She had managed to provoke him very cunningly, and he wanted to end the conversation that instant.

"All you do is tell me lies," she said. "I know I didn't kill Breno. And I know what you're capable of. You're a *monster!*"

Teo punched her. Then he realized it was the worst thing he could have done, because it made him look like the bad guy. He apologized, wallowing in resentment. He had saved her life. If Breno had been there, what would he have done? *Would he have played Antonín Dvořák's Symphony no. 9 to suture her wounds?*

Teo was indignant; he felt as if he'd been robbed. He held her arms and shook her hard. He denied having done anything to Breno or her. He denied it again. Clarice shouldn't have called him a monster. She had no *right* to. He wasn't a monster. And he desperately needed her to believe it.

27

They didn't talk to each other for two days. It was hotter now, and Teo imagined the papers announcing the hottest day of the year, the harshest summer of the decade, things like that. They'd blame deforestation and the depletion of the ozone layer. Due to the heat, he was eating less and had lost some weight. His face thinned out when he lost weight. Patricia would notice the difference, possibly Clarice too. But Teo made a point of treating her with indifference, as if he hadn't noticed that she was acting strange.

Her calling him a *monster* was still tormenting him, and for the first time, it seemed obvious that they'd never stay together. Clarice was stupid, incapable of seeing anything more than a hand's length from her own face, and *she* questioned *his* character? After the fight, Teo had left some books on her bedside table, as well as biscuits and a plastic bottle of water. He'd dryly told her to call him if she needed anything.

Teo used the time apart to study. He spent most of the day in the kitchen or outside the cottage. He slept in the other room and avoided contact with Clarice. She hadn't called him once. On the Friday morning (if he wasn't mistaken it was Friday), Teo was in the kitchen when he heard her crying behind the closed door. Normally, he would have left her to cry (it was all she did), but something guttural and very specific in her voice made him decide to go talk to her. Clarice was hunched over with her bare arms wrapped around her. The smell was bad.

"I told you to call me if you needed to go to the bathroom."

She looked like a frightened animal peering out of its burrow.

"I can't feel anything."

He looked at her, trying to understand. Her voice was melancholic.

When she cast her eyes about the wet mattress, he finally understood but felt too uncomfortable to say anything. Her spinal injury meant she couldn't control the urge to go to the bathroom. Teo chided himself for having forgotten that detail: Clarice would have to wear diapers.

He heated up two full pots of water, as he didn't want to wet Clarice's head in the cold shower. He rinsed her hair and massaged her temples. He ran his fingers down her neck, working out knots in her shoulders, and reached her ankles. As he touched her, he realized just how much he liked her. The war of silences was maddening. He wanted to say something to stifle the sorrow that was building up in him.

"The owner will be back in two days."

He didn't want to mention that they had to leave, but he thought Clarice would be interested in numbers. She remained quiet, allowing him to massage her. Her breathing was discreet—almost nonexistent—and Teo thought that, like an electronic device, Clarice was wearing out.

He asked if she wanted to sit in the sun. The weather was pleasant, and there was a refreshing breeze. She answered no and said she wanted to go back to bed. Teo didn't believe she really preferred the bed—there was a heavy negative charge in the room—but he'd given up trying to understand her whims. He turned the mattress over and laid her on the bed. If he left the room that instant, he'd miss his only chance to make peace with her.

"I don't want to fight with you."

"Leave me alone."

"Please—I can't bear that you blame me for everything that's happened. I didn't go after Breno. He was the one who—"

"Go fuck yourself, Teo. I don't want to hear it."

He pulled up a chair, as he didn't want to sit too close to her. "I'm not a bad guy, Clarice. I'm sorry I handcuffed you. . . . There were times when I felt you liked me. I want to go home, but I can't lose you. I told my mother about us, and she can't wait to have you over for dinner. I think your mother likes me too. It's all so perfect. But I need you to want me, and I don't know how to make it happen. I'm lost. You insist on finding fault with everything I do, no matter how hard I try."

"That's your problem! You forced your way into my life!"

"I've already said sorry."

"I don't care what you do for me. I was held prisoner, sedated with that shit . . ." She started crying again. "You can beat me, tie me up, kill me. I'm crippled, and I couldn't give a fuck what happens to me anymore."

"I saved your life. Come on, you have to give me that."

She gave him a serious look. Teo thought she looked like she wanted to eat him alive, a hungry wildcat.

"You're not in your right mind and want to transfer your own blame onto me!" he went on. "I know it's horrible, but . . . I didn't want you to get hurt. And it's not my fault Breno came after us with a knife. He caused all this."

Clarice was leaning forward slapping her legs. What was left of her was right there in front of him, and even if her chances were remote, he sincerely hoped she'd recover.

"I feel self-destructive. Because of you, I'm actually afraid of myself. I'm a worse person than I used to be."

"Because of me?" He wanted to throw it all in her face. "Are you're forgetting that I found you drunk, lying in a doorway in Lapa, after kissing a disgusting lesbian? You were throwing your future down the drain. I pulled you out of it!"

"You didn't even ask me if I wanted out."

"You were living a fantasy, Clarice. Breno was jealous and ignorant. A violinist without a penny to his name! Your mother had good reason not to like him."

"I loved Breno."

"Oh, come on, stop it! You helped me finish him off! And even though you're trying to blame me, you know—deep down you know—that you helped me! We're in this together, Clarice." Their conversations had a certain intensity that was always the same. "You call me a monster, but you refuse to acknowledge everything I've done. The first version of *Perfect Days* was crap. Thanks to our conversations, your screenplay is better now, and someone might actually take an interest in it."

"I'm not talking about screenplays."

"But I am. I've always supported your artistic endeavors. I've always been concerned about your health too. I may have gone a little overboard banning cigarettes, but I didn't do it to hurt you. I've never done you any *real* harm, Clarice. I didn't bring any ammunition for the revolver because I'm incapable of hurting you."

"You left me paralyzed!"

"The truth is, you think you're so superior to everyone else. You think you're untouchable, capable of anything. Maybe now you'll eat some humble pie."

"I don't believe—"

"I have a handicapped mother, and I know it's a drastic change," said Teo. "Looking after her means renouncing a little of myself, of my life. It isn't for everyone."

He touched Clarice's arm. Her skin was deathly cold.

"I try to be the best man I can. I don't care if you smoke or can't walk—I want to take care of you. I want you to write your screenplays and for us to go to your film premieres together. I think you've got talent, and this new condition might be your edge. It might give your texts an original voice."

"Teo, I—"

"I don't want you to say anything. In two days we're going to Paraty. If you want, you'll be free to live your life and find someone else, someone willing to put up with your condition," he said, feeling cruel. "It's really tiring, a burden. Not many people can do it."

Teo stood up, certain he'd said everything that needed to be said. When he left the bedroom, he couldn't remember the expression on Clarice's face, but he felt he'd made an impression on her. It was obvious that she'd choose the solidity of a stable relationship. She didn't have a lot of talent, and there wasn't much left of her. She needed someone who would encourage her, not people who dragged her down, like Breno and Laura.

That afternoon, as he tidied the cottage and swept the sand out of the kitchen, Teo remembered the few short-lived relationships his mother had had since the accident—with middle-aged losers—and concluded that Clarice would be headed for the same if she gave up on him.

. . .

Because he didn't know what time the old woman was coming, Teo sedated Clarice in the morning. He took the opportunity to remove the stitches from the wounds that had already healed. He rearranged items in the toiletry bag and satchel and folded the dry sheets. The ampoule of Thyolax was almost empty, and it was the last one, but he wasn't worried. When they got to Paraty, he'd figure something out. The days had been slow, but he'd perked up mentally the day before. He'd happily give up life in the anatomy lab for an uncertain life with Clarice. He saw his face reflected in the bathroom mirror. He was tanned and more handsome. There was a taste of salt on his lips. His hair had grown a lot, and the curls gave him a good-natured demeanor.

The old woman arrived shortly before midday. Clarice and their clothes were already packed. After a quick look around, the cottage was closed and the boat took off. Teo asked the woman if she could take him straight to the mainland, but she mumbled something unintelligible and said she was going to Abraão Beach. Her expression was humorless, and Teo wondered if his photograph had appeared in the newspaper. Even though he was in the right, he knew people would never understand what had happened with Breno. They were all obsessed with codes and rules and he'd have no defense, even if he tried.

As they approached the coast, the feeling that the police were waiting for him at the port intensified, and he threw up in the water. As he disembarked, he was ashamed of his own overreaction. He bought a ticket to the mainland on a ferry that left in eight minutes. On the ferry, overcome with curiosity, he tried to turn on Clarice's cell. The battery had lost its charge. He turned on his own cell knowing he'd received lots of calls from Patricia and Helena. He made a bet with himself: more than thirty, less than forty. There was no reception on the water, so the result of his bet was delayed.

When they docked, his cell beeped: eighty-seven calls and countless messages—he didn't go to the trouble of seeing how many. He was so bewildered that he turned down all offers of help with his bags and carried them to the car himself. It was an awkward situation. He concluded that the biggest problem with middle-class Brazilian mothers was that they didn't have anything to do. How could they be so invasive?

He laid the Samsonite on the backseat and, with some effort, put Clarice in the front passenger seat. She was deeply sedated, and her body flopped forward onto the glove compartment. Teo buckled her in and started the car.

He drove in silence, listening only to Clarice's deep breathing. She was moving her head slowly, eyes tightly shut. Every so often she'd halt in a position of suicidal immobility, a bitter expression would flash across her face, and she'd start moving again. Teo imagined she was having a nightmare and wanted to pull over, but there was no shoulder on that part of the road. He glanced in the rearview mirror and slowed down a little, but a car behind him honked its horn instead of overtaking. He thought about shouting something out the window. Clarice's sleep became even more agitated, and he tried to wake her up. He poked her arm, to no avail.

It happened very quickly. One minute Clarice was slumped over in the passenger seat; the next, she was hugging him tightly, preventing him from holding the wheel. The road curved, but the car went straight ahead. Teo felt the impact with the retaining wall, his body being thrown forward and tons of metal tumbling through the air with him in it. Then he didn't feel anything at all.

28

Teo didn't know if it was late, but everything was dark. There was a beeping coming from somewhere, and it grew faster, accompanying his heartbeat. It jabbed his brain through his right ear. He wanted it to stop but couldn't make it. His hands clenched something soft. He was dizzy. A sliver of light shone under the door. The smell of hospital alcohol made his eyes want to close. He could hear footsteps and shushed voices behind the door. On the other side of the bed, the beeping continued. His head was raised on a thick pillow, and several blankets were keeping his legs warm. A frustrated attempt to make him comfortable.

When his eyes adjusted to the half-light, he looked at his body. Electrodes on his chest, thermometer under his left arm, oxygen saturation, blood pressure gauge, intravenous catheter in his jugular. He felt calmer, although it was odd to be the patient. The urinary catheter in his urethra stung. The tips of his toes and the soles of his feet were numb. The beeping grew louder.

Someone opened the door, bringing light and noise into the room. "Can you see me?"

He shook his head, and then he saw the doctor. "Now I can."

The man was old and gray-haired. He was studying the vital signs monitor and barely gave Teo the time of day. "What's your name?"

It took him a few seconds to answer. "Teodoro."

"Do you remember what happened?"

He was immersed in a cauldron of confusing sensations.

"A car accident," said the doctor, without giving him any time. "You lost a lot of blood."

The images came back painfully. He remembered the road and some of his thoughts as he was driving. Death, screams, needles, iron, open wounds. He remembered Clarice. He glanced around the room: there were no flowers or cards or colorful balloons. There were no police officers either.

"How long have I been here?"

"Two days. I don't know where your friend is." The doctor nodded at a long bench with a light blanket on it next to the bed. Someone had visited him.

"What about Clarice?"

"Who?"

"The woman who was with me in the car."

"I don't know. You were transferred here. Wait for your companion to come back." He made some notes on the bedside file. "You hit your head, but you'll be fine. If you need anything, press here." There was a button near Teo's free arm.

Teo suddenly understood that Clarice was dead. The sterile environment, the doctor's objectivity, and the lack of police confirmed it. Clarice was fragile and hadn't made it. He remembered the impact at the moment of the crash, the metal against his chest. It hurt as if it were happening all over again. He'd been in hospital for two days, and Clarice would have been buried by now. The thought emptied him out.

He was lost in thought when the door opened again.

"You're awake!"

Patricia wheeled herself over and held his hand, squeezing it tightly. She started to cry.

"I was desperate. You don't know how much I prayed—"

"I want to know what happened to Clarice, Mother."

Teo noticed that her eyes reddened, and the bitter taste of medicine on his tongue seemed stronger.

"She's in the ICU," said Patricia in a wisp of a voice.

Teo didn't really know how to react, so he said nothing.

"I'm so sorry."

"I need to see Clarice."

"She was taken to another hospital. And you need to rest. Maybe tomorrow."

After so long without seeing his mother, Teo realized he didn't have much to say to her. Patricia was wearing a dress as crumpled and old as herself. Her happiness at his recovery hadn't been enough to erase her weariness. She tried to smile, but it was a sad smile.

"I spend the whole day here, and when I go to the toilet, you wake up! Marli came to see you. She really likes you."

He couldn't be bothered thinking about Marli and the negative energy she brought with her. He remembered his tiny bedroom, the smell of mold, and its abandoned appearance. He didn't miss his bed, the furniture, or his medical books. He didn't want to go back to that life, and yet suddenly, there he was.

"I'm so glad, son. I prayed to God so much. I went to . . ." Patricia kept talking for several minutes. She took some bead necklaces out of her bag and showed him, saying that Marli had taught her how to make them. She had already sold three of them at church. Then she talked about the latest happenings at church and Marli's exhibitions in downtown Rio and Niterói. Teo was glad she wouldn't stop talking. The trivia comforted him.

"Now you say something," she said finally. "Tell me about the crash."

Teo racked his brains, searching his memory, but the images were vague. He tried to recall odors, urges, impressions. He remembered his state of mind—it wasn't that different from what he was feeling at that moment. The number of missed calls on his cell had alarmed him, and truth be told, he hadn't been paying a lot of attention to the road.

And there was Clarice's embrace—he remembered that too. But he wasn't certain about the intention behind it. Had Clarice awakened and launched herself at him, deliberately causing him to lose control of the car? Or had it been a reaction to her bad dream and his poking her? He saw her with clenched teeth, eyes wide open in a cruel gaze, as she held his arms so he'd crash the Vectra. But he knew it was just his imagination.

"It was an accident," said Teo. "Clarice was asleep and had a bad dream. She was frightened and grabbed me. She didn't see what she was doing."

"Oh my God!" Patricia put the necklaces back into her bag.

Teo realized he hadn't said anything about them. To be honest, he thought they were pretty ugly.

"I hope she recovers quickly. Were you really happy?"

"Very."

Patricia's watery gaze came to rest on a point above Teo's head, and when he looked up, he saw a clock there. It was almost three o'clock in the morning.

"'Love is only beautiful when we find someone who makes us the best we can be,'" Patricia said. "It's by Mário Quintana."

Teo didn't care for poetry, but he liked hearing it.

"Do you think this girl's made you into something better?"

With Clarice, he'd felt things he couldn't believe. Compassion. Reticence. Guilt. Regret. Love. She had made him human.

"I love Clarice, Mother."

"I don't think she's the right person for you. But that's all I'll say."

Patricia shrugged and turned her wheelchair. She looked like a jittery cockroach limping about the room.

"I don't have anything against her. But remember that dream I told you about? I dreamed that something bad was going to happen. Samson died. You were in this accident. And Clarice's ex-boyfriend seems to have gone missing too."

"So I heard."

The subject didn't interest him. He was very certain of what he had to say, which was almost nothing.

"The detective handling the case stopped by yesterday morning. He wanted to talk to you."

"To me?"

"Yes."

Teo was annoyed that he had to talk about Breno. It was as if an invisible thread had bound their lives together in a tacky soap opera plot.

"I don't know how I can help."

"It all started with that girl, son. Don't you see?"

"No."

"I still can't swallow what happened to Samson. And now you've gone and got engaged. It worries me."

Teo looked at his hand and saw the engagement ring he had bought. Perhaps it had been a little too much, but he didn't say anything. He wanted his mother to disappear right there and then. It was very mulish of her to interrogate him in his hospital bed. What did Samson's death matter at that moment?

Patricia wheeled herself toward the door. "I'm going to get some juice. Do you want anything?"

Teo realized that the conversation had become unbearable for both of them. "I don't want anything."

"Then rest," she said. "Tomorrow's going to be a long day."

H e didn't fall asleep immediately. He wanted to get up and run away, but being stuck in the hospital room had its advantages. Except for Patricia pestering him, it was better to be isolated than not. Just imagining Helena's stupid expression and all the questions she would ask exhausted him. His thoughts wandered, deliberately wavering between the real and the impossible— he went so far as to think: *What if Breno had never been born?* He reveled in the idea.

Teo mused that Clarice hadn't shouted anything at him and therefore came to the conclusion that it really had been an accident. She'd had a bad dream—perhaps about Breno—and had sought comfort in his arms. Now she was in a coma somewhere, needing help: his help. He was vaguely satisfied and drifted into a pleasant sleep, as if he were lying on clouds.

When he opened his eyes, it was daytime. There was light in the room and a landscape of dilapidated buildings could be seen through the window. He recognized his mother's voice. She was talking to a man.

"The detective would like to talk to you," said Patricia, sounding strangely cheerful. When he looked at the man, Teo understood: she was attracted to him. He was bald and very thin, like his late father. There was something in his smile, a kindness for which Patricia was thirsty.

"Please, I'd prefer to talk to Teo in private," the detective said.

There was a tone of candor and also a certain decorum in his voice. "Thank you for keeping me company."

Patricia left the room immediately. The detective continued to smile as he approached the bed. He was wearing jeans and a flannel shirt. Outside the hospital air-conditioning, Rio de Janeiro was boiling.

"I'm Detective Inspector Aquino from the Twelfth Police District here in Copacabana, but you can call me Aquino."

Teo was surprised Patricia hadn't mentioned that they were so close to home. It was comforting.

"I know you woke up during the night and are recovering," said the detective. "I don't want to impose, but I need to ask a few questions. Is that okay?"

"Yes, of course."

"I'm investigating the disappearance of Breno Santana Cavalcante. Do you know who he is?"

"Clarice's ex-boyfriend."

"That's right, son."

The detective took a photograph out of his pocket. It had been cropped from a larger image and showed a happy Breno, wearing a jacket and wool scarf. His smile looked like as if it had been drawn on, and Teo understood why his parents had chosen that photo to give to the police. Breno looked especially good in it, and the disappearance of someone good-looking elicits pity.

He waited for the detective to ask something.

"Do you know Breno?"

"Clarice mentioned him, but I've never met him. Actually, I didn't know what he looked like until now."

"What do you think about him?"

"A typical ex. A bit inconvenient perhaps."

"Did he bother you?"

"Clarice made it clear that they'd broken up, and that was enough for me."

"Do you know why they broke up?"

"I'm not sure, as we didn't talk about that kind of thing. But I think he was kind of domineering."

"Domineering?"

"I read some of his messages on Clarice's cell. They were manipulative, looking for pity. At some point, she stopped answering them."

"When was that?"

"November last year. End of November, I think."

"Breno's cell is missing too, but we are trying to recover his call history," said the detective. Teo noticed that his dead-fish eyes didn't miss a thing. "How did you and Clarice meet?"

"At a barbecue. A few days later she went to Teresópolis and took me with her."

"Did you decide to take off out of the blue?"

"No. It was arranged in advance. Clarice's a screenwriter. We went to a hotel where she likes to write."

"Dwarf Lake Farm Hotel."

Teo had avoided mentioning the name of the hotel and was unsettled that the detective had the information on the tip of his tongue.

"After that, where did you go?"

"We slept in a motel and then went to Ilha Grande."

"Why the change of plans?"

"There wasn't a change. Clarice is writing a screenplay for a road movie called *Perfect Days*. The characters travel to Teresópolis, Ilha Grande, and Paraty. They spend the night in a motel too. We followed the same itinerary as in the screenplay."

The detective's face was impassive. The story sounded surreal, even though it was true.

"Did you know Breno had disappeared?"

"Helena mentioned it to me over the phone after you talked to her."

"And what did Clarice think about it?"

"I didn't tell her. She was writing her screenplay, on a kind of retreat."

"That's the reason you didn't tell her anything?"

Teo didn't like the tone the conversation was taking. He hadn't told Clarice anything because he didn't want to involve Breno in their relationship and because he didn't think anyone would take the story seriously for very long.

"I didn't even know Breno," he snapped. "I had no reason to worry about him. I thought maybe he'd decided to take off for a while, go chill out somewhere."

"I called your cells several times."

"There was no phone reception in Teresópolis or on Ilha Grande. To be honest, I thought Breno was going to turn up quickly."

"He still hasn't turned up, son."

Teo hated that the detective was calling him *son*.

"Breno went missing on the first of December. Where were you and Clarice that day?"

"At the hotel in Teresópolis, I think."

"It'd be nice if you were sure."

Teo snorted a kind of laugh. "No one pays attention to dates when they're on vacation, do they?"

"It may be important."

"Are we suspected of something?"

"Oh, no, nothing like that!" The detective gestured vaguely with his hands. "As soon as Clarice wakes up, we'll talk to her too. I've been stopping by there every day."

"How is she?"

"In a coma, as I think you know. It looks like she's stabilizing. I certainly hope so."

The detective gave him his best smile, and Teo was obliged to smile too.

"Clarice's doctor told me she had some stitches on her body from before the accident. And some fresh scars."

"She hurt herself on Ilha Grande. She hit a rock when she was swimming." Teo had already thought about the answer to that question.

"Anything serious?"

"Not really. I'm a medical student. I sutured the cuts. We were on a deserted beach, and there wasn't anything else I could do."

"How did you get to the deserted beach?"

"We contacted a local woman who had a cottage to rent. She took us there on a boat."

"Do you know the woman's name? Where can I find her?"

"Gertrude," said Teo. He felt ridiculously vulnerable now. He thought about his friend Gertrude and the comfort she would have brought him at that moment. He decided never to tell anyone else about her. Their relationship was in the past, and it was something private. He regretted having mentioned her to Clarice when they were in Teresópolis. "I don't know where she lives."

"Okay. What were Clarice's injuries on the rock?"

"A few cuts on her back and feet. A really deep one in her left buttock."

The detective took notes. There was such an uncomfortable silence that Teo thought he'd finished, or that he was thinking about something else.

"Two accidents in a short period of time. That's a lot of bad luck, don't you think?"

"I don't believe in bad luck." Teo spoke slowly, as if he were very sure of what he was saying and didn't care what anyone else thought. Nevertheless he had to face the fact that the detective might suspect something, and the idea was making him nervous.

"I see that you and Clarice are engaged. I hope things get sorted out and you get married soon."

"Thank you."

"You're going to have to buy a new ring. I noticed yesterday that Clarice's is missing."

"What happened?" asked Teo before the detective could. Clarice had no doubt thrown it away on Ilha Grande, and he hadn't noticed.

"I thought you knew."

"I don't think it's got anything to do with Breno."

"Let's see, son. Let's see."

They talked for a few more minutes. The detective wanted details about the car accident and Clarice's screenplay. He also asked for the name of the motel. Finally, he said he might be back the next day and left a card with his phone number at the police station.

Teo's body felt very flushed and his self-consciousness about his physical reaction made him even more exasperated. He said good-bye dryly, even though he didn't want to be rude.

Patricia had the tact not to ask any questions. She made bead necklaces in silence all afternoon. Teo's mind was awhirl. He came to the conclusion that he hadn't done so badly. After all, what did the detective have on him? It was strange that Aquino hadn't mentioned the handcuffs and arm and leg separators, but that didn't mean much. Teo closed his eyes, still depressed but unflustered. He had a feeling no one was going to catch him, no matter what.

29

T he detective didn't show up the next morning, which seemed to disappoint Patricia. Shortly after lunch, Teo was released. He still felt pain in his legs and torso, as if his body had been put through a grinder, but he didn't complain. He wanted to visit Clarice. Patricia refused vehemently, and he agreed to go home. They took a taxi, which made Teo remember the Vectra.

"Totaled," his mother said.

The sun was coming through the window, illuminating the wrinkles on Patricia's face. Teo was amazed that the world was exactly the same as before. As he walked into the flat, he cast his eyes over the furniture, unconsciously expecting Samson to appear and come sniff his legs. Depression hit him.

He headed for the kitchen, convinced that if he went into his room, he'd be returning to his boring life. Soon he'd be cleaning windows and pushing Patricia to church in her wheelchair again. The thought made him feel a little desperate. He drank a glass of water, opened and closed the refrigerator. He undressed and climbed into the shower. The water was very cold. All he could think about was his old life and the life he'd had with Clarice. He also thought about the fact that she was full of tubes somewhere, and that Patricia refused to take him to see her, and that made him feel even worse.

He lay down in the dark, remembering the time he'd spent in the bed with Clarice. It was very different now. There was a smell of imminent tragedy in the air—feelings had specific odors, and he was able to detect them sometimes.

Patricia ordered a pizza. Teo ate only two slices and watched TV, but the soap opera dramas made him impatient.

"You look worried," said Patricia.

"I am a bit."

"I'll take you to see her tomorrow."

He thanked her and fibbed that he was tired.

He thought about what to say to Helena when he saw her. They'd met only once, but he had spoken to her on the phone enough to want to avoid her. He considered visiting Clarice when Helena wasn't there, but she was probably by her daughter's side the whole time, and at any rate he had no way of knowing when she wasn't there. He tossed and turned in bed, and his sense of foreboding didn't leave him for a second.

The biggest pain in the neck when caring for a disabled person was that the disability slowed everything down. It took them ten minutes to change a pair of trousers, fifteen to go to the toilet, and more than half an hour to get a taxi with wheelchair access. Visiting hours had started an hour earlier, and Teo walked up the hospital ramp pushing Patricia's wheelchair as she said something about a news item on highway accidents that she'd seen on TV. It was getting harder and harder to smile at her. He realized his reactions were delayed, but realizing it didn't make any difference. He still felt awful. He fiddled with the ring on his finger and told the receptionist he was the patient's fiancée.

"Only one more person can go in," she told him, handing him a visitor's ID.

The hospital was very organized, with tight security and fingerprint identification. Clarice must have been transferred there right after the accident, he observed. The Manhães family wouldn't have left their daughter in a public hospital for very long. Teo had to park Patricia in a corner, but she'd brought her bead necklaces.

He walked down the corridor, very alert. His love of medicine came flooding back to him. How was it possible that he'd forgotten that feeling and been able to think only about Clarice? He walked into the ICU and spotted her cubicle a few yards away.

He could barely see her, lying under sheets, hooked up to monitors and an oxygen panel, but he recognized Helena. She looked defeated and exhausted, slumped over her daughter's bed. Teo's eyes widened, and he shook slightly, although he knew his fear didn't make any sense: Helena was just a desperate mother.

He thought about leaving, but she lifted her head and fixed her eyes on him.

"What did you do to my daughter?"

It was hard to get his thoughts in order. Without realizing it, he took three steps back. There was a man with Helena who he assumed was Clarice's father. Those were the people responsible for giving life to the woman he loved. Both of them looked completely spent. The man hugged Helena from behind and patted her shoulders.

"Stay calm, hon."

"I can't . . ." Helena's voice failed her. She hunched even further over her bare arms, and Teo began to find her pathetic behavior exasperating. He came closer, prepared for any hostility.

He had the right to visit his fiancée and couldn't care less what Helena thought of him.

Clarice looked like a china doll that had fallen to the ground and broken. The doctors were now trying to put the pieces together again as best they could: cardiac monitor, aspirator, drips. Bending over the bed, Teo gazed at the contours of the body he had once found svelte and exciting. The sight of Clarice's physical deterioration was ruining his mood; he began to think it had been a stupid idea to come here. Helena was weeping silently in her husband's arms. He started to rehearse an apology but lost track of his thoughts halfway through it.

The scars on Clarice's body were stigmata on Teo's back. He could see the fury under her quivering eyelashes, the repudiation on her dry lips, and was afraid, even though she was sedated.

"I want you to leave," said Helena.

On the mechanical ventilator trolley was a picture of Clarice when she was younger, maybe fifteen. She was at a table set for a birthday party, hugging her parents and wearing a colorful dress. Teo wished he were in the photo. Maybe Helena would let him put a photo of them as a couple on the ventilator trolley too. First he would have to be nice.

"I'm so sorry," he said very sincerely, as he really did lament that things had come to that.

"This is your fault!"

"It was an accident. There was nothing I could do."

"An accident? I haven't spoken to my daughter in months! And now . . ."

Teo trod lightly. The tiredness bearing down on his shoulders hadn't let up in twenty-four hours. "I'm still confused. I—"

"I want you to explain now." Helena's hands shook. "I can't bear any more of your stalling."

"Let him speak, hon," said her husband.

Helena looked pale and haggard. Teo noticed how alike she and Clarice were in their mannerisms: the same primitive fear, the same vigorous attempts to intimidate him. At the moment, Helena's expression was identical to Clarice's when she found out Breno was dead.

"I don't want you to lie to me!" she said.

Teo surmised that he and Helena's husband played similar roles in their relationships: the rational counterpart to their partners' emotional melodrama. He didn't want to come across as insensitive, but he used a pragmatic tone of voice to narrate the moments leading up to the car accident, adding details that sprang to mind as he spoke.

He explained that Clarice had hurt herself on some rocks while swimming off Ilha Grande. He felt more comfortable talking about it now and was able to lie more easily. Helena was very upset and tried to say something.

"I'm so worried that Clarice—" Suddenly, her throat tightened and she couldn't speak.

"Clarice's going to be fine," Teo said, although he didn't really believe it.

Helena sighed and waved him over. Her smile moved Teo in a way that Patricia hadn't been able to. Her hand was cold but comforting. He was careful not to stare at her, as he didn't want to make her uncomfortable.

"Sorry to offload on you. It's just that I feel like the worst mother in the world," she said. She started crying again.

He wanted to feel empathy, be moved by her pain, but all he could manage was slightly watery eyes. He had an impulse to tell her the whole truth about Breno, and about Clarice's attempted suicide, but it quickly abated.

"Would you get me a coffee, please?" Helena asked her husband.

As he left, Teo thought they'd share a poignant moment hugging, sharing hopes and crying on each other's shoulders, but Helena dried her eyes and her expression changed.

"Tell me about Breno."

"I didn't see Breno. And Clarice never said much about—"

"Stop lying." Helena stared at him, anxious but far from hysterical. She had recovered the air of superiority that he feared. "Our family has been going to that hotel for years. I know Breno was there that day. Gulliver told me."

Teo leaned on Clarice's bed and lowered his eyes. His head spun, reexamining facts without coming to a conclusion. He thought about punching Helena and nicking her jugular with a scalpel, but they were in a private hospital, and it would be hard to get away with it. He needed to deal with the fact that she knew. She knew a lot more than he had given her credit for, and it was quite possible that she knew everything.

"Right after he stopped by our place, Breno went to Teresópolis," she said with the same smile as Clarice, the same protruding teeth. "Gulliver said he saw a man arriving at your chalet that night, but thought it was you. Was it?"

"Yes, possibly."

He felt like he was going to pass out.

"The next morning Gulliver found the padlock on the gate open. Someone had entered on foot."

"And what does that prove?"

"Breno is dead. And you killed him."

Teo wanted to leave. It was ridiculous, offensive, vulgar.

"I'll tell you what I did," Helena went on. "I'm a lawyer, as you know. That detective has been sniffing around and seems to have a bee in his bonnet about you and Clarice. I don't want my daughter involved in a scandal. To be honest, I don't care if Breno is dead. I don't care that you killed that waste of space."

"I didn't—"

"I asked Gulliver to change your departure date on their records to the twenty-ninth of November. Breno disappeared on December 1. I'm on your side, but I want you to tell me the truth."

Teo sighed, staring at Helena. The conversation felt unreal. He knew that anything he said was of the utmost importance, and he couldn't say the wrong thing.

"Breno showed up in Teresópolis that night. He was completely unstable and had brought a knife to force Clarice to go back with him. He'd been drinking too. He stank of *cachaça*. We got into a fight, and before we knew it, he was . . . lying on the ground . . . dead. We didn't mean to do it. Clarice was desperate. I was too. Neither of us is a murderer."

An insane feeling of mirth made Teo smile slightly.

"We buried Breno in the forest behind the hotel. It was all very quick. It felt like a dream. But it really got to Clarice. She shut down, didn't want to talk to anyone. She refused to go back to Rio. She didn't want to talk to you, as she said you wouldn't understand."

Teo noticed that Helena's shoulders tensed slightly.

"Clarice lost it. She started saying it was my fault. She was sure we were being followed, but she was imagining things. At one point, she even said she hadn't invited me to Teresópolis and that she wanted me to leave her alone. She'd gone back to smoking and was missing someone by the name of Laura. . . . She was always repeating her name."

Teo made a point of mentioning Laura's name, as he presumed Helena didn't like her either.

"The last few days . . ." He sounded offended. "The last few days she even accused me—she said I was holding her prisoner."

"Prisoner?"

"Yes, I—I admit I did it twice. It was only twice, Helena.

She'd lost it. It was on Ilha Grande. Clarice was really depressed and . . . do you think it was wrong? I needed to set some limits. She didn't hurt herself by accident on Ilha Grande. She actually threw herself into the sea trying to take her own life."

Helena raised her bony hand to her mouth.

"I was just trying to take care of her. I stopped the bleeding, stitched her up. But she'd get worked up so easily. She wanted to turn herself in to the police. It's all so sad. The woman I love. The woman who said she'd marry me."

Teo pretended to wipe a tear off his cheek.

"I tried to spare you all this."

"What about the car accident?"

"I don't know." He was relieved to be able to open up to someone, even if it was only a crack. "I've thought a lot about it. Sometimes I'm sure it was an accident. Not long before that, Clarice and I had made up. She seemed healthier, she'd stopped smoking again and had come to accept that Breno's death had been *necessary*."

"Do you think she might have made the car crash on purpose?"

"Clarice had already tried to kill herself once, on Ilha Grande. Even though she was better, I thought she might have had a relapse . . . gone back to thinking about Breno, Laura, cigarettes— all the things that kept her away from a more wholesome life."

Helena continued to stare at him, and he got ready for a new onslaught of questions. Clarice's father came back with coffee for everyone. Teo thanked him for his thoughtfulness. Helena had donned her terrified expression again and was clinging to her husband. At that instant, he understood that all mothers were like her: false, self-seeking, and very cunning when protecting their offspring.

Teo said good-bye and left. The conversation would keep

him buzzing for the next few hours. He concluded that Helena was on his side and would continue to support him. It was a victory, albeit a provisional one. When Clarice woke up, perhaps he'd be labeled a liar or a coward. He wanted Clarice back, full of life, spontaneity, and sarcasm; but all he had to do was think a little to come to the conclusion that it really would be better if she didn't wake up.

30

Six days passed. Teo would go to the hospital in the morning and would leave only at night, when visiting hours were over. He sat near Clarice's bed. Patricia went with him once or twice but gave up when she realized the detective wasn't coming anymore. Clarice remained in a stable condition, with no improvement.

Teo got closer to Clarice's father. His name was Gustavo, and he was pretty ugly, very different from his daughter, but very knowledgeable. They talked about his Houston-based employer's oil platforms, as well as economics, medicine, and politics. Teo liked him a lot; he wished his own father were alive and as good a man as Gustavo.

Helena didn't talk much to Teo. She was friendly, but he didn't know what to make of her. Sometimes it seemed that she believed him and even liked him, but the rest of the time Teo had the feeling she didn't think that highly of him and that her judgment was merely on hold. He felt that the things he'd told Helena were very plausible and fit into his own reading of Clarice's actions over the last few months. She had gone crazy, attempted suicide, and the episode with Breno had just been bad luck. That was the truth. He tried to present the facts another way but got lost, as there were huge blanks that couldn't be explained away. It wasn't possible, for example, that Clarice had thrown herself into the sea merely because of Breno. In his assessment, misguided feelings and a personality weakened by other problems had created the fatal chemistry.

On Friday, Teo took two medical books to read at the hospital, as Gustavo had gone to a meeting in São Paulo and there wouldn't be anyone to talk to. Besides, Clarice's silence, punctuated by electronic beeps, created a pleasant rhythm for reading—and he especially liked studying surgical procedures while sitting in an ICU. Shortly after midday, the doctor came to say that Clarice had improved slightly overnight. The news was enough to cheer up Helena.

She invited Teo to lunch at a nearby Arabic restaurant. She seemed to be making an effort to be nice. She mentioned that Gustavo really liked him, and she told him stories from Clarice's childhood. (Once she'd hit a classmate who'd called her Rabbit.)

Then she started in with the questions. She was particularly interested in her daughter's psychological state.

"She was living in another reality," said Teo for the thousandth time. "The shock of what had happened unhinged her. There were days when she didn't seem to remember Breno, and others when she'd start the day up in arms saying horrible things to me."

Helena told him that Clarice had seen a psychologist for seven years as a teenager.

Teo put down his bread, wiped his fingers on the napkin, and looked up at her. "I really care for your daughter."

They ordered rice with lentils and cheese *sfihas*. She insisted that they share some lamb *kaftas*, but Teo explained that he was a vegetarian. He felt welcomed by the Manhães family and was already very much at home with them—he said things like "I want to have two or three children," and "I fully support Clarice's artistic career, but I think she needs a job that gives her some financial stability," and "Cigarettes are a deplorable addiction. All addictions are deplorable, for that matter."

Helena smiled at him. "When did the two of you get engaged?"

"On the twenty-fourth of November. I'll never forget it. We were sitting on one of those benches by the lake at the hotel. We talked about having children and decided on surnames. Manhães is her maternal surname, isn't it?" he said, taking a stab in the dark.

"Yes, it's from my father's side."

"Mine is Avelar Guimarães. Manhães Guimarães doesn't work." He laughed heartily.

Helena looked at him. "Any relation to Judge Avelar Guimarães?"

"His son," said Teo, a little ashamed, but it quickly passed. Helena knew who his father was and admired him. She had read some of his books on civil procedure and didn't seem to care about the scandal in which he'd been involved. Teo noticed that status was important to her and talked about his plans as a doctor.

The conversation came back around to Clarice. Helena asked where they'd left the rug to be washed, and Teo had to make up an excuse: he said they'd forgotten it in the trunk and later used it to carry Breno's body to the grave in the middle of the forest. He felt like a character in a crime novel.

Teo assumed she didn't know about the handcuffs and separators in the suitcase. Maybe the detective hadn't divulged the information. He wasn't afraid of being suspected of something, as he'd bought it all in a sex shop, but the thought that someone might think he was perverted bothered him.

"Are you going back to the hospital?" she asked.

"Yes."

Teo glanced at his watch. They'd forgotten their problems for an hour and a half.

Helena said she had something to do that afternoon and insisted on paying the bill. As they were saying good-bye, she said, "I hope this nightmare is over soon. It'll be great to have an Avelar Guimarães as a son-in-law."

Teo thought about the pleasant time he'd had and was surprised to find Detective Aquino sitting next to Clarice's bed. He was flicking through a notepad, but when he saw Teo, he stood and greeted him with a nod. He said he'd stopped by and thought it odd that no one was with Clarice.

"Helena and I went to get lunch," said Teo. There was something dishonest about the friendliness in the detective's gaze.

"I managed to find that Gertrude you mentioned."

For a minute, Teo was confused and thought he was talking about his Gertrude.

"Is this her?" The detective showed him a very bad photograph of the toothless old woman.

Teo looked at it but didn't touch it. It was offensive that that woman and his friend had the same name. He still hadn't grown used to the idea.

"Yep, that's her."

The detective put the photo back in his pocket and sighed. "Something doesn't add up. I talked to Gertrude, and—"

"Would you mind not calling her Gertrude?"

"What's the problem?"

"I'm just asking." Teo wished he could leave the conversation. Couldn't he have any peace?

"The woman said there was no one with you on the boat. She said you went to the deserted beach alone."

"The old woman's potty," he said with a smile. "Did you believe her?"

"I don't know."

"I don't have any reason to lie."

The woman might have mentioned that she'd seen someone with him on the beach. Or maybe she hadn't said anything because that was what he'd asked her to say. She was a complete idiot, and he couldn't think like an idiot.

"Are you sure this is the woman who took you and Clarice on the boat?"

"Yep, that's what I said."

Teo was finding it all very tiresome. It was his word against that of an illiterate old woman.

"She must have been mistaken, then," said the detective.

"Sorry I can't be of any more help."

"There's something else that I find curious. There was an empty suitcase in your car."

"Clarice was the one who packed everything. It doesn't make any sense that she'd leave one empty."

"Well, that's what happened."

"Maybe you should talk to the first responders. They must have taken some stuff."

"If they were going to take something, they'd have taken your cells, don't you think?" The detective's animosity was growing, and Teo was secretly pleased.

"Dunno."

"I've requested authorization to get your and Clarice's cell phone records. We're trying to recover the content of her laptop too. It was damaged in the crash, but we've got technicians working on it."

"I don't see what that has to do with Breno being missing."

"It'd be great if you could tell me why the suitcase was empty."

"I agree, it'd be great."

This conversation didn't make the slightest bit of sense to him.

"Breno was a nice young man," said the detective. "He didn't have any enemies. I wonder who could have done this. What do you think?"

"Maybe he killed himself."

"Helena thinks the same thing, but I don't agree." The detective shrugged. "You're going to be summoned to report to the police station."

Teo wanted to say something, but a cavernous sigh came out of his mouth. He felt too weak to answer back, move, or leave. It was like revenge, a nightmare that was becoming real.

"I don't want to talk to you anymore," he finally managed to say.

"Okay, son." The detective smiled and gave him two little pats on the shoulder before disappearing down the corridor.

Teo realized his hands were shaking and closed his eyes. He wanted to chase after the detective, but couldn't think of anything else to say. When he opened his eyes again, he looked at Clarice—so pale—and murmured, his voice full of bitterness, "I won't be caught, I *can't* be caught . . ."

He stopped at a bar near the hospital and ordered two shots of whiskey with no ice. He thought about what would happen if he didn't do anything and what could happen if he did. Looking at things from the police's perspective, he'd seemed guilty from the start. Unanswered calls, a car accident, and Clarice hurt—it was all very obvious and led the detective straight to him. He felt antagonistic and helpless at the same time. He

chided himself for not having turned on Clarice's laptop after
they left Ilha Grande. He didn't know what she had written
while he was handcuffed to the bed, but she had probably written about the handcuffs, the Thyolax, or worse—a message full
of resentment and lies.

He saw his reflection in the tabletop, his downturned mouth
and desolate eyes. He had been stupid and he despised stupidity
more than anything. At the end of the day, he was guilty. He had
risked so much to have Clarice; from the moment they'd met,
he'd felt as if she were already his.

He understood the situation perfectly: Clarice didn't care for
him. It was vaguely consoling that Helena and Gustavo were
behind him, but it wasn't enough for him to feel at peace. Clarice
had never wanted anything to do with him—that was the truth.
Their time together, his dedication and effort, it was all going to
go down the drain. If she stayed in a coma for months, perhaps
years, she still wouldn't belong to him. If she woke up, she'd tell
the police everything. Either way Teo couldn't see anything but
defeat. Imagining her dead was less painful.

He paid the bill half drunk. He moved easily, feeling brave
enough to do what had to be done. He walked straight into the
hospital because he hadn't returned his visitor's ID when he left.
When he got to the ICU, he already felt different, a little odd but
happy, as if nothing were real. He often felt as if he were living
in a film, with people on the other side of the world watching
his every move via cameras that were left on twenty-four hours
a day.

The hospital seemed emptier at that hour. Visiting hours were
almost over, and the doctors were changing shifts. The lights in
the corridor cast a milky-white beam of light into Clarice's ward.
Teo looked around before closing the curtain. The beeping was
bothering him and seemed louder now. He was a little dizzy but

focused his attention on the machines that were keeping Clarice alive, fed by dozens of wires attached to her arms, nostrils, and neck.

He silenced the vital signs alarm and mechanical ventilator. He leaned over, stroked her face—her skin was cold—and disconnected the ventilator. The silence perturbed him for a moment, but her heart rate sped up on the monitor.

Clarice writhed. She breathed in agony, lashed out with her arms. It was horrible to watch—his penance, he thought.

He was gripped by a feeling he'd never experienced before, and he realized he couldn't go through with it. Clarice wasn't like Breno. He reconnected the ventilator and turned up the fraction of inspired oxygen to one hundred percent.

The alarms sounded loudly and doctors hurried in, pushing him aside. "Respiratory failure!" one of them shouted.

Teo didn't hear anything else. His body obliged him to move. He left the hospital, walked through the streets, and before he knew it, he was home. He locked himself in his room, where he cried a lot, not really knowing why. Patricia knocked on his door. He didn't want to talk to her or anyone else. Gustavo, Helena, Aquino, or Breno. If he'd had a loaded gun right then, he'd have put a bullet through his head just to be free.

When his mother finally let him be, Teo raced to the bathroom and swallowed a Hypnolid tablet. His whole body twitched as if his soul were doing somersaults in the air, but he knew he needed to rest. He fell asleep thinking that everything was completely and utterly wrong.

31

His head hurt. The detective's questions had really gotten to him, and he'd ended up doing the wrong thing, he concluded. He felt as if he were rotting on the inside. His desire to kill Clarice had been petty, and he had given in to it all too easily. He'd been drinking, but that was no excuse. There were probably security cameras in the hospital corridors, and by now everyone would know what he'd done. He imagined the desolate expression on Helena's face and Patricia's reaction—his mother's life depended on him, and now all was lost.

He didn't even know if Clarice was still alive. He hoped so. There was no way he could call the hospital or Helena. He'd been so distressed that he barely knew the facts. What would he say? He didn't know if there were cameras or what state Clarice was in. He had a noose around his neck. The image amused him.

He got dressed, and when he opened the door, he found Patricia brimming with questions and advice. He stepped around her, pushed the wheelchair into a corner, and left, feeling free, savoring the importance of the gesture. Patricia was a dead weight and didn't know it. She needed to know it and to rethink the way she treated him. It was the only way they'd ever be able to live in harmony.

The day was cloudy and cool. Teo walked along heedlessly, taking the same route as he had the day before. He made it to the hospital in twenty minutes. Helena and Gustavo smiled at him— or was it just his imagination? They were talking to a doctor. Clarice was still in her bed covered in wires.

"You saved her life," said Helena, giving him a kiss on the cheek.

Gustavo greeted him too, and Teo was perplexed. He thought he was surrounded by madmen. The doctor explained that they had noticed he'd increased Clarice's fraction of oxygen during her episode of respiratory failure and that it had saved her from becoming a vegetable—and perhaps even death. Gustavo and Helena were very happy with him, and even the doctor congratulated him. It was nice to have people fawning over him.

Teo was so happy that even if Clarice stayed in a coma forever, it wouldn't be a bad thing. He could visit her once or twice a week and imagine all the things they'd do together.

"After yesterday's fright, Clarice's condition has improved," said the doctor. "She should recover in a few days."

Helena decided that Teo should have lunch with her again, this time with Gustavo. She was the kind of person who demonstrated her happiness by eating. She chose a very expensive restaurant in Leblon and ordered wine. At the table, Teo had to make up a last-minute story about the previous day. He tried to be discreet, since his heroic deed was already impressive in and of itself. He was tired and came to the conclusion that he didn't want to lie, deceive, or pretend anymore. It was possible that Clarice would

wake up in a few days, and it barely mattered to him. He'd enjoy
the Manhães family while he could. Later, if they all hated him
and wanted to see him behind bars, what did it matter? He didn't
regret what he'd done. He'd done everything for Clarice, and it
was up to her to appreciate it. If she preferred to turn him in, fine.
He'd know she was well, and that was enough. If she were dead,
he'd have nothing.

Teo excused himself to answer his cell. They had already finished their main course, and only Helena had wanted des-
sert. It was Patricia, giving him a tongue-lashing. She said she
didn't recognize this new Teo. He loved the expression. He
thought about replying that he was very happy as this *new Teo*
but merely apologized for having left so quickly and told her the
news. Patricia was taken aback. She said she was proud of him,
but still upset. Teo promised to cook for her later.

When he returned to the table, Helena was alone and had
already paid for lunch.

"Gustavo's gone to get the car."

Teo sat down and put his cell in his pocket.

"The detective is suspicious of Clarice and me," he said. He
had wanted to tell her when they first sat down but had felt inhib-
ited in Gustavo's presence. There was no one else around now,
and the waiters were chatting near the cash register.

"Nothing will happen."

Teo wished he could be as sure as Helena.

She ate the last spoonful of her *petit gateau* and looked at him.
"Why are you so worried?"

"The detective let on that he was sure. He said I'd be summoned."

"He doesn't have anything on you and is just trying to bait

you. You'd think Rio de Janeiro was a peaceful city and he didn't have anything better to do."

"What if he summons me?"

She chuckled. "You just go and tell them your story."

"Does Gustavo know the truth?"

"You've never seen Breno, and Breno never went to our place after he and Clarice broke up. My husband knows that truth."

Teo felt pathetic. It was actually quite funny that he was so bothered by the detective, while Clarice's possible recovery didn't worry him in the slightest.

Gustavo came in to say the car was outside. They were back at the hospital in thirteen minutes. Gustavo looked at Teo affectionately.

Teo was annoyed that he couldn't tell him the truth. Ethically speaking, he didn't see any problem with what he'd done: accidentally killing Breno, who had forced his way into their chalet holding a knife. He understood that it was reprehensible—even criminal—from the police's point of view, but Gustavo was very different from the police. Teo would be ashamed to tell him, not because of what he'd done but because he'd lied about it. But his fear was justifiable, as well as his contempt for Breno's actions. He imagined Gustavo would be shocked at first but would eventually understand and forgive him.

Teo stood next to the bed thinking about how to broach the subject, but didn't get around to saying anything because he saw Laura coming down the corridor, and his stomach tightened. He recognized her immediately. He'd never forget the disgusting almond-shaped eyes that had persuaded Clarice to do outrageous things. She was holding four ugly roses wrapped in colorful paper. She eyed Teo curiously. He tried to control himself, but it was impossible. It took a lot of cheek and falseness to show her face after everything that had happened.

He walked up to her and grabbed her arm forcefully. "Come with me."

Teo didn't know how she'd managed to get in; after all, Clarice already had the maximum number of visitors allowed by the hospital. Nonetheless, Laura had somehow got herself a visitor's ID. She was definitely the sort who got what she wanted by devious means.

"What are you doing?" shouted Laura when they were halfway down the corridor. She was small, like Clarice, but nasty. She wore her black hair plaited like an Indian, which made her look even more pathetic. Teo didn't want to talk to her, but forced himself to say, "Get out of here, and don't come back."

"Who are you to—"

"I'm Clarice's fiancé." He waved his ring at her. "You don't need to introduce yourself. I know who you are and what you did with her. She's put all that behind her now."

People in the hospital were staring at them, some concerned, others amused.

"I read your text messages, and Clarice told me what happened in Lapa. You should go look for a husband." Teo went back to the ICU.

Laura didn't dare put in another appearance, which made him happy. She was a terrible influence. He was certain he'd done the right thing by kicking her out. Helena and Gustavo didn't say anything, but it was clear to Teo that they agreed with him.

Dinner with Patricia was silent and subtly pleasant. He tried to make cordial conversation, which was the cue for Patricia to bring up the new Teo and how she was disappointed with the choices he'd been making. She went so far as to say that she'd hoped for a studious son, not a skirt-chasing fool.

Teo left the table. Couldn't she at least be grateful for the dinner?

A few minutes later Patricia came to the door of his room. "I'm sorry. I know you're suffering."

He accepted her apology and told her what had happened at the hospital earlier.

Patricia laughed a lot. "I still don't understand why you kicked the girl out. What did she do to Clarice?"

Teo couldn't tell her that Clarice was homosexual, bisexual, or whatever she was—he'd given up trying to figure it out. "I don't know. Clarice didn't like her."

"Aren't you curious to know why?"

"No."

"When Clarice wakes up, try to find out. I know you don't like it when I say it, but I've still got that bad feeling. The girl still bothers me."

"When Clarice wakes up, I'm going to marry her and live my life," he said, really hoping he was right.

Patricia left the room in a huff.

Teo reflected that since his father's death, she had been a well of bitterness. There was all that talk about feelings and premonitions and her trying to persuade him to do what she wanted. First the incident with Breno, then Clarice's suicide attempt, and then the car accident. What else could happen?

It was Tuesday morning. Teo was in the hospital cafeteria with Gustavo, talking about soccer, a subject about which he knew very little. Gustavo's cell rang, and he answered it in a hurry. It was Helena.

"She's awake, she's awake!" Teo heard. Gustavo didn't need to say a thing.

They hurried down the corridors to the ICU. Clarice was beautiful, very pale, her face sleepy, her eyes half closed. Helena was crying, holding her daughter's hands, and Gustavo ran to embrace them.

At that instant, Teo understood that it was the end of the road for him, but he was satisfied knowing he would love her forever. He wasn't nervous; all he felt was a light pain at the nape of his neck.

When Clarice looked up at him, the pain in his neck left him too. She stared at him with unprecedented interest. She glanced briefly at Helena and Gustavo and then back at Teo, a little confused.

"I'm sorry, but . . . who are you?"

32

Clarice knew her name but was confused about her age. She was very upset when Helena told her about the car accident. She couldn't remember having seen Teo before, or what had happened in the previous month or year. She had very fresh memories of her childhood, her parents, and her Catholic high school, but recent events had been completely erased: the *Perfect Days* screenplay, her studies in art history, and the death of her paternal grandfather two years earlier. She seemed truly perplexed that she was engaged.

The questions were many and came from all sides. He was afraid that Clarice would remember everything and accuse him, but her expression was so hesitant that Teo could tell she was being sincere. He wanted to kiss her and massage her shoulders but held back. Helena was still crying a lot. Everyone was shocked to learn that Clarice's legs had been paralyzed in the car accident.

Clarice received a lot of presents and visitors. The presents came accompanied by cards that got on Teo's nerves, signed by friends he'd never heard of. How was it possible that she knew so many people? He didn't even like to touch the cards. He tore them up without showing them to anyone.

When Clarice was released, they fell into a routine. They spent a lot of time together at her parents' place in Jardim Botânico. She was shy at first, but he gave her space, and they talked a lot to recover their intimacy. Almost every night Teo would come over with a present for her: a book, a pair of sunglasses, or a bottle of perfume. They talked about cinema and theater and watched lots of films together. Her interests remained basically the same, although she hadn't shown any taste for cigarettes or women. She loved *Little Miss Sunshine*, which was now her favorite film.

Little by little he and Clarice grew closer, and it was lovely, as Clarice was really making an effort to like him. She laughed at the things he said and liked hearing about his plans for the future. She kissed him on the lips of her own free will. She didn't ask a lot, just questions to satisfy her female curiosity: how they'd met, when he'd asked her to marry him, what the trip to Teresópolis had been like, things like that. The advantage of her lack of memory was that he could tell her whatever he wanted; he exaggerated the details in order to make it all sound poetic and inevitable. They had fallen deeply in love and were destined to be together.

Teo was required to report to the police station one Friday morning. He answered the same questions as before and left satisfied, feeling that Detective Inspector Aquino was completely lost. It had been impossible to recover the content of the broken laptop, their cell phone records didn't indicate anything, and well, what exactly was the problem with transporting an empty suitcase in the trunk? Clarice was summoned too, but Helena obtained a court order granting her permission not to participate in the inquiry, since she was in no condition psychologically to participate. Teo thought Detective Aquino would insist on her testimony, but he didn't.

A few weeks later Breno's disappearance had been forgotten. Other mysteries came along to occupy the police—mysteries with bodies. Breno's disappearance would go down on that list of stories that begin to sound like fables with the passing years: the violinist who went missing after being dumped by his girlfriend. Many would assume he was somewhere else in the world—in Rome or Florence—performing in public squares. Others might think Teo had murdered him. But there was no proof. And no one seemed terribly interested in the matter now.

Helena didn't bring up the subject, and the detective himself never showed up again—in September of that year, Teo saw him in a TV interview collaborating on a case in which a group of young people had committed suicide in a gruesome manner. He had turned off the television without paying much attention to the story. He wasn't in the mood to hear about misfortune and tragedy. Clarice didn't mention Breno, which was great: he began to allow himself to feel that he was truly dead and buried.

Over the next few months, she underwent a whole battery of exams, consulted countless neurologists and physical therapists, and attended sessions that included hydrotherapy and kinesio-therapy to recover the movement in her legs. Teo went with her and helped her repeat the exercises at home to stimulate circulation and stop her limbs from atrophying. Her progress was slow, they commented at the dinner table, when in fact it was null. Clarice had gained more mobility in her body and had learned to drive her electric wheelchair, and the pain in her back had diminished, but her legs were still motionless and would remain so—her spinal injury was strangely deep and straight.

They needed to accept that they were expending a lot of effort and money on Clarice's recovery in vain. To compensate for that defeat, Gustavo took it into his head to hire a specialist in functional neuroimaging to investigate Clarice's memory.

The neuropsychologist paid them a house call on a Monday afternoon and conducted tests well into the evening. "The brain is very complex," the doctor said. "Human beings have a short-term memory and a long-term memory, which are controlled by different regions of the brain. Clarice was affected in such a way that she is capable of remembering past events, but her memory of more recent events has been seriously compromised. This kind of amnesia is the most common. After suffering a car accident, the person might not remember the accident or the months leading up to it. We can begin treatment to try to gradually recover these memories."

Teo was against any kind of treatment. He had made up a much better version of everything. He felt sick just thinking about the past. Helena was against it too, but Gustavo insisted on it, saying that stopping Clarice from retrieving her memory was akin to paralyzing her personality, which Teo thought was a bit much. He liked Gustavo less after that.

At any rate, the sessions with the neuropsychologist proved fruitless. Clarice could remember only what Teo had told her, with the wealth of details he'd told her and the way he'd told her. According to the neuropsychologist, Clarice's most recent memory was her graduation from high school. Her case was somewhat unusual, as amnesia usually affected only shorter periods of time, weeks or months.

Clarice applied for university again, this time to study fashion design. Her new friends were as unpleasant as her old ones, but at least she didn't stay out late at bars or listen to samba in Lapa. Nor could she dance with other men. At any rate, there weren't

as many of them now. Teo went out of his way to make sure that
Clarice felt good, even if she almost always had a vacant or bored
expression on her face.

Sometimes he'd catch her observing him. Her eyes would lin-
ger on him, but he had no idea what she was thinking. When it
happened, he felt stupid and impotent.

Clarice wrote in a notebook every day. Teo imagined it was
the draft of a novel or a new screenplay.

"The doctor asked me to write everything down, trying to
separate what I actually remember from what I think I remember because you or my mother told me," she said. "Lots of people
with amnesia have done similar things and it usually works."

From that day on, Teo began to pay extra attention to the
things he said to Clarice and did with her. He avoided beaches,
motels, and orchestra recitals. He didn't mention Gertrude,
because Clarice would ask to meet her. Just listening to a violin
gave him goose bumps. She was somewhat addicted to sex,
although she had to find pleasure in other erogenous zones—she
especially liked it when Teo licked her ears. They had sex almost
every day, but he refused immediately when, on one occasion, she
asked to be handcuffed to the bed.

Teo graduated in medicine and did his residency in psychia-
try. He had become interested in the subject in his fourth year,
and it had redefined his career. Helena and Gustavo bought them
a flat in the district of Catete and helped out with the bills. They
also paid Clarice's university fees. The flat was pleasant, with
wide doorways and a large bathroom to accommodate the wheelchair. Teo discovered that the previous owner had been quad-
riplegic.

Though Breno's body was never found, Teo remained in the
habit of scouring the newspapers every day and ended up devel-
oping an interest in international economics. When she gradu-

ated from university, Clarice went into business with a friend. She worked from home, updating her Web site and sewing custom-made items. Nuances of her personality resurfaced, but he was already so used to them that he didn't mind. He knew Clarice was unstable and emotive, and when they fought, it was always for silly reasons, like the color of the new casserole dish or the position of the sofa in the living room.

Clarice's inability to control her bodily functions continued to be an inconvenience. He bought her geriatric diapers and helped her change them. Sometimes she'd have nightmares and would wake up thinking she was fourteen or fifteen years old. Those were sad moments. It bothered Teo to see her suffering the consequences of her own irresponsibility after so long. This Clarice, obscure and intractable, always caught him off guard.

Patricia insisted on trying to understand Samson's death and gave Clarice a hard time. The time they spent in each other's presence was always punctuated by subtle insults, but only once was the exchange of accusations so serious that Teo had to intervene. Patricia accused Clarice of having killed her dog.

Clarice defended herself saying she couldn't remember the dog. "If I were going to kill someone, I'd have killed you," she said.

That December Patricia had a heart attack while having dinner at their place.

After his mother's death, Teo felt a growing need to start a family of his own.

They got married at São Bento Monastery on a lovely January morning. It was a very beautiful church, with a delightful view of Guanabara Bay. Teo was already familiar with the traditional Benedictine boys' school next to the monastery and decided that their son was going to study there. He had recently got a job at the Instituto Philippe Pinel psychiatric hospital and could afford the school fees now.

Clarice was beautiful in her white dress. Happy and tearful, she was wheeled to the altar by Gustavo. Marli attended their wedding, and that was the last time Teo saw her. He felt that his mother's death had severed his ties to the past, and now there was only the future. A future of promise and hope.

Clarice was having fewer nightmares, although sometimes she'd still wake up acting strangely, and it was very distressing— she'd shout and break plates of food against the wall, saying they'd been poisoned. Maybe their marriage wasn't perfect, but there were much worse ones out there—plagued by betrayal, lies, violence, alcohol, and illness.

Clarice's pregnancy took him by surprise. Teo had been so involved in his master's that it took him a while to recognize the signs: her missed periods, frequent nausea, and unusual cravings.

She had done a few exams, and he took time off work to go with her to the doctor's appointment.

"Congratulations—you're four months pregnant. It's a girl," said the doctor. "Have you given any thought to names?"

They hadn't talked about it, as they had both been sure it would be a boy. At any rate, Teo was happy, and Clarice appeared to be too. He realized that this was one of the most important moments of his life. He loved Clarice and the child she was expecting. He opened his mouth to reply that they hadn't thought of anything yet, but Clarice interrupted him. She was sitting up straight and stroking her belly, which was beginning to bulge. She smiled at Teo and said, "A beautiful name came to me just now. Gertrude. What do you think, my love?"

NOTE FROM THE AUTHOR

Hypnolid and Thyolax are fictitious names; however, a range of similar medications whose active ingredients are midazolam or sodium thiopental produce the same effects. Unfortunately, the ease with which one can obtain such drugs isn't fiction. Also, it is perfectly possible to hide a petite woman in a large suitcase with wheels. I have tried it and it works.

ACKNOWLEDGMENTS

For personal reasons, I didn't include acknowledgments at the end of my first novel, *Suicides*. Nevertheless, with that book and this one, a number of people helped me keep my mind on the job and get to the end with some sanity. For this reason, I would like to thank those who attended the *Suicides* launches in Rio de Janeiro and São Paulo. More than four hundred friends and readers came to help me toast the beginning of it all.

Cici, always.

My grandmothers, Emília and Teresinha, for being more than perfect.

My grandfather, a shirtless wise man.

My father, who prefers not to read what I write but encourages me.

My aunts, uncles, and cousins.

Pedro Terra, first and best reader.

Victor Schlude, for believing in this story.

Cliff Landers, dear friend and adoptive grandfather.

Daniel Ribas, icon of the literary world.

Thales Guaracy, who made the ship weigh anchor.

Bernardo Relvas, Natália Couto Azevedo, Gabriel Quintella, Bernardo Harboe, and Paulo Pepulim, whom I consulted exhaustively on medical matters while writing *Perfect Days*. Naturally, any error is my responsibility.

Thuanne Baptista, Santiago Nazarian, Fabiane Guimarães,

Kássia Monteiro, Luisa Geisler, Erica Schlude, Igor Dias, Amanda Regina, Emanuelle Stein, Luiz Biajoni, Lucas Rocha, Josué Oliveira, Jéssica Seabra, Leandro Rodrigues, Rafael Ferreira, Félix Fraga, Fernando Barreto, Georges Spyrides, Alessandro Thomé, Vivian Pizzinga, Dirceu José Fernandes, Janda Montenegro, Mateus Pinheiro, and Gabriel Leitão, for reading and commenting on my novels as I wrote them.

Friends from the former BPGM Advogados, who were there at the beginning of my career to share in the excitement; friends from the reading club at the secondhand bookstore Baratos da Ribeiro, for the codfish cakes, beer, and literature; and the students of Colégio de São Bento, for our small brotherhood.

My good friends Nylda Helena, Sonia Campos, and Norma Passos.

Clarice Cudischevitch, for getting into the suitcase.

Débora Guterman, for being so sweet.

Christina Baum, Renata Megale, and the directors of the AASP (São Paulo Lawyers Association), for believing in me.

Carola Saavedra, for her careful reading and kindness from the outset.

Luciana Villas-Boas, the best literary agent, and Anna Cardoso, her incredible assistant.

Luiz Schwarcz, Otávio Costa, and Flavio Moura, for welcoming me so well at my new publishing house.

Alison Entrekin, who took such great care translating this story into English.

Booksellers everywhere, who help make it worthwhile.

Readers everywhere, who make it worthwhile.

Finally, I would like to thank my mother. She was quite shocked after reading *Suicides* and asked, "Why do you write about such violent things? Try to write a love story."

Perfect Days is the result of her request.